Hell Holes

Gail P. Robertson

Hell Holes

ISBN: 978-0-9921203-7-5

Other books by Gail P. Robertson:

When the Need is Great
Hour House
The Whimsical Crime of Rhythm and Rhyme

This book is dedicated to
my beloved mother, Paulette Davies,
for her loving heart and total candor.

HELL HOLES

CHAPTER 1

"OWWEEEE!"

Ablakan sucked his punctured finger and glared in mock severity at the long-haired calico kitten.

"No, Shnook, don't bite." He shook the finger from a safer distance at the unrepentent furball. She twitched her tail in response, fever-bright eyes never leaving the digit just beyond her reach.

He smiled fatuously at Shalaii's only feline. Schnookums had been a birthday present from his dearest human friend, Jan Brody. From the moment he laid eyes on a tricolored domesticated cat, during a visit to Earth, he'd dreamed of having one of these magnificently independent creatures come live with him. Of course, he could not inflict such a destructive whirlwind on a palaceful of irreplaceable treasures. But now that he was in his own complex on Pantai, he could indulge his desire.

Ablakan opened the cleanser door in the ante room and extracted a suitable-sized dressing to cover the tiny wounds. The wide mirror reflected his beige leathery arm, the skin criss-crossed with tiny lines from the quilted cushion on which it had rested. The handmade gift was from Earth's second 'porting telepath, Brenda Foxworth. He noticed that his sun-gold mane, which flowed from its apex at the back of his head to halfway down his spine, was at the moment a shag which resembled the tangleweed he had removed from the garden path yesterday. Shnookums found it almost as irresistible as fingers.

Ablakan cast an indulgent smile at the troublesome cat and brushed his mane back into place. He carefully checked his eyes. Fortunately, the kitten's claws had not left a mark as they attempted to capture the tiny pupils which moved independently of each other in his eyebanks. The breathing slits underneath had not fared as well, and Ablakan dabbed at small beads of half-dried blood. As a final check, he opened his ovoid mouth, baring his twin rows of sparkling teeth.

1

Satisfied at last that the features of his horizontally-oblong head were still in place, Ablakan re-entered his sleep chamber.

A gentle knock on his door sent the kitten scurrying toward the sound.

"Come in," Ablakan called, and the door opened a crack.

"Is *SHE* inside?"

As if in reply, a small paw, needle-sharp claws extended, insinuated itself into the gap and tap-tapped around the corner in an effort to reach the body which went with that voice.

"Shnook, no!" Ablakan scooped up the protesting feline before she could get into more trouble.

"I've got her, Saymin," he assured his valet, who opened the door gingerly.

His elder by three decades (that he would admit to), today Saymin wore notably incongruous attire. His uncharacteristically short warmers had been rolled down on his right leg to expose the bottom third, just above the ankle. The otherwise bare skin sported an enormous bandage held in place with what appeared to be leagues of tape. Saymin deposited his load of clothing on the bed and walked toward the closet with a decided limp.

Ablakan had seen the damage Shnook inflicted on him the day before – three miniature scratches which barely succeeded in breaking the top layer of skin. But if Saymin needed to play the martyr, Ablakan wasn't about to deny him the pleasure. At least while distracted by the cat, his valet wasn't trying to matchmake for Ablakan. Being a boy one day and Shalaii's most eligible bachelor the next was quite disconcerting.

"How is your leg?" First Ablakan of Pantai inquired, knowing Saymin would expect a fuss to be made over his 'war wound', as he called it.

"I have learned to live with the pain, sir." The valet favored the kitten with an aggrieved scowl. "The medic assured me it is not life-threatening."

"I am relieved to hear that. Are you settling into your quarters well? Have you everything you need?"

"It is perfect," Saymin assured him. "Primary Tweno was indeed generous in the arrangements – well, mine, anyway. I have not seen anyone else's yet. And such a view!"

2

"I'm not surprised. We are so fortunate to have him as our ruler."

Ablakan blinked rapidly and turned away, his eyebanks becoming sodden. Despite the magnificent surroundings and plush accommodations Tweno had arranged for him and his staff, Ablakan was feeling overwhelmingly homesick.

As usual, Saymin noticed the mood change and placed a hand on his employer's shoulder.

"I miss them all, too, sir, and you can be sure they miss you as well. There is still much daylight left. I am certain you would lift his heart if you 'ported over and challenged the Primary to a game."

"They won't be eating for a while yet," Ablakan agreed, cheered by the prospect.

"Why not give him a call right now?" Saymin quietly left the room as Ablakan closed his eyebanks to mentally 'knock' in Tweno's mind. The Primary opened to him instantly, unable (or perhaps not trying) to hide his pleasure.

I was wondering if you have found replacements willing to let you win at golf? Ablakan needled.

No, they're all poor sports here. They don't want to look bad when I beat them, so they refuse to play. Use all sorts of lame excuses, like family or having to work – you know how it is. Are you offering?

I need the exercise. And, Ablakan added, as honesty got the better of him. *I miss the company.*

Then let's not waste any more time.

A moment later, Ablakan appeared before his mentor. They grinned at each other knowingly, for each had felt the loneliness in the other during that brief contact. Tweno was now barely taller than Ablakan, who stood 6'6", according to Jan's measurements, but Tweno doubled him in mass. Ablakan hoped in time to also put on weight to offset his gangly length, but everything he ate seemed to translate into height.

Carts in hand, Ablakan 'ported them to the first tee with the offhandedness of old habit. He watched as Tweno, who had been to him more surrogate father than ruler over the years, sent his ball in a devastatingly accurate trajectory to land three feet from the cup.

"Are you sure you haven't been practicing?"

Tweno smirked but said nothing.

Ablakan's shot had a slight curve to it, and his ball stopped at the far edge of the green.

"The first week is always the hardest," Tweno said as they sauntered towards their respective balls. "Soon after I moved into the skyzone tower in Tabix, I almost quit. The honor of governing our largest continent just didn't make up for the homelife I had left behind, even with my mother having just died. I wasn't much older than you when I took on the job. And I didn't have the ability to 'port myself home when the loneliness got too sharp."

Ablakan felt his skin pink, but not because of Tweno's remark. He remembered someone he should have been missing even more. "How is Epash handling it?"

Annoyance flickered across Tweno's face. "She is playing the heartbroken mother to the hilt, and the staff are flocking to buy her wares out of sympathy. But when I went to see how she was feeling, she almost brushed me off when she saw I hadn't come to buy. I certainly wouldn't worry about her."

"It was generous of you to let her continue running the palace gift shop, now that I'm no longer there." Ablakan felt his gratitude stronger than his words conveyed. The alternative would have had Epash living with him, probably trying to run Pantai instead of letting her son do his job.

"The staff have grown surprisingly fond of her," Tweno murmured, as he pulled the putter from his bag. He neatly sunk the ball in one tap.

Ablakan took two strokes to do the same. With a sigh of contentment, he retrieved his ball.

It was as they approached the second tee that a hole of a different sort appeared, no larger than a pinprick in the fabric of space. Nearby particles of cosmic dust abruptly veered toward it, to disappear an instant later. The vortex grew, and more debris, this time from further away, fell prey to its growing appetite.

As usual, they chatted only sporadically during the game, for the most part enjoying each other's company in companionable silence. The quietude gave Ablakan much-needed time to review recent events, in familiar surroundings, and put them in perspective.

It had been almost eight years (he thought in Earth time now, as did most of those heavily involved in trade and commerce within the alliance) since he and Jan Brody had telepathically 'met'. Her husband, Tom, had become fixated on Shalaii's sun, empathically picking up feelings, though he initially discounted Jan's suggestion that he was doing so. When, a couple months later, they all heard a psychic scream from the crashed Orowan astronaut Moohri, it set off a maelstrom of events. Jan was the first to learn to teleport items, in an effort to get food to the starving alien. Over time, a deep bond of friendship grew between the three planets, initially through Ablakan, Jan and Shownae, the 'porting telempaths on each world, and of course, Moohri. But eventually it included each planet's major political leaders. Once Moohri was proven disease-free and returned home, high-level meetings between world leaders set the stage for trade and interplanetary travel.

The Orowans' provision of their pristine moon, Shyr, to be used as a recreation and trade destination by and for all three species, had been the icing on the cake, as the humans called it. Hard to believe there were now seven planets in the alliance.

Ablakan smiled indulgently, remembering his fearfilled early attempts to enlist his government's aid in the rescue mission. It had taken some doing, because his people at that time did not believe there was other life in the universe. His efforts had culminated in a terrifying encounter with their insane elderly Primary, who ordered him put to death for treason. Fortunately, then-First Tweno and his counterparts from the other two continents – Lisham of Tunan and Konapi of Enaxat – declared her mentally unfit to govern, and voted in Tweno as Shalaii's new Primary. Even after all these years, it still seemed incredible that they had chosen him, Ablakan, to become First of Pantai when he reached the Age of Arrival – about 17 in human years.

In the interim, he had held the title of Interpreter and Interplanetary Ambassador. Ablakan had worked hard to teach Tweno and Shownae to speak English, as this was the only language all three species could vocalize. Over time, he was besieged with people wanting language training or his services in 'porting goods to and from Shalaii. When the telepathic welder Kyollan finally came on board, Ablakan was able to relieve

Tweno of some of his former duties as a First. At that time, Tix, the three-year-old 'path, had been a pleasant drain on Ablakan's time, but much too young to be of help.

Ablakan's life at the palace on the island paradise across from Tabix had been idyllic. As his eyebanks swept the familiar terrain near the 16th hole, many fond memories came to mind. The golf supplies and training had been a delightful gift from their human colleagues many years ago, and both Ablakan and the Primary loved the game.

Tweno broke in on his musings. "How are you settling in? Was there anything I missed?"

"Not a thing I can think of."

Ablakan shook his head in amazement. Even with 10-year-old Tix dampening his curiosity the past few months, how had Tweno managed to pull off such an enormous surprise without Ablakan tumbling to it? Instead of occupying the top floor of a skyzone tower in Tabix, as Tweno had done while a First, Ablakan and his staff (which included some handpicked favorites among the palace crew) now enjoyed the facilities Tweno had had constructed on the site of the old observatory. The aging structure had been moved two years before to the crest of Troyell, a nearby hill. Beside Ablakan's luxurious mansion were spacious staff quarters, an office complex complete with decontamination room (to ensure pathogens would not be transported between planets), and several guest cottages. Each building faced the ocean, with the Primary's island sitting on the horizon like an emerald jewel. The backs of the buildings looked out over Tabix, Pantai's largest city. In between were extensive sloping forestlands perfect for tranquil walks. The one amenity notably missing was a golf course. Tweno had informed him with a wicked grin that this had been deliberately left out to ensure Ablakan would visit him often.

"I don't think I properly thanked you for the ceremony, sir," Ablakan realized. "I was so astonished by the new home you provided . . . "

Tweno chuckled as they trudged towards the 17th green. As usual, Ablakan's ball was off to the side – always the same side, he noted. Maybe if he twisted his body a bit?

"That was quite a get-together," Tweno said. "There were literally thousands of people, from all seven worlds, who wanted to come. You sure made a lot of friends over the years."

"Wonderful friends," Ablakan agreed. He lined up the ball with his club. This time he matched his mentor and sunk it in one stroke.

The celebration of his reaching Age of Arrival, and his inauguration as First of Pantai, had been exciting but also an eye-opener. Some of his dearest friends had been there – Jan and Tom Brody, and Jack and Brenda Foxworth, along with the Orowan contingent which included Shownae, Trikon and Moohri. The latter two shared the Orowan title of Lead Spacefarer. Ablakan had also been honored by the presence of the President of the United States and the new Secretary-General of Earth's United Nations.

So much of what had happened that momentous day were a happy blur in his memory, but a few events stood out with crystal clarity. One humorous exchange involved the U.S. President.

"Primary, I thought your people didn't go in for torture," the President harangued Tweno at one point.

"We don't." Tweno blinked in surprise. "Why do you ask?"

"How else do you explain Ablakan being a foot taller than I remember him?"

Merriment twinkled in Tweno's eyebanks. "We have a much subtler way to accomplish that. I had the cooks lace all those muchipans he's been eating with growth hormone." Tweno grinned at Ablakan, for the youth's weakness for that delicacy was legendary.

"Umm, you wouldn't have a bit of that hormone to spare, would you?" Jan asked ingratiatingly as she sidled up to Tweno. "Say, a gallon or two?" Behind her, Tom smothered a laugh. They all knew how much she hated being short.

Tweno sighed regretfully. "I'm afraid Ablakan used up our planet's entire stock."

Ablakan smiled on his way to the 18th tee, remembering Jan's feigned pout.

Later that morning had come the one incident he truly regretted. The proceedings had been fairly long and stuffy, but he had come through it without any obvious blunders. When Tweno clipped the shining crests onto the shoulder pads of his dress uniform, then draped the sash of office across his torso and declared him a First, Ablakan had been so relieved it was over that, when they left the stage, he had made a bee-line for Jan. She had stepped forward, arms outstretched to hug him.

Ablakan gulped, experiencing the terrible moment afresh: him standing there, frozen in dismay, as he watched his mother plow forward to intercept him, elbowing her way through the crowd of well-wishers.

"Ablakan, surely your guests can wait until you have been properly congratulated by your own mother," Epash informed him sharply.

"Of course, Mother. Please forgive me." Ablakan tried to extend his arms around her in a hug, but they did not quite reach.

"Humph," she said, making a big production of hugging and rocking him from side to side for much longer than convention required. Ablakan felt himself flush, but dared not break the contact, having already publicly embarrassed her. At length, her prerogative pointly discharged, Epash released him and stepped back into the crowd with a withering glare at Jan.

Ablakan hesitated, realizing all eyes were on him. He wanted to apologize to Jan, but under the circumstances, he would have to keep his distance.

At that moment, Tweno placed a hand on his shoulder and steered him towards the human delegation, one member of which, of course, was Jan. Carefully, the Primary negotiated Ablakan between the President and NASA's Administrator, Dr. Lesley Saunders, which just 'happened' to put him directly across from Jan. Ablakan gave his boss a quick glance of appreciation.

I'm so sorry, dear, Jan told Ablakan mentally, while appearing to be listening intently to something Dr. Saunders was telling the First Lady. *That was my fault.*

No, Jan, you have done nothing wrong. As I told you years ago, you have been more of a mother to me than Epash ever was. The sad truth is, I see her very seldom, and I simply forgot she was here. His tone turned bitter in self-rebuke. *I humiliated her in front of some of the most important people in the galaxy, and after all the time Tweno spent drilling me in protocol. And I embarrassed you, and probably Tweno as well.*

8

Jan turned her eyes toward the First Lady, who was now speaking. To Ablakan Jan said, *Dear friend, we all make blunders. I have made some doozies – just ask Tom. But we apologize and then put it behind us and go on. Don't forget, this is just your first day as an adult. Anyway, look at Epash. She's socializing with the matrons over there, see? Probably forgot about it already.*

Craning his neck, Ablakan spotted his mother. Ever so carefully, he touched her emotional aura and was relieved to find she was indeed enjoying herself.

Thanks, Jan. And you are right. I must interact with my guests as a First and an adult, not like a boy who has been chastized by his mother.

Exactly. He felt Jan's projected approval.

After lunch, there will be a two-hour relaxation period. Most of the visitors will be out on the golf course. Would you join me then for a quiet walk along the lake? It will probably be my last for a long time.

Love to. Jan turned away, for their small group was dispersing to socialize with other dignitaries.

A bit later, Juneli, his best friend among the palace staff, pointed the way to a diplomatic resolution of his *faux pas*. She stretched her willowy frame to whisper in his ear as he entered the dining lounge. He gave her hand a quick squeeze of gratitude before proceeding to his place at the table. Each platter held a place card on which a name had been emblazoned. Ablakan remained standing until he spotted Epash waddle into the room and begin looking at each card to find her seat. Ablakan caught her eye and motioned her over, indicating her chair.

Once she was close enough to read that she was to be seated on Ablakan's right, but three seats down, he switched the name cards so that she would sit next to him. He held out the chair for her. It took no small effort for Ablakan to push it back in place once she was seated, but he managed to do so without the exertion becoming too obvious. During the luncheon, he made a point of conversing with her as much as with anyone else.

When the feast was over, his mother was one of the first to excuse herself from the head table. As she arose, Epash leaned over and whispered to him, "You have redeemed yourself,

9

Ablakan. But always remember hierarchy; it is the cornerstone of diplomacy."

Ablakan stared at her in surprise. That was a most un-Epashlike comment, and one he intended to remember.

"Thank you, Mother. That is very true." He inclined his head in respect, which he had not done towards her in many years.

But later, when Jan joined him for their stroll along the tree-lined lake, Ablakan walked in silence.

"You look like a man with a weight on his shoulders," Jan remarked. "Surely those medallions don't weigh that much."

Ablakan sighed. "It is what they represent that troubles me."

"Why?"

He slowed his pace, trying to put his feelings into words. "Until now, I have always known what needed to be done. First it was to rescue Moohri, and make sure there was a 'porting telepath on each of the three planets. Then we had to arrange negotiations between the leaders and set up trade. After that, there was Shyr to transform, new 'paths to train, new species to bring into our alliance. But now –"

"Now it's just keeping everything running smoothly," Jan finished for him.

He nodded and looked down at his feet. "Perhaps I am wrong, but without strong goals to work toward, I fear we will become lazy and complacent. Eventually, all we have worked so hard to create could break down."

"Tom and I had the same concern not long ago. As you say, stagnation is the first step towards decay. But don't forget, dear, every new species that joins us changes the mix, revitalizing us. And it also challenges us to become even more flexible in our thinking and how we do things." She placed a hand on his shoulder. "I don't think that's what's really bothering you, though, is it?"

"No," Ablakan frowned. "It is part of it, but I can't seem to get at the real problem."

"Perhaps I can help." Jan turned to face him, and he stopped, regarding her solemnly.

"Since we met, you've been focused on interplanetary events and their effects, right?"

He nodded. "Pretty much."

"Today you reached the Age of Arrival. You are legally an adult in your society, and you have become one of the four most important people on your planet: a First."

Ablakan's expression twisted in a grimace, as he started to see what she was getting at. "So until now, I was a child playing a role in galactic affairs. Today I became an adult in charge of one continent on one planet, with far less time for the offworlders, what with the 'path and 'porter help we now have."

"Sort of like a space jockey becoming deskbound," Jan agreed. "And at such a young age. Small wonder you're having mixed feelings. But I'm going to tell you something in strict confidence: It will not be as it seems right now. That's all I can tell you. Just trust me on this, okay?"

Ablakan squeezed her hand. "I would trust you on anything. And thank you for understanding. I was miserable and didn't know why."

"Glad I could help."

And, of course, Jan had been right. As several of the guests joined him and Tweno for their maiden tour of Ablakan's new facilities, Tweno's final two surprises of the day had come when Ablakan opened his private office. There was one of his all-time favorite people. Her flowing yellow mane gleamed in the sunlight streaming in from one of the many bay windows imported from Earth. She was leaning impishly against the huge redwood desk Tweno had had commissioned for Ablakan.

"I believe you know your new assistant?" Tweno said blandly.

"*Juneli!*" Ablakan twirled her around in his arms in a most unbosslike manner, so great was his delight.

"I'm sorry, June," he said. "I'm just so glad to see you."

She gave him the warmest smile. "What is there to forgive in so hearty a greeting?"

"Juneli has been upgrading on her own time. You will find her well-versed in all aspects of being a First's Assistant. I personally composed and graded all her exams to ensure she could handle all routine elements. For yours will not be strictly a First's job, though that will be a good part of it."

A wild hope surged through Ablakan's heart, and he saw Tweno nod knowingly. "You are too valuable to us, and to our offworld allies, to spare you in your old capacity as Offworld Ambassador, 'porter and 'path."

"Yes," Ablakan sighed happily, as he now putted his ball into the cup on the 18th hole. "That was the party of a lifetime, but almost more excitement than I could handle. I look forward to a little boring routine."

* * *

Dru Hepiak, piloting Lowen's fastest cruiser toward Shyr for his meeting three days hence with the ambassadors of the allied planets, had little reason to smile just then. Several tiny asteroids streaked towards his craft, and he had to perform some creative manoeuvers to avoid them.

Hepiak frowned. What are they doing here? He consulted his charts again. They should have been well away from his flight path. His speed seemed to diminish momentarily, then resumed normal acceleration. Hepiak's sharp eyes probed his instrument panel, but nothing looked out of the ordinary. His rear portals offered no answers, either.

After briefly noting the phenomenon in his log, Hepiak turned his attention to his planned side trip to visit 'School' and the upcoming negotiation for acceptance as one of the aligned worlds.

Behind him, the space debris disappeared from view, permanently. The second black hole created that day accepted its latest tribute and increased its size to accommodate the next offering.

CHAPTER 2

Jan Brody stuck her head around the door of Jack Foxworth's bedroom. He lay propped up on a mountain of pillows, with one hand holding a compress to his forehead.

She carefully balanced the tray of temptations she hoped to get down his swollen throat, and asked brightly, "How are you feeling now?"

"Better, thanks." Jack swallowed, then grimaced at the pain it caused.

Jan let the lie pass without comment. He was eyeing the assorted tasties as though they were cruel punishments. "Most kind of you, Jan, but I'm not hungry just yet."

His stomach rumbled traitorously. Jack gave her a sheepish grin and reached for the mug of broth on the tray. "Perhaps just the soup."

"Mom," a juvenile voice croaked from the room next door.

Jan raised her voice. "She's at work, dear, remember? I'll be right there." She placed the tray on Jack's night stand and hurried to Billy's room. She hadn't counted on them awakening from their afternoon nap so soon, and both at the same time.

"How are you feeling?" she asked Jack's stepson.

"My throat hurts real bad," the boy whispered hoarsely.

"I know, Billy. Mumps are no fun, that's for sure."

Jan brushed back the nine-year-old's shoulder-length brown hair with her hand and felt his forehead. His temperature was down from what it had been earlier, but he still felt hot to the touch.

"I'll get you some soup. Be right back."

The boy croaked, "Just water – no, make that ice cream. Please?"

Jan sighed as she went to the kitchen to fill his order. How would they recover if she couldn't get them to eat? Jan hadn't played nursemaid in a long time; she'd forgotten how exhausting it was. But today was her turn, and she was determined to be pleasant about it.

"And I thought work was hectic," she muttered softly a while later during one short respite. She plucked a cushion from the couch on which to rest her tired feet, and caught sight of her reflection in the ornamental living room mirror.

Could I be shrinking? Jan worried, then realized she was slouching. It's bad enough being five foot one without making yourself look even shorter, she chided herself. She sank back onto the couch with a sigh of relief and perched her feet on the now doubly-cushioned footstool. Rest was one commodity that always seemed in short supply.

Jan and Tom shared spacious accommodations on NASA's Ames Research Centre land with Jack and Brenda Foxworth and Brenda's son, Billy. Patchwork though their 'family' was, it was the happiest Jan had ever known. And it became even more cohesive when Brenda and Jack beamingly announced their engagement. Not long afterwards, Billy had looked so dashing in his tiny tuxedo, as he gave his mom away to the man he'd been calling 'daddy' for the past two years. Jan blinked. They've been married four years already?

A coughing jag and low moan brought Jan to her feet. Mumps to a man in his early 40's is no joke, she reminded herself, and hurried into Jack's room.

"How about a little ice cream to coat your throat?" she suggested.

He nodded gratefully, hacking. Jan scooted for the near-empty box in the freezer. She made a mental note to call Tom and have him pick up more on his way home. Jack's coughing set off Billy, so Jan rushed back with the boy's bowl to refill it, too. After fussing with their respective pillows and checking their temperatures, Jan returned to the couch, feeling like she'd run a marathon.

The framed picture of Ablakan, taken at his inauguration three weeks before, coaxed Jan into happy reverie, but the escape was short-lived as another spate of coughing erupted, this time initiated by Billy but soon copied by Jack. She just had them settled again when Tom arrived home, earlier than expected.

"Am I glad to see you!" Jan stood on tiptoes as Tom leaned over to kiss her lips. To Jan, he hadn't aged a day since they arrived at Ames, although his hair was now unanimously gray. Which makes him look even more sexy, Jan thought. Odd that fatigue seemed to heighten her libido, rather than diminish it.

From behind his back, Tom produced a gallon drum of Tutti Frutti ice cream.

"How did you know?" Jan grabbing the precious comestible. "I was going to call you to pick some up." She peered sharply into his eyes. "Has Brenda been giving you telepathy lessons?"

"Don't I wish! About all I can manage is an occasional projection. No, Eric told me we should keep a lot of this on hand, so I got it just in case."

Jan silently thanked nobody in particular that Dr. Eric Rhodes, their grandfatherly boss, had been hauled out of retirement to become Director of Interplanetary Relations.

"You look right worn out, love. Why don't you go lie down? I'll take over for a while."

"That's okay, thanks. Don't forget, you've got your stint on the Hale Telescope tonight."

"No, I don't. Eric gave me the night off. Told me to go home and take care of the 'little missus and the sickies'."

"For real? He said that?"

"Scout's honor," Tom declared, raising the wrong hand in a Scout salute.

"Remind me to hug the stuffing out of him."

Tom gently clasped her shoulders and turned her towards their bedroom. A little push sent her in that direction. "Go rest. Brenda'll be home soon, anyway".

As Jan headed down the hallway, Tom went to check on 'his' patients.

Feeling mildly guilty, Jan nestled her slender body under the covers of their king-size bed. Muffled coughs could be heard down the hall. She shook her head, sheepishly recalling their naïvety six years before in declaring that the world of viruses had been defeated. True, a decontamination process developed by the three original allied worlds had permitted Moohri to return home and now ensured interplanetary travel could be accomplished without fear of spreading disease pathogens. But for medical use, the few chambers on each planet meant months-long medical waiting lists, and the cost of their use was high. Serious viral ailments were being eradicated, but humans remained at the mercy of unpleasantries such as the common cold and mumps.

15

Sleep put an end to further musings, and Tom closed the door to their room soon afterwards so that no sound would disturb her slumber.

On the other side of Earth's sun, a third black pinprick appeared – this time, between Mars and Earth's orbit. Not even space dust was in the vicinity, so the rupture remained virtually undetectable.

* * *

Ablakan was enjoying a hearty breakfast on the balcony when Juneli appeared at his elbow. He looked up in surprise, for she seldom arose this early.

"I don't know," she said, before he could ask. "I just woke up with a funny feeling, like something's about to happen."

Juneli had no measurable telepathic bend, but she had an uncanny sense of anything unusual or out of place. Though she was seldom able to pinpoint the source, Ablakan welcomed any kind of advance warning he could get.

"Person or event?"

"It doesn't feel like a mind" She frowned in her effort to put definition to the feeling.

"I'll put Tix on it, then." Ablakan motioned toward the chair next to his. With a distracted sigh, Juneli accordioned herself down onto it.

"Thanks for the alert, June."

"Just *once* I'd like to get something concrete."

"Perhaps one day you will." Ablakan reached over to pat her clenched fist. "But for now, you're providing something none of us can – a forewarning."

Ablakan winced as a loud knock echoed through his mind.

"Tix is calling," he informed Juneli before opening to the child.

Sir, School wants you to call them as soon as possible.

The multiple life form known as 'School' would telepathically assimilate from anyone who came within range every memory and experience that person had. In return, School transferred data they felt the person could most use. As such, they were an incredible well of knowledge, though as stationary beings they could only interact mentally.

Ablakan thanked her and signed off, relaying the message to Juneli. "School has never sent for anyone – not that I've heard,

16

anyway. It must be important. Think that's what you were picking up on?"

"I don't think so," Juneli replied, looking perplexed. "Though it feels connected somehow."

"I'd better see what they want."

Ablakan hastily gobbled down the last of his breakfast and composed himself in the chair for what might be a lengthy mental conversation. He positioned his focus a discreet distance from School's homeworld and signalled his presence – an unnecessary practice with School, but just barging in felt rude.

A slight tingling sensation just behind the eyebanks told Ablakan his identity was being verified. The feeling disappeared, to be replaced by the mental voice of the multiplicity.

We had a most pleasant visit with Dru Hepiak of Lowen. A very practical species, the Lowens. They will make a great addition to your alliance.

Ablakan listened in surprise. School was a forthright group of egos; idle chatter was the last thing he expected from them. An Earth expression presented itself: 'break it to him gently'. Ablakan tensed, wondering what could be so wrong they could not tell him outright.

Reading this, School projected amusement. *We are striving to learn 'tact'. But perhaps we should practice it on newcomers.* A slight hesitation, then *Dru Hepiak's mind held a puzzle – an encounter with asteroid material where it should not have been, traveling at an incongruous speed and trajectory. We found, just beyond his coordinates, a small singularity – what your human friends call a 'black hole' – which had not been there before.*

Coordinates flashed into Ablakan's mind, and he quickly jotted them down, as School continued.

We have extended our mind in a great search, and among your allied planets, there are sixteen tiny holes in space that we believe were not there until very recently. They feel new, but where matter is being assimilated, they are growing rapidly.

A swarm of butterflies beseiged Ablakan's stomach. This would be his first major 'situation' as a First. *Do you know what is causing them?*

No.

Is there anything about them you have discovered, other than their existence?

Only that there do not appear to be any new ones outside of the areas travelled among your planets.

Ablakan blinked. It sounded like their space travel was somehow causing the anomaly. A disquieting thought niggled. Could teleporting be the culprit? Or even telepathy?

We do not know, School responded, unable to distinguish between Ablakan's personal thoughts and those he was projecting to them. Systematically, School transmitted the coordinates for all sixteen spacial holes.

Thank you for warning us, Ablakan said. *You'll let us know if you find out anything more, won't you?*

Of course.

School's final words faded from Ablakan's mind as they severed the connection.

Juneli listened attentively as he told her what he'd just learned.

Ablakan scratched his neck mane worriedly. "Sixteen. How do you remove multiple singularities?" He wrinkled his nasal-slits at the inadvertent pun.

"Don't feed them?"

"That might slow them down. If it's one of our modes of travel that's causing them, we have to isolate it and make sure it is stopped at once. I'd better tell Tweno." Ablakan regarded his assistant for a moment. "That's what you were picking up on, wasn't it?"

She didn't reply immediately, her eyes attaining a strange, faraway look. When she did speak, her voice was barely audible. "We haven't seen the problem yet, just the footprint that it leaves."

Ablakan had the uncanny feeling he had just heard the prophetic understatement of his life. Closing his eyes, he contacted Tweno, Kyollan and Tix, giving them what little information he had.

Do you know of anyone on any planet who is knowledgeable about black holes? Tweno asked.

No, sir. The humans have some theories, I understand, and may have done some research, but I don't think they know nearly enough for what we're dealing with. But I'll put out an alert through the links.

The 'porting telempaths on each planet – referred to as 'links' because they mentally connected each planet to the others – usually worked for their world's space department. That was also the logical starting place to seek people with an understanding of singularities.

Keep me informed. Tweno signed off.

Ablakan knew Tweno shared his concern, but their Primary was not one to fret. He would deal with a problem once its nature was sufficiently known to suggest a course of action. Till then, he would watch and wait. Ablakan envied Tweno his patience and aplomb, for right now Ablakan was very worried.

Jan was his first port of call. She took in the 'heads up', as she called it, with the same sense of foreboding he had felt from Juneli.

Our scientific types have gotten a lot of data on black holes, but I don't think they have any idea what causes them or how to collapse them, she said, confirming Ablakan's assessment. *I'll get the specialists on it right away, though. What are the coordinates of those holes?*

Ablakan listed them off and projected a sense of reassurance he didn't feel before breaking contact.

Shownae was next on his list. The Orowan doubted they had anything to offer that the humans wouldn't have already discovered, but promised to send Ablakan whatever they had.

The other three allied planets held out little hope of enlightenment from their respective space agencies, but also said they would check.

Finally, Ablakan called on the two planets who were negotiating for entry into their alliance, and even informed the two who had been refused entry. The latter two had been so unpleasant and uncooperative, even at the opening negotiations, that no headway could be made, and they were unanimously voted out of any active trade with the allied planets. Still, they might have vital information on these holes in space, and at the very least, needed to be made aware of the problem and the location of these hazards.

From the start, the conversation with the Aq'Narl did not go well.

Why should we help you? the Regent asked belligerently through his psychic interpreter, when informed of the problem. *Your problem means nothing to us.*

Perhaps not, but singularities do not care what – or who – they pull in. If you choose not to share your knowledge, that is your right, of course. But we at least can tell you where the holes are that we know of.

Proceed, Regent Maxxift said with poor grace. Ablakan listed the coordinates.

That is the last?

Yes, sir, Ablakan confirmed. The Aq'Narl link immediately severed the connection between them.

Ablakan muttered under his breath in disgust. The other non-member summarily refused contact. Ablakan shrugged, leaving them to their uninformed solitude.

Juneli was sitting there, still as a statue, when he opened his eyes. At first he thought she was trying not to distract him, then realized she was tranced herself. A word Jan taught him as a possible description for Juneli's talents came to mind: precognition. He had never heard of it before Jan explained it to him. Could his assistant be Shalaii's first known precog? At length her eyes focused on his face, and she took a deep breath.

"Did you see anything?" Ablakan leaned forward.

She nodded. "A great many holes, and later – it had to be later, because those same holes were suddenly very much bigger – later a bunch of them very close together. And then still later, it was one large funnel in space. Ablakan, I don't like this; I don't like it at all." Her face was unnaturally pale, and Ablakan noticed her hands were trembling.

"I don't either, June, but once again, you have given us a preview of what is to come. That could make a big difference in how we handle it. You didn't see what we were doing about it, did you?"

"No, just those horrible holes. Oh, and the big hole was very close to Shalaii. Much too close."

"June, think carefully. It's not there now?"

"No, I don't believe so."

"Mind if I twin with you? I want to see exactly where it will appear, and if possible, when."

"Yes, of course." Juneli opened her mind like a flower.

Ablakan read her experience of a few moments before. The scenario played out very much as she had described it. Ablakan returned to the beginning, trying to access what happened before the advent of the holes, but could not. Next he strove for a time sense of when the large hole would appear. A vague timeline niggled tantalizingly just beyond reach. Disappointed, Ablakan withdrew, consoling himself that at least now he knew where they would occur, if not when.

Ablakan recorded the locations, then thanked his assistant, adding, "I'd better get on this right away."

"I'll reschedule your appointments. Any too important, I'll ask the Primary or Kyollan to handle."

"I don't know what I'd do without you." Ablakan smiled his gratitude.

"Hopefully, we'll never find out," Juneli said, and disappeared into the house to change.

With a sigh, Ablakan accordioned out of the chair and headed for the office.

* * *

Juneli leaned against her desk, trying to quell the longing and resentment which threatened to overwhelm her. Will he never see me? She ached to tell him how much she loved him, had always loved him. But what right had she, a lowly assistant, to tell the First of Pantai, Shalaii's premier teleporter, that she yearned for him with all her being? Her mouth curled in final judgment: None at all.

* * *

The table between Lead Spacefarers Moohri and Trikon seemed to hold a lot of reports and charts, none of which shed any light on the current situation. Moohri pushed back his chair in defeat. "There's nothing here that can help us."

"Shownae reported from Ablakan that there is a hole that will appear a quarter lightyear from here. If we position sensors all around those coordinates, they may give us some useful data," Trikon suggested.

"Let's hope so." Moohri nodded. "I believe the Shalaians and humans are planning to do the same thing with other holes. Between our findings and theirs, maybe we'll get some answers."

For a minute, neither one spoke, each lost in his own thoughts. Moohri was the elder by three years. Both he and Trikon had the classic Orowan male physique – leathery, pearl-skinned and barrel-chested. Their slender physique near the hips were an asset which permitted rapid movement on all-fours, although the preferred walking stance was upright. Their heads were round and tubular, with single ovoid eyes on three sides. Trikon's pupils were a deep chestnut, and the corners of his eyes slanted upward, a feature the females considered most attractive, to the chagrin of the confirmed bachelor. Moohri's eyes were the more traditional black, and his humanoid mouth, though devoid of lips as all Orowans were, had a sensual pout to it.

Trikon drummed his five stubby flattish digits on the tabletop. "If Ablakan is correct in thinking they are being created by space travel, we might actually cause that hole by 'porting the probes around where it will be."

"That's a possibility," Moohri admitted. "Maybe we should set probes around a distant site, just in case. Then, if we keep everyone away from where this hole is supposed to appear, maybe it won't happen."

Trikon nodded. "It's worth a try."

* * *

Jan had just entered her studylike office at Ames when the phone rang. Eric Rhodes wanted to see her immediately, not his usual 'when you have a minute'.

Must be about those holes, Jan realized as she hurried down the hall to his office. Eric's door, as usual, was open, and she plunked herself down in one of the comfy chairs which were scattered around the room.

"What's up?"

Eric raised a finger, then closed the door behind her and pressed the button on the speaker phone. "She's here, Mr. President."

"Good. Jan, I understand there's been some disturbing escalations in the number of black holes?"

"Not yet, sir. But if Juneli is correct – and so far, she's always been – there will be. We have no idea of the time frame, though."

"So how many are we talking?" A moderate southern drawl crept into the President's tone. It became more pronounced when he was worried.

"As near as Juneli and Ablakan could determine, about 78. Some of them will be quite large – especially the one near Shalaii."

"And they're all along travel routes?"

"Yes, sir."

There was a lengthy silence on the voicebox. "So if we use any form of travel or transport to set up test equipment in the vicinity, we could be creating the holes, not just chronicling them."

"That's the theory," Eric said. "And we can't rule out 'porting or even telepathic transmissions as the culprit."

"So why haven't they shown up before this?" the President asked. "There hasn't been any new travel methods used in the last eight years, leastwise none that I know of. So why now?"

Eric nodded. "It does beg the question. Every member planet is choosing, for their monitors, future holes as near as possible to the furthest edge of their space. If we're lucky, maybe we'll get some answers before too many of these turkeys occur. Trouble is, of course, we don't know which ones will appear first."

"Surely you could figure that out from the size they were when Juneli 'saw' them?" the President asked.

"No, sir," Jan interjected. "According to Tix's latest information from School, they grow in proportion to the amount, or possibly the size, of the matter they ingest."

"You make them sound like they're alive," the President grumbled. He was not in the best of moods, Jan noted, but then, neither was she.

"There's no evidence to support that supposition," Jan told him glibly, ignoring Eric's look of reproach. "But removing all matter within their gravitational pull does seem to be a valid delaying tactic." She blinked before continuing, "Assuming what we're using to clear the area isn't the transport method that produces them."

Unexpectedly, the President chuckled. "Why don't you feed them something they'll choke on?"

Jan's eyes widened, but not at his anthromorphization. "I wonder if that would work. Especially with the very small ones. Like a cork in a bottle."

"Keep me informed of your progress."

"Yes, sir," Jan and Eric replied, almost in unison, just before the President hung up.

"You think it would work?" Eric asked, inclining his head towards the phone.

"Why don't we find out? Where's our furthest tiny one again?"

Silently, Eric located it on the star chart behind his desk, using the coordinates Ablakan had provided.

"Now?" Jan asked hopefully.

"Might as well."

Jan settled herself in the plush chair and closed her eyes. With great care, she positioned her focus in the vicinity of the hole. Although she couldn't see it, her attention immediately zeroed in on a point that felt somehow a lot denser than the surrounding darkness. She approached with caution, even though it was only with her mind. As close as Jan could tell, its aperture was less than a quarter of an inch across.

Splitting her focus the way Ablakan had taught her to do years before, Jan searched nearby space for a suitable 'plug'. A rock, perhaps a foot long, seemed perfect for the job. It had a pointed end, rapidly increasing in diameter to about nine inches at its widest.

Jan positioned the rock so the point would go straight into the opening. Even holding it in place with her mind, she could feel the inexorable pull the hole exacted on the object. Jan guided the rock, doing her best to keep it aligned as the gravitational pull increased. When she could no longer control it, she let it go and it jammed itself into the hole.

She backed off a bit and watched opposing cosmic forces at work. The hole had stretched to perhaps three-quarters of an inch across, but that was as wide as it could go. Jan waited, but the rock showed no evidence of crumbling. Satisfied at last, she returned her focus to Eric's office.

Her boss lifted a querying eyebrow.

"It's plugged and seems stable that way, at least for now. I'll keep an eye on it, though."

24

"Do that. It's a lot simpler than trying to keep space debris out of its way. You going to let the others know?"

"Why don't we wait till tomorrow? If it's still in place and hasn't grown, I'll tell them and start plugging all the smaller holes in our area. Maybe even try the same with the bigger ones, d'you think?"

"*Distant* bigger ones," Eric cautioned.

Jan nodded. "Definitely. And I'd like to peek at where that big hole will appear, see if there's anything of interest in the vicinity."

"Find out what you can, and keep me apprised. Saunders is riding my case for answers."

Jan could believe it. Saunders ran NASA with a fair but iron hand.

Eric began shuffling papers, an obvious cue the meeting was over. Jan excused herself and returned to her office. Something niggled at her mind; something about where the big hole would be. What had Ablakan said? A bunch of tiny holes close together. That would suggest repeated stops at that site by whatever travel method was causing them. The hole was to appear very near Shalaii, but somewhat outside the route between Shalaii and Orowa.

Jan studied her star chart of the location. There was nothing of interest in that vicinity. Most people avoided it, in fact, because of the asteriods that littered the area.

Could someone be *mining* the asteroid field? If so, and if their form of travel was causing singularities where they stopped, that would explain why there would be so many holes so close together. Perhaps those rocks were worth a closer look.

At that moment, Tom stuck his head through the doorway.

"Hi, hon. Am I interrupting?" he asked.

"No, you're just the person I need, in more ways than one." Jan grinned at him, and they shared a quick kiss. "I just had an idea, but I'd like to run it by you first in case I'm missing something obvious."

"Don't know how I can help. You're the expert in these areas."

"Not in asteroids," Jan pointed out.

"Me neither. What's the question?"

Jan explained what she had been thinking.

Tom pursed his lips, looking thoughtful. "You could be right. That pretty well leaves out Earth and Orowa. Neither go in for mechanical travel; they just 'port wherever they want to go. And they wouldn't be mining asteroids on the sly; they'd clear it with Shalaii first."

"But if a special-interest group somewhere thinks Shalaii wouldn't give them permission, they might just mine it on the q.t." Jan considered first one then another of the newer member planets. "Something valuable they want all to themselves."

"Doesn't have to be a member planet," Tom noted. "We know the forms of travel they use, and a bit about what the two planets negotiating for entry have. But the two rejects kept theirs to themselves, remember."

Jan grimaced. Despite their behavior, calling the disqualified candidates 'rejects' seemed a bit harsh.

"Why don't you check with School, see if they ever shared knowledge with an Aq'Narl or Shrylter? They might know."

"There's a thought." Jan leaned back and sent her mind into a parking orbit above School. A tingling moment inside her skull was replaced with a happy feeling from the planet below.

Jan, you are welcome. You have a question for us?

Thank you, yes. Jan projected to them her speculations, then waited quietly while the grouped minds sorted through their mountain of data.

There has only been one contact with an Aq'Narl – a renegade who was near death after his ship was almost destroyed in his escape. But that was centuries ago. He died before we could assist him. No Shrylter has ever approached our world.

Pity, Jan sighed.

There are presently two holes close to the asteroid field. If you hide a sensor in the field, you may learn what you seek.

We may at that, Jan smiled, perversely pleased to find School had a devious side to them.

We learn from our contacts, School said goodnaturedly, in obvious reference to her thoughts.

Jan thanked them and withdrew.

"Anything?" Tom asked when her eyes opened.

26

"Neither species ever exchanged knowledge with School – big surprise. But School, if you can believe it, suggested we hide a probe in the debris field and see who, if anyone, comes around."

Tom's jaw dropped most satisfyingly. "You're kidding? School said that?"

"Or words to that effect. There's hope for them yet," Jan smirked.

"Well, I'll be!" Tom was silent for a moment, then his face took on an uncharacteristically malevolent grin. "Why don't you snatch one of the smaller asteroids, and we can have the technical guys here hollow it out and put the probe inside? Just leave suitable holes for the sensors."

"I wouldn't mind finding out what's so interesting about those rocks, anyway," Jan agreed. She pressed a button on her phone system and a disembodied voice said, "Decontam". Jan asked if she could 'port an asteroid into the chamber, and was told there was no previously-scheduled traffic for the next half-hour.

"What size and shape is the probe?" Jan asked Tom. "And what kind of information can it gather?"

"Don't know. But I can find out pretty fast. While I do, why don't you clear this with Eric, just to stay on his good side?"

"Will do." They left the room, headed in opposite directions.

"We'd better check with our member planets first," Eric said, vetoing immediate 'porting of an asteroid.

Jan opened her mouth to object, but he raised a hand. "I know; the leaders may not know if someone on their world is playing fast and loose in Shalaian territory. Just let them know what you're planning. You can ask them to sit tight, and assure them you'll report whatever you find out."

Jan looked skeptical, but Eric was adamant.

"They'll agree, Jan. They have as much at stake as we do."

"That's true. I'll call Ablakan first, as it's their rock I'd be poaching."

Eric nodded. "Remember what Epash told Ablakan: 'Hierarchy is the cornerstone of diplomacy'."

Jan's expression turned sheepish. "Not exactly my long suit, is it?"

"Nope." He softened the comment with a smile.

"Maybe one day I'll learn it from School."

* * *

Tix was not having a good day. First it was School awakening her at an uncouth hour – and the message wasn't even for her. Worse, they declined to tell her what it was about. She sniffed in disapproval. For a ridiculously advanced lifeform, they sure knew little about fair play and natural curiosity. And now, to top it off, the Primary and all the Shalaian links except her were in a meeting. She had been asked to manage all by herself. That was 10 minutes ago and already she was being bombarded from all sides by 'porting requests.

Swallowing her pique, Tix sorted through the waiting traffic, prioritized them and began 'porting cargo to its destination as courteously as she could.

In his office, Primary Tweno was also trying not to frown. *But who would do such a thing? Even if those asteroids were valuable, there are enumerable rocks throughout the galaxy. Why come all the way out here to get some?*

I have no idea, Jan said. *I may be dead wrong on this, but if they are being mined, hollowing out a rock would give us two things: It might tell us why someone would want them in the first place, and with a probe inside, we could get solid evidence – pictures and such – of who's invading your space.*

Why don't we each take a few of them and test them out, then compare notes? Ablakan suggested. *What would be worthless rock to one of us might be treasure to the other, and we'd miss the significance if only one of us is testing it.*

Good point, Jan said.

Then it is agreed. Thank you, Jan. Tweno withdrew from the link and signalled Kyollan, who followed suit. *Kyollan, please put me through to the other links. I need to talk to my counterparts. Perhaps they know who might be interested in those asteroids.*

Meanwhile, Ablakan was shaking his head in dismay. *I was just remembering the location of the other holes, Jan. If you're right, it also means that that species has been – or will be, in many cases, if Juneli's visions are accurate – traveling all around each of our solar systems without making their presence known. There can't be asteroids in every one of those locations. In fact, I know for sure there aren't in at least six of them. So what are the*

28

*travellers doing there? They're expending time, fuel, manpower –
for what?*

*I wish I knew. Perhaps we'd better start scanning our regions,
see if we pick up anyone dropping by unannounced.*

*The other links and leaders should be forewarned. I'd better
call Tweno back before he talks to them,* Ablakan said, about to
close the connection.

*Oh, when he does, maybe he could mention a little experiment I
just tried. It's still too early to tell if it'll work long-term, but they
may want to do the same around their solar systems.* Jan
proceeded to describe her 'hole-plugging' exercise.

Your President thought of it? Ablakan asked in disbelief.

Yup. Surprised me, too.

* * *

Dru Hepiak sat in his space cruiser, uncertain what to do next.
He had just received a most disturbing call from Lowen's
Supreme Commander, informing him of the singularities and the
possibility their new cold-fusion drive was causing the holes. The
message, chasing him across space, had taken all day to reach
Dru. Now, still a day away from his meeting on Shyr, he had been
instructed to cut engines and await further instructions.

Dru absently chewed a blunt webbed forefinger spike. It
certainly wouldn't help their efforts to join the alliance if they
were causing holes all over the known galaxy. He punched a
series of buttons on his com oval, and moments later a
disembodied voice announced he'd reached Shyr
Communications.

This is Dru Hepiak of Lowen, he told the voice. *May I be
connected with Link Shownae as soon as possible? There has
been a . . . development.*

I will contact him, the voice replied.

Dru silently thanked School for having taught him English
through mental transference. It would certainly make negotiations
a lot easier.

A quiet knocking interrupted Dru's thoughts. Since this was his
first direct experience with long-range telepathy, Dru opened up
with great care.

Greetings, sir, Shownae said cheerfully in the Lowen's mind.

Greetings, Shownae. I am sorry to disturb you. I am to negotiate on Shyr tomorrow but our Supreme Commander, Pel Taefek, said I must shut off my engines in case they are creating holes in space.

I could 'port you and your ship to Shyr, if you like.

That would be very helpful. Abruptly, Dru found himself blinking in the unaccustomed sunlight reflecting off the spaceport's glistening surface. *Thank you.*

My pleasure.

Dru felt the Orowan split his focus to contact the receiving tower, assuring them Dru was there with permission.

I will join you inside, Shownae said before disengaging.

That surprised the Lowen. He had not expected Shownae to meet him personally. Dru extricated his slender body from the cockpit and stretched out the kinks. He wore no clothing, for his thick silver fur made outerwear unnecessary except in extreme conditions. His chest, stomach and abdomenal areas were divided into three flattened, semi-separate globes, each protected underneath with a remarkably strong band of muscle. Lowen physiology might appear fragile because of their small bones, but Dru knew from personal experience how resilient his dense bone and muscle could be.

It had perplexed him the first time he shook hands with people from these allied worlds. In every instance, they had clasped his hand carefully, as though afraid to shatter it. Surprisingly, they seemed undisturbed by his split-hemisphere head, the chasm extending down to just above his nose. His had been the only species he had seen thus far to sport this particular feature. He was rather proud that he also had not gawked at some of the peculiar anatomies he had seen during the initial visit.

The green light flashed on in the decontamination room, putting an end to his idle thoughts. Dru stepped out into the waiting area and gripped the Orowan's hand without hesitation.

"Would you mind if we reconvene on Orowa? Our Lead Spacefarers are eager to talk with you," Shownae explained. They entered the receiving lounge beyond the chamber. Through the window, Dru could see his cruiser being lowered into the parking area, to make room for the next ship waiting to land.

"I am here to answer." Dru bobbed his head twice. "But I have only just learned of these holes."

"Will you hold my wrist for a moment?"

Dru complied, and was immediately inside another decontam chamber, with Shownae beside him. At the end of the procedure, they stepped out into the Orowan receiving room. Shownae pressed a series of numbers on a wall unit and spoke quietly in his own language before turning back to Dru.

"Lead Spacefarers Moohri and Trikon will be available shortly. Can I offer you refreshments?"

Dru swallowed, realizing his mouth was indeed dry. "Thank you."

Shownae's eyes (well, the two that were visible to Dru from this angle) glazed over slightly, presumably to telepathically place an order.

"Actually, you may have been the first person to have come across one of these holes, other than, presumably, whoever made them," Shownae told him while they waited. "School picked up on the anomaly you recorded two days ago."

"You mean the asteroids?" Dru asked, suddenly realizing the significance of that event.

"Yes. There was a small hole quite close by, but you were probably going fast enough and at a sharp enough angle that you didn't notice."

"There was a small slowing," Dru admitted. "But nothing showed on my instruments."

"We all owe you much for that information," Shownae inclined his head. "Time may be a big factor. The more knowledge we can gather, the better."

Dru squirmed in his seat, uncomfortably aware that his people might be responsible for what was happening. A tan-uniformed Orowan arrived, bearing a tray on which were an impressive array of foods and beverages. Some of them were unfamiliar to Dru, so he chose the ones he had sampled during his previous visit. He smiled his appreciation to his host and the server.

They ate in silence, for which Dru was also grateful. It seemed the Orowans were aware of Lowen disinclination to speak while consuming foodstuffs. It was good of Shownae to respect Dru's custom. They were nearly finished when the wall com unit tingled for attention.

Shownae pressed a button. A brief exchange followed.

"Moohri and Trikon are free whenever you are," Shownae said.

"When you are finished." Dru had cleaned his plate, but Shownae's snack was only partially consumed.

"I had a bite earlier." Shownae gestured towards the hallway on their right. Dru slowed his gait, noting that Shownae was struggling to keep up. Dru grinned inwardly. He was considered short by Lowen standards, having reached only eight feet before his growth had inexplicably stopped. But considering Orowan ceiling heights, perhaps it was just as well.

Shownae indicated a conference room, to which the door was open. Dru ducked his head and entered. He kept his head lowered in a bow to the two occupants of the room.

"Captain Hepiak, we are honored by your presence," Moohri said as they shook hands.

"It is good of you to meet with us on such short notice," Trikon added, unwittingly stealing the very words the Lowen had intended to say.

"Thank you both," Dru replied.

The requisite offer of beverages was turned down with thanks, leaving them free to get down to business.

Moohri clasped his hands together, evidently choosing his words with care. "Captain Hepiak —"

"Please call me 'Dru'." The Lowen smiled to show he meant no disrespect.

"Thank you," Moohri bowed slightly. "Dru, we do not know what is causing these holes, or the ones that we have reason to believe will soon appear. But as we told your government, we suspect it is caused by some form of transport. It could be mental (like teleportation) or physical (like propulsion systems). At this point, we simply don't know. And we are not trying to pry into what kind of drive you use. But if you could find out where in this sector your people have gone lately, we could see if the list matches up with the location of the known holes."

"I will check. We have a new drive, but we will not use it until we know." Dru's stomach muscles were painfully tight. How could his people remove those holes if it turned out the Lowens had been causing them?

Moohri and Trikon exchanged glances.

"Shownae could put you through to your Supreme Commander now, if that is acceptable."

Dru nodded assent. Presently, the Orowan's faraway look changed to a quiet smile.

"Your telempath, Sat Frundal, is getting Commander Taefek now," Shownae informed him. Then Dru felt himself being linked, and Frundal and Tefek were verbally there, as tangibly as if they were in the same room with him.

Supreme Commander, deep apologies for the interruption, Dru began respectfully in their own language, but Taepek waved it aside.

We must speak frankly and quickly, Taepek said. *Have the Orowans asked to inspect our new drive?*

No, Commander. They ask only if we can tell them where our cruisers have been, so they can check if those places now have spacial holes.

Perhaps they already know about the drive from School.

I did not get that impression. They have honored our customs and I feel no guile or insincerity among those I have spoken to, Dru reported. All Lowens were at least partially empathic, and many were telepathic as well. Dru was in training to increase his innate abilities, but doubted he would ever approach the range of their main telempath, Frundal.

I would agree, Commander, Sat Frundal interjected. *Shownae's mind and feelings are completely open, and he has full trust in the Spacefarers. I believe they are as they seem.*

Then for now, we will assume that they are, Taepek decided. *Captain, if the situation requires it, allow them to investigate your drive. But only if evidence is found linking it to those holes. Frundal will call Shownae with our travel itineraries.*

Thank you, Commander, Dru said, his heart much lightened. Then in English, he told Shownae the discussion was over, and the link was ended.

Dru turned to the Orowans. "We will provide a list of where in Alliance space Lowens have traveled."

33

Moohri inclined his head. "We are grateful, Dru. And please be assured that, even if it turns out the new drive created the holes, we understand it was not intentional. It will have no effect on our negotiations with your world. Of that I am certain."

"That is most kind." Dru felt his muscles relax a bit.

"The negotiators from the other planets will not arrive until tomorrow," Trikon remembered. "Would you stay at my home overnight? I was planning to attend a ricari performance, and I would welcome the company."

"Thank you, yes!" Lowens admired athletic prowess, and Dru had been deeply impressed by his one exposure to ricari.

* * *

In the asteroid belt near Shalaii, a small cargo ship activated its suction field. Slowly at first, then with greater speed, several large rocks within its sphere of influence were drawn inexorably toward the open maw in the ship's underbelly. Once the objects were aboard, the door sealed shut and the vessel covertly accelerated towards its next destination.

Behind it, a pucker formed at the exact spot where the suction field had been most intense. In time, the pucker became a minute bubble pushing outward into space, to silently explode an instant later into a black hole. At the moment of its appearance, the direction of the flow reversed. But this new hole had the misfortune of attracting an asteroid far too large for it to accommodate. The rock plugged it firmly, and the hole had no choice but to hold it fast.

CHAPTER 3

"I need a softer covering," a dispassionate part of Ablakan realized, as he painfully extricated his legs from his office furniture preparatory to picking himself up off the floor. To his left, an aggrieved Shnookums licked a patch of hair back into place, eyeing his owner balefully. She had only wished to capture one of those long, fast-moving legs of his. He didn't have to go sprawling like that, almost squashing her in the process. Pointedly, Shnookums turned her back on him, her tail twitching in disapproval.

The sound of running feet caught her attention.

"Sir, are you alright?"

"Yes, but be careful of —"

"*Aaaaaaaa!*"

Ablakan desperately scrambled to one side as the janitor's enormous bulk hurtled towards him at an impossible angle. The floor reverberated as the servant landed with a resounding thud.

"*Shnook!* Stop that!" Ablakan yelled at the marauding feline. "I'm sorry, Bennan. I don't know how she got here; I locked her in the house before I left."

"It was my fault, sir," the janitor said, disentangling one of his legs from Ablakan's. "I did not close the door quickly enough when I left your quarters, and she ran out between my legs. I have been trying to find her ever since, but I see you found her first."

"More like she found me," Ablakan said, rubbing his bruised knee. "I will have to make suitable arrangements for her, I see. I had not realized cats were so – resourceful."

Juneli appeared at the door, taking in the pair's disheveled appearance. Shnookums made a dash for her legs, and Juneli scooped her up neatly, holding her at eye level but out of reach of her claws.

"No you don't, little one," she told the kitten sternly. "You've caused enough trouble for one day." Juneli turned her quizzical eyebanks toward Ablakan. "Same place?"

"For now, yes," Ablakan said, thanking her with a smile. "Till I can come up with another solution."

Bennan and Juneli departed, the latter carrying the squirming cat.

35

Ablakan settled himself behind his magnificent desk and sent his focus into the asteroid field that was, or would become, the site of multiple black holes. He frowned. Where there had been two, now three holes were present. They would have to work fast if they wished to prevent the large hole he had viewed through Juneli's memory from forming. There was no shortage of rock samples, so Ablakan chose an asteroid at random. It was just over two feet long and a foot-and-a-half wide. He transported it directly into the decontamination chamber, then 'ported himself into the adjoining room to press the button automating the decontam sequence. Once complete, the rock would be ready for analysis.

One of the lights immediately began flashing red – an indication that radiation levels were well above normal. He checked the readout and gulped. Not just above normal; far beyond safe. Ablakan quickly 'ported it back from whence it came, then 'pathed a call to Dr. Saunders at NASA headquarters.

Ablakan? Is something wrong? Saunders asked, his surprise evident in feelings as well as speech. In eight years, this was only the third time Ablakan had called him directly, using the technique Brenda had taught them for speaking inside a non-telepath's mind.

I have a little problem. I 'ported a rock from our asteroid field into my decontam chamber, only to find the radiation level was almost off the scale, so I sent it back. Now I have to find a way to decontaminate the chamber itself. I was hoping you might have some ideas.

Interesting, Saunders said. *Could you identify the radioactive element?*

No, the chamber's not set up for that – yet.

I'll send a mop-up crew over if you like, Saunders offered.

I'd appreciate that, Ablakan told him, adding, *There is a third hole in the field now. I found it just before I brought in the sample.*

So the field is being mined. With radiation levels that high, you won't be able to use sensors to find who's doing it, either. Saunders was silent for a few moments. *It would be a drain on everyone, but I suggest you set up round-the-clock 'pathic surveillance of that field. You can count on my links to help out, and I suspect the Orowans will volunteer theirs, too, if you make up a schedule.*

Excellent idea. I'll check with the Orowans and put it together immediately. Oh, and please remind Jan not to 'port to Earth any asteroids. He withdrew from Saunders' mind and called Shownae, with a request that he link Moohri and Trikon so Ablakan could speak to them altogether. Once they were in mental contact, Ablakan related his discovery and the conversation he'd had with Saunders.

A rapid-fire exchange ensued among the Orowans.

Count on our links to help, Trikon stated. *Shownae, when you have the timetable, you'll set it up among your people?*

Gladly.

We have one possible development at this end, Moohri volunteered, and described events concerning Dru Hepiak and the Lowen's new drive. *We're awaiting their travel logs.*

Ablakan thought a moment, then said, *Why not ask him to let you 'port his ship someplace out of harm's way, fire up his drive and do anything he can think of that might conceivably cause a hole to appear, then monitor the site for a while?*

I never thought of that, Moohri said.

Me neither, admitted Trikon. *He's staying with me till tomorrow. I'll ask him right away. Thanks.*

Juneli does the same for me sometimes, when I get too caught up in a problem. Ablakan smiled, knowing how they felt.

Ablakan's final call was to Tweno, to give him an update. Like Ablakan, Tweno was shocked by the radioactive nature of the field so near their homeworld.

Ablakan had just signed off when he smelled the subtle aroma of Juneli's perfume. He opened his eyes with a welcoming smile.

"There is a young lady asking for an appointment," Juneli told him. "A very *attractive* young lady, I am told."

"Told by whom?"

"Saymin. He said this lady asked him to check if she could see you."

Ablakan frowned reflectively. "Saymin, hmm? Can you recall his exact words?"

Juneli's pupils shot to the roof of her eyebanks as she played back her memory of the conversation. " 'Can you get this very attractive young lady in to see the boss, maybe late this afternoon?' Those were his exact words. Now she is on the hear-other, asking for an appointment."

"I thought so," Ablakan nodded grimly. "He's trying to set me up. He's mate-hunting again."

"He means well," Juneli stated, but Ablakan noticed she looked none too happy about it.

"Alright, find out if she has a legitimate need to see me on some professional matter, and if so, give her an appointment. Otherwise, just cite my heavy workload and so on."

"Will do." Juneli turned smartly towards her office with a tiny smile.

It sure is wonderful having Juneli to pinch-hit for me, on top of what a good business mind she has, Ablakan thought. Her precognitive abilities was an added bonus he'd had no right to expect. He sniffed appreciatively of her waning fragrance in the room. She was indeed one in a million.

* * *

Dru looked up in surprise as Moohri and Trikon came toward him. He was being given a tour of the Spacefarer Academy and hadn't expected to see the Spacefarers until much later.

"Can you spare us a few minutes?"

"Certainly." Dru smiled an apology to the tour guide and followed the pair. Once out of earshot, Trikon told Dru about Ablakan's suggestion.

"What movements might make a black hole?"

"I have no idea, not knowing what capabilities your craft has," Moohri began. "But if a ship is mining that asteroid belt near Shalaii, they'd have to use some sort of field to bring the rocks on board. And perhaps some scanning device to identify the elements they want. Or maybe it's just sitting in space with the capture field on that is causing it. Who knows? We would appreciate any experiments you could think to try."

"I could go now," Dru offered.

In a surprisingly short time, Dru found himself in his cockpit, his cruiser 13 lightyears from Orowan space.

"What I wouldn't give to learn to teleport," Dru murmured, as he set about performing a series of manoeuvres which he hoped would not cause any holes and would prove their drive system was harmless to space. The experiments took the better part of an hour, for 'parking over time under energy-drain' was a test in itself. Also, his little craft was impressively versatile, and it took a while to exhaust its repertoire.

Finally, Dru signalled the Orowans he had done all he could think of, and he and the ship once again sat on the parking base on Shyr. He went through the mandatory physical clearances, and Shownae 'ported him back to Moohri's office, where Trikon and Moohri awaited.

"We thank you for your efforts," Moohri said. "Now all we can do is monitor the area to ensure no one else goes there, and see if any holes appear. Personally, I don't believe they will. Whoever is mining Shalaii's asteroid field obviously wants that radioactive element, and from what I gather, your people have no use for such things."

"None that I know of," Dru corrected. "But I do not know all that goes on on my planet."

"Too true," Trikon chuckled. "With the huge amount of trade among the allied worlds now, I can't keep up with the new developments." He turned a querying look on Moohri, while continuing to address Dru. "If there's nothing else we're needed for, why don't we have an early dinner, then take in the ricari event?"

"Nothing more here," Moohri said blandly. "Have a good time."

Dru nodded with a happy smile, relieved the tests were over for the day. He bowed to Moohri, and followed Trikon out the door.

"I've made a reservation for us at one of our better restaurants," Trikon was saying. "I couldn't risk an interplanetary incident by poisoning their ambassador with my cooking."

"Then we have something in common," Dru hummed. "My mate will not let me near the cooker, either. Too dangerous."

* * *

Ablakan sighed gratefully. The day's work, at least officially, was over, and he looked forward to a quiet evening. Or as much of one as Shnookums would allow him to have. Fond as he was of the kitten, he found himself wondering if the cat should be construed as a gift or one of Jan's humorous tricks.

The internal com link on his hear-other began flashing, making its discreet burping sound. Fearing the worst – that Shnookums was again on the loose and wreaking havoc – Ablakan pressed the button. The disembodied voice of the complex supervisor addressed him diffidently.

"Sir, there is a young lady here to see you. She believes you forgot to give her an appointment, and she hopes to see you anyway. Should I schedule her for another day?"

Ablakan sighed in annoyance. Undoubtedly, this would be the 'attractive young lady'. He couldn't decide whether to consider her persistence a virtue or impudence.

"Sir?" the voicebox prompted.

"I'll see her now. Please send her up." Ablakan glanced around the office. It was somewhat cluttered but not really messy. Anyway, he had no desire to impress her.

In less than five minutes, the supervisor and a tallish woman came into view. Ablakan had to admit the term 'attractive' seemed to have been coined with her in mind.

"Wiki to see you, sir." The supervisor bowed and left.

"Greetings, Wiki. Please be seated. How might I help you?"

"First Ablakan, it is good of you to see me without a formal appointment," she began, putting the tiniest emphasis on 'formal'. Her voice was delightfully musical, and Ablakan found himself becoming fully attentive.

"I have many talents of which you could avail yourself."

Talents? Ablakan's interest quickened. Might she be a 'path? Or a precog, like Juneli?

"Not *those* kinds of talents." She smiled, accurately interpreting his expression. "But I have remarkable organizational skills, I am told. I have managed the Chani Museum for the past two years, and the Kraxa complex before that."

Ablakan eyebanks widened in recognition. Running either of those operations would be a monumental task, he knew.

"But why would you wish to work here? After all, our facilities would be less of a challenge than what you have been doing."

He noticed he was leaning forward, eager to hear her reasons. Ablakan made a point of leaning back in his chair.

"You are far too modest, First," she said, flashing him a radiant smile. "The facility itself may be smaller, but you have your finger on the pulse of the known universe. I have had much contact with our otherworldly business interests, but working for such an influential person as you would be a great honor."

With an effort, Ablakan pulled his eyes away from her radiant face. Immediately, the room dimmed noticeably.

"If you would leave me your employment profile, I will give it my earliest attention," Ablakan said. "But I cannot promise anything. I already have a wonderful assistant who runs the office for me."

Wiki rested her hand on Ablakan's for an instant.

"You misunderstand, sir. I have absolutely no wish to replace anyone, only to . . . augment your existing staff." She rose in one fluid motion. "Perhaps we could meet at another time, after you have read my profile."

She reached into her carry-all and produced a slim, exquisitely-bound document which she placed on the desk before him.

"My code is in there as well," she said, flashing one more devastating smile in Ablakan's direction.

She left then, but the office flatly refused to dissipate the sensual aroma of her perfume.

For a long time, Ablakan just sat there, gazing in the direction of her departure. Somehow, 'attractive' seemed too mild a description of her. A part of him longed to have that beautiful creature on staff in any capacity which would allow him to bask in her smile. But if he thought Shnookums could turn his life upside-down, Ablakan had no doubt Wiki could do so tenfold.

* * *

"I'm tired of these mindless shows," Jack Foxworth said plaintively. "What I'd really like is to go for a walk. I can't lie around here forever."

Brenda beamed at her husband. Yes, he was definitely improving. But the doctor had insisted he and Billy stay in until the physician came to check on them the following day. Brenda intended to see to it both 'her' patients complied. But as their health returned, it brought with it an understandable urge to break out of their quarantine. Or house arrest, as Jack preferred to call it.

"Tomorrow." Brenda leaned forward to check Jack's forehead, and grinned. A most unpatientlike gleam had sprung into Jack's eyes as her loose-fitting blouse shifted to reveal two of her finest physical assets.

"As long as I must stay in," he began.

"You're definitely going to live," Brenda smiled. "And your temperature is nicely down. Let's keep it that way, shall we? I promise; as soon as the doc gives the word . . . " Her grin finished the sentence for her.

"Okay, Warden," Jack replied with feined petulance.

"Anyway, right now I have to split my focus between you and that asteroid field. When you get the 'all clear' from Doc Morrison, I want all my focus to be on you."

Jack reached up to capture her hand. "I'll hold you to that, milady."

* * *

"How was your day, sir?" Saymin asked, as he helped Ablakan out of his office clothes and into loungewear.

"Confusing." Which was an understatement.

"I hear you had an unusual visitor."

Ablakan glanced sharply at his valet. "You wouldn't have had something to do with that, would you?"

"I may have mentioned to Wiki how overworked you and Juneli are," Saymin admitted. His hands expertly adjusted the garment to leave the mane free, the way Ablakan preferred it.

"Anything else you 'just happened' to tell her about us?" Ablakan demanded irritably. Sometimes Saymin could be a royal pain.

The valet's manner turned apologetic. "I may have said you seem lonely here in this big complex by yourself, with just the staff for company."

"Saymin –"

The hear-other chose that moment to bleep for attention, and Ablakan snatched it up in exasperation.

"First." He winced, realizing how belligerent he must sound, so he added, "How may I help you?"

"Can you send someone to get your cat out of my seejak tree, sir? Please?" asked a plaintive voice Ablakan recognized as belonging to his next-door neighbor. "It has been knocking down fruit and now it is tearing the bark off the limbs."

"Yes, I'm sorry. I will send someone right away."

Ablakan hung up the instrument and dropped his head in his hands with a groan.

Mercifully, when Ablakan opened his eyebanks the next morning, Schnookums was still curled up in a ball by his feet. He smiled at the diminutive troublemaker, tempted to make efforts to confine it Priority One. Black holes were frightening, but Schnook was a menace.

The timememometer showed it was still quite early, but Ablakan was wide awake. He threw back the blankets and prepared to face the challenges of another day. This time, he had dressed himself before Saymin realized he was up. The valet gave him a reproachful look when he saw that his services wouldn't be needed that morning.

"I couldn't sleep any more," Ablakan told him in a conciliatory manner, while wondering why he should feel the need to justify getting up early and dressing himself.

"Yes, sir." Saymin withdrew with a small bow.

At least this time Schnook hadn't attacked the valet.

Ablakan 'ported himself to the kitchen and consumed a hasty meal. An idea was forming that he wanted to try out before Juneli awakened. His office seemed the natural location from which to test his hypothesis. He placed himself there, settled into his cushiony chair, and closed his eyes in concentration.

Immediately, his focus located the three holes in the asteroid field. None had grown appreciably overnight, so Ablakan surmised there had been no materials within range of their limited influence. His focus expanded to include all of the rocks that made up the Shalaian asteroid field, then he mentally 'tagged' each rock so that any change of location would immediately draw his attention.

Satisfied, Ablakan withdrew. It should no longer be necessary for all the 'paths to take turns monitoring the field. He placed a call to Jan, who had taken up the habit of rising early.

Good morning, Jan, Ablakan smiled. *How are Jack and Billy?*

Much better today, thanks. The doctor is letting them come and go as their energy permits. Which means, no more babysitting.

To Ablakan, she sounded greatly relieved.

Have there been any more hell holes in your asteroid belt? Jan asked.

Hell holes?

Well, we're going to have a helluva time collapsing them, now that they're here, not to mention those Juneli foresaw, Jan replied.

Hell holes. Ablakan savored the term. *That's a good description for them. Just the new one yesterday. But I had an idea.*

He explained what he had done, and added *I need you to remove a rock and 'port it anywhere you like, so I can see if I can track it.*

How about this? Jan asked, a smile in her mental tone.

Ablakan had felt the rock change position. Now he searched for that mote of 'him-focus' that he had attached to it and found it nestled behind Uranus. He 'ported it back in place.

It works, he announced unnecessarily. *Thanks, Jan. I'll let everyone know they don't have to watch the field any more.*

What field? she inquired drolly. *Oh, you mean that little rock garden you have in your back yard?*

Very radioactive *rock garden,* Ablakan pointed out. *You might even call them 'hot rocks'.* He closed with a chuckle. It wasn't often he could beat Jan at her own game of bad puns.

Juneli appeared in the doorway as he was opening his eyebanks. "Getting an early start?"

"I found a more direct way to track our miners." He gave her the details. "Would you get Tix to pull all the 'paths off guard duty? Remind her to thank them all for us."

Juneli scribbled the notation on her 'scriber for later. Ablakan knew that Tix wouldn't be up yet, or if she was, she'd be stuffing her face. With my muchipans from the palace kitchen, no doubt, he thought enviously. Delicious as his chef's pastries were, they just couldn't measure up to those he remembered. His new location came at a heavy price.

"I hear you had a visitor after I left," Juneli said nonchalantly as she placed the day's itinerary before him.

"Saymin's doing again, but this one was above average. Well above average," he amended reminiscently.

Juneli's gaze turned wary. "What did she want, if you don't mind my asking? The usual?"

"Perhaps. She has held some impressive positions, and said she's looking for a challenge, like organizing this office." Ablakan saw his assistant bristle, and raised a hasty hand. "As an adjunct to you, so you could assist me more closely with the offworlders."

Juneli didn't seem convinced. "What did you say to that?"

"Nothing, really. She just left her resume, and I told her I'd get to it when I could."

That seemed to mollify Juneli somewhat.

"You can go through it if you like. I don't know when I'd have the time."

Juneli picked up the document and tucked it behind her 'scriber. "What's on tap for today, besides finding out who's making those holes?"

Ablakan smiled inwardly. Along with basic English, Juneli was picking up slang human terms and using them every chance she got.

He handed her a thick folder. "It's in order of importance, but it doesn't all need to be done today. Mostly routine stuff."

She was leafing through it as she strolled into her own office.

Now that they had a means of, hopefully, learning who was mining their asteroids, the next order of business was figuring out how to collapse those holes which had already formed. Ablakan placed his awareness near School. If anyone would know, it should be them.

School opened to him with a warm, flowing welcome.

You come about the holes, they discerned. *We do not have the information you seek, but perhaps understanding them and the nature of space would help you.*

The tickling sensation lasted several seconds, during which Ablakan would have sworn his head expanded to twice its size.

What can I offer you in exchange? Ablakan asked, once his mind had settled from the experience.

If you find the solution, let us know of it.

You have my word. And thanks.

He sat for a long time, pulling back what he had been given, and committing it to the 'scriber. It was the finest Shalaii had to offer, and allowed him to enter the details verbally. When he had dredged up the last of the implanted data, Ablakan read it back, trying to see the 'big picture'.

Not for the first time, Ablakan wondered if information he received from School was accurate. Their view of space was so

45

foreign to currently-held beliefs that he found it suspect. But if they were right . . .

Ablakan was still sifting through the ramifications when a gentle knock sounded in his mind.

Greetings, Ablakan, Shownae began. *We had Dru Hepiak of the Lowens try every way he could to make holes in space –*

Jan calls them 'hell holes', Ablakan interjected with a chuckle.

Hmm, they might as well be, Shownae agreed. *Anyway, no holes appeared, so I think we can assume their new drive is not to blame.*

They must be relieved.

Indeed they are. I was just talking to Jan, and she told me about your tagged rocks. I must try that sometime; it sounds like a handy skill. Have there been any other developments in your area?

No new holes since yesterday, Ablakan said, assuming that was what Shownae meant. *However, School gave me a bewildering description of space, and the origins of black holes and stars. I don't know what to make of it. But if they're right, it may help us find a solution.*

Do you have it written up?

Yes, I'm just printing it now. I'll 'port it to each main link, and after our leaders have had a chance to read it, I suggest we set up a conference call for them.

I'll pass it on to Administrator Wiltanus as soon as you send it, Shownae promised. He seemed about to add something, but apparently changed his mind, for the Orowan projected a hand-clasp and disconnected.

Ablakan frowned. He had felt the worry Shownae tried to hide – a quiet fear that had nothing to do with black holes. Ablakan toyed with the idea of calling him back, then decided against it. He had no right to pry into something Shownae chose to keep to himself.

* * *

'. . . you have escaped justice for too long. It has caught up with you. I have caught up with you! Now you will pay for your treachery, and all your skills and all the Fates cannot help you. I am Justice. You have been found guilty, and you shall die . . .'

The second death-threat Shownae had received that week went on to suggest he make peace with his Fates before he would join them. As with the first, it had been slid under his door in the middle of the night, and he had never awakened. How could someone have such deadly intentions and Shownae not pick up on that person's presence?

*　*　*

"The contents of Ablakan's talk with School just arrived," Jan told Eric. "Wait till you read this."

Her boss looked up, a quizzical expression on his face. "So? Give me the short form."

"Uh-uh. This you have to read for yourself. It should raise a few eyebrows in academic circles."

Eric eyed her sharply, and grunted as he reached for the report.

She was tempted to stick around and watch his face change as he digested it, but her workload wouldn't permit the indulgence. Jan returned to her office, grinning. Accurate or not, leave it to School to turn human notions of space upside down.

A large shipment of bedding plants and seedlings destined for their most distant member planet, La'oell, took her the better part of an hour to transport, as each portion had to be sent to a different address on the planet, along with its unique nutritional supplement. When she finished and opened her eyes with a sigh of relief, she saw that the message-waiting light was flashing on her answering machine. She had the sound turned off, so it wouldn't break her concentration while she was working.

Jan played back the cryptic message. "When you're available," was all Eric had recorded. This should be good, she smiled to herself on her way to his office.

"What did you think of it?" Jan asked when she got there. Eric's face was having trouble keeping up with his range of opinions.

"Either they're way out to lunch, or they've handed us a goldmine," he said. "Trouble is, I don't know which."

Jan nodded sympathetically. She felt equally ambivalent about the material.

"Have you told Saunders yet?"

"No. I wanted you and the others here for it," Eric replied.

47

Right on cue, Jack, followed by Tom, Brenda and their other 'porter, shaman Richard Ironhorse, filed into the office and settled themselves in the chairs fanning out on the other side of Eric's desk.

"Now what's happened?" Jack asked pessimistically.

"School's either pulling our leg, or we've all just gone back to school," Eric quipped. "I've made a copy of this for each of you to study. It's a transcript of Ablakan's input from School this morning. But for the purposes of this discussion, I'll just hit the high points."

Jan leaned forward in her chair to watch the faces of her colleagues.

Eric cleared his throat. "According to School, space isn't space; it's plasma."

Jack stared at Eric in disbelief. He opened his mouth, but Eric shook his head.

"There'll be plenty of time for comments afterward. Let me get through this first."

Jan glanced at Tom, who snorted derisively. Richard merely shrugged, poker-faced.

Eric's finger traced a zigzag line through the notes, then he frowned, changing his mind. "I'd better read this to you verbatim."

Black holes are regions of vacuum in space plasma. Because of space's nature of pushing outward from all points surrounding any solid object (hence what you perceive as gravity), and since there is no such pushing outward influence in the vicinity of a black hole on the side of the black hole facing an object, space on all other sides will push the object towards the vacuum which, because of its own nature, will attempt to fill that void, hence also pulling in toward the vacuum's center.

The vacuum is a funnel-of-sorts. It is a 'door' between two dimensions. What funnels through this dimension flows – or more properly, is propelled – into the other, which is what you would call an antimatter system. Where one and the other interface there must be a 'door', otherwise the two systems would rapidly cancel out each other.

There are corresponding 'black holes' on the other side which funnel back into this dimension the other way. In other words, what was in the other dimension at that point is being funnelled into this one. The (from your point of view) interesting thing is that what is mostly being 'recycled' is space plasma, and that space plasma is exactly the same in both systems (i.e., it is neither this-dimension-specific nor the other-dimension-specific, but an integral part of both – the common element in both).

When enough, and large enough, space bodies have been recycled through this funnel (which is in fact more a tunnel than a funnel, as it does not narrow), and when enough energy build-up has accumulated, the collection of matter and antimatter materials meeting on one side or the other of the dimension line will cause a tremendous explosion, and conversion over time of the atoms from one type to the other (matter to antimatter, or vice versa).

The outer perimeter reflects this tremendous energy change as heat and light, and the pressure inward as well as outward of this metamorphosis keeps the inner materials from transforming until enough pressure of the outer reaction has eased to permit them to explosively change inward and outward, thus compressing and holding in stasis those beneath them towards the core, and so on, continuously. As you realize, what I am describing is the birth and continued functioning of a star.

Your theorists believe the universe is expanding outward and is also being slowly swallowed up by black holes. What you now realize is that all-that-is in your dimension continuously flows in the space plasma, and that black holes are the two systems just described's method of recycling themselves and each other so that they would not 'burn themselves out' over time. What you may also now be recognizing is that the two dimensions are (form) one ecosystem.

Eric looked up to survey the effects on his listeners of what he had read out. Their faces showed much the same range of emotions as Eric's had, Jan was amused to note.

"That is easily the biggest pile of hogwash I've ever heard," Jack stated, then looked at the others and his boss. "Isn't it?"

"Is it? I don't know." Eric shook his head. "Not so long ago, our best minds truly believed we were the center of the universe and alone in it, and that the Earth was flat. I'm not willing to discount School's perspectives so quickly."

He turned to Jan, directing his first question at her. "*If* this is accurate, does it suggest a way to get rid of those artificially-created holes?"

That took her off-guard. She had been so eager to watch her colleagues' reactions, she hadn't given any thought to the material itself.

"I'd like to discuss it with the other links first," Jan hedged.

"Alright. Get on it soonest." His expression told her he hadn't been fooled, and Jan flushed guiltily. She had become complacent of late.

"Any comments, or questions I *can* answer?" Eric looked from face to face.

"Just for Jan." Richard turned towards her. "Did Ablakan say School thinks this is the only way stars are created?"

"He didn't say either way, but School doesn't give extraneous information when you ask for something. It would be 'black hole-specific'. They know our minds don't have the capacity theirs do."

"Just wondered," Richard murmured, his eyes contemplative.

"Something?" Eric prodded.

Richard searched in his copy of the notes, finding the passage he wanted.

"By 'the collection of matter and antimatter materials meeting on one side or the other of the dimension line will cause a tremendous explosion, and conversion over time of the atoms from one type to the other', that would suggest there are two types of stars in our universe: ones that produce energy through nuclear conversion, like our sun does, and others that use the matter/antimatter conversion for fuel; the latter coming about through black holes exiting into that universe. So my question is, what happens to black holes on one side when a sun is created on the other side? Is it closed by the explosion?"

Eric shrugged. "If so, instead of plugging them, maybe we should be feeding them."

Brenda leaned forward and laced her fingers together. "But what if there's a nearby planet on the other side? We could be destroying it if we deliberately create a sun. I don't know if there even *is* an antimatter universe, but if so, it could have the same planets in the same positions as we have in this one, couldn't it? Or is that just in science fiction?"

"Haven't a clue," Eric said blandly.

"I wonder if School has an antimatter counterpart they converse with, and that's how they get their knowledge of the universe, by comparing notes," Tom mused, half-joking.

Jan sat bolt-upright. "I never thought of that. Telepathy crosses space without the restriction of time. Maybe it can cross *any* type of space. When we finish here, I think I'll pay School a visit."

Eric blinked. "Huh. Wouldn't that put a whole new spin on 'first contact'?" Then he levelled a warning glare at Jan. "Don't even think of trying something like that on your own. For now, just see what School has to say about it."

"Alright," she replied meekly. She would wait, but oh, what a new vista of understanding this would open for everyone if . . .

"Anything else?" When no one seemed to have anything more to say, Eric nodded. "Alright. I'll e-mail this to Saunders, and no doubt he'll run it by the Big Boys. I might as well add what we've been thinking, give them more food for thought."

Tom was eyeing Jan suspiciously as they filed out of Eric's office. Jan was angling towards the cafeteria.

"Promise," Tom instructed cryptically.

"I'll go by the book on this one," Jan agreed. "But you have to admit, it fairly begs exploration."

"Don't forget, School could be wrong," Jack pointed out. "In fact, I'm betting on it."

"Either way, that doesn't discount other universes or the possibility telepathy can bridge them." Jan could almost taste the adventures involved, and her eyes must have shown it, for the wariness never left Tom's face. She gathered food items onto her plate and ate mostly in silence, letting the others carry the conversational ball. There were so many tantalizing aspects to the idea that her mind just wouldn't leave them alone.

"– Jan?"

"Pardon?" Belatedly, Jan realized Brenda had been talking to her.

"A dog with a bone." Brenda shook her head. "But Tom brought up another interesting point with his comment. If School didn't get this view of the universe and black holes and suns and such firsthand, who did they get it from? No species I know. In all the years we've been talking to them, I don't think any of us thought to ask for an intro to other lifeforms they've run across who might be friendly."

"Ohhhhh!" Jan groaned. "You're right."

"What really surprises me is that no one brought it up, on any of the worlds we've spoken to," Brenda continued. "That borders on the unbelievable."

"Yes, it does, now that you mention it. And School is probably brimming with first contacts." Jan looked at her colleagues with mock concern. "Am I drooling?"

Tom extracted an invisible handkerchief from his pocket and dabbed at the corners of her mouth.

Jan wolfed down the last bite of sandwich and waved goodbye to the others, her mouth too full to speak. She 'ported herself to her office, almost missing the chair in her eagerness to send out her mental call to School.

Jan, we have been expecting you. School projected a smile without anything around it – the proverbial Cheshire Cat *sans* cat.

You certainly gave us a lot to think about, she remarked tactfully. *How did you learn all this?*

We watch and we listen, was the enigmatic reply.

Have you actually seen any suns form that way? Jan remembered Tix's comment that they didn't know how to die. Presumably, then, they had had a very long time to observe the workings of the universe.

In part. Other beings carried experiences that added to what we had discovered or surmised.

That brings up another point. You've obviously had a lot of contact with different species over time. Would you be willing to help us contact others who would be friendly and might like to join our trade alliance?

Many no longer exist. There was resigned sadness in that statement. *We have spanned much time, and some lifeforms you would have enjoyed meeting . . . have not.*

But some have? Jan didn't want to seem pushy, but the opportunity was too good to pass up.

We will ask those we can contact directly who we believe would welcome your friendship, School promised.

That would be great. Thank you very much. Jan closed with a grin of delight.

When she opened her eyes, she let out a whoop of joy. And to think, when she first met School, she had considered voting against further contact with them!

* * *

Ablakan was enjoying a brief respite from his work, watching Schnookums explore the new playroom his staff had just finished setting up for the kitten. A pet store on Earth had provided much of the diversions, and had also talked him into accepting, as their gift, a second beautifully-marked calico kitten almost the same age as Schnookums. They had made a valid point. Schnook was far more interested in her live playmate than in the most imaginative toys the store had been able to provide.

Ablakan watched the furballs stalk and pounce on each other with mock ferocity. Better them than his legs. At least they would keep one another company during his long workdays. In time, Jan assured him, the kittens would be mature enough to be given the run of the mansion, and even unrestricted access to the parklike surroundings. But for now it seemed an equitable solution to her – now their – marauding instincts.

As he got up to leave, Ablakan became aware of a 'shifting' sensation in his mind, and instantly realized what was happening. One of the rocks he had tagged in the asteroid field was being moved.

Within moments, he found the vessel, its underbelly open, drawing a small group of rocks inexorably toward its cargo bay. Ablakan couldn't recognize the markings on the ship, but the freighter was unmistakably Aq'Narlian.

Making note of its exact location, Ablakan waited till it powered up its engines, then followed the ship and its tagged cargo as it sped away towards deep space. With great care, he touched the captain's mind and that of the first mate, and gleaned both name and destination in that momentary contact.

When Ablakan again focused on the spot in the asteroid field which had just been mined, he found precisely what he had expected: A fourth hole marked the exact position where the ship's open bay had been.

* * *

53

"Aq'Narls. It *would* have to be them." Tweno's lip curled in contempt.

Their one contact with that race had left a bad impression. Ablakan had felt the painful death of an Aq'Narl child, no older than Tix had been when she came to them. The girl had just been spaced alive by a passing cruiser. When the incident was reported to the Aq'Narl government through Jan, since Earth was the only member planet which had had contact with that race, she had been told not to interfere in Aq'Narl punishment. Disobedience was not tolerated, no matter what the age.

Which didn't augur well for resolution of the holing problem.

Tweno shook his head in resignation. "I'll have Kyollan pass it along through the links. You're following them?"

"Yes. I know where they're going, but I also want to see what they want those rocks for. I didn't dare pry long enough to find out. I'm hoping whatever it is is illegal from their government's point of view, and maybe their ruler will work with us to stop it."

"Maybe." The cast to Tweno's face showed he considered that highly unlikely. "Get as much information on their operation as you can, but try not to get caught. I want them to think they're getting away with it for now."

"Will do."

Ablakan knew that if anything happened to the rocks in the cargo bay, he would instantly know it. Until that happened, his only source of information would be the crew itself, and he dared not do more than momentary checks lest they becoming aware they were being scanned.

At the freighter's present speed, their objective was almost nine hours away, according to the timetable the first mate had had in mind, so that left Ablakan free to explore other avenues. He would have liked to probe the thoughts of Regent Maxxift, who ran Aq'Narl, but he had no mindprint to use to find him. Then he remembered Jan had had dealings with the Regent, albeit briefly. Ablakan could find Maxxift's mental signature through her memory of it.

The Aq'Narl? Jan said when he told her his discovery. *They're surly to the extreme, but I didn't think they were thieves.*

The freighter may be working alone, Ablakan pointed out, in an attempt to be fair. *I'd like to peek at the Regent's memory, see if he knows about them.*

Jan grimaced. *That's not exactly ethical, but we* do *have to know.*

Ablakan opened his mind a little wider as Jan brought up the memory of her mental encounters with that individual. Surly? He would call Maxxift downright nasty! No wonder the vote to refuse Aq'Narl membership in the alliance had been unanimous.

Say, about School's ideas on black holes and such, Jan said. *What was Tweno's take on it?*

Ablakan smiled, remembering. *I believe his exact words – translated, of course – were 'They're kidding, right?'. I found the postscripted comments from the links most intriguing, especially the possibility of contacting antimatter worlds. If Tweno hadn't stopped me –*

Eric warned me off trying yet, too, Jan sighed. *Maybe when this 'hole' business is over . . .*

I hope so. It's more tempting than muchipans. Ablakan closed with a grin.

Thanks to Jan's memory, he had no trouble locating the Aq'Narl Regent's mind. It fairly radiated smug satisfaction. In the brief moment of contact, Ablakan realized the Regent not only knew of the holers, he had sent them. And now Ablakan also knew why the Regent so badly wanted the asteroids' uranium.

* * *

Shownae was catching a much-needed afternoon nap after being pulled off asteroid field watch by Ablakan during the wee hours of the morning. Suddenly, the window of his bedroom concussed explosively. A disgusting-looking slimy substance oozed down the window.

Shownae dashed outside in the hopes of physically spotting the perpetrator, but to no avail. He surveyed the scene before him. The whole side of his new house was covered with the thick goo, as was his lawn and ornamental shrub-bushes from Earth. The remnants of a metallic cylinder were scattered around the area. On his back walkway, a large stone sat atop a sheet of paper – the human product that countless Shalaian merchants now stocked.

Shaking with reaction, Shownae 'ported the stone into space and picked up the note.

'Next time, it will not be industrial waste.'

Shownae crushed the sheet into a tiny ball and stormed back into the house.

"May the Fates disown him!" he snarled. Then he shook himself. *You cannot fight hatred with hate,* he reminded himself sternly, and made a concerted effort to calm down. What he needed was to *find* his tormentor.

As he had done many times before, Shownae mentally sought the culprit. He sent his focus around the outskirts of his home in an ever-expanding circle, but no matter how thoroughly he scanned, he could find no corresponding experience or vindictive feelings towards him. Shownae scowled in frustration. How could that be? *Could my enemy be mechanical, not a being at all?* At least, that would explain why he couldn't pick up on it.

Shownae needed help; there was no doubt about it. But like him, his fellow 'porters already had their hands full with the black hole problem and whoever was causing them. He'd just have to resolve this one on his own.

A memory surfaced. Many years before, he had made the same decision not to bother his friends when he detected danger awaiting him in or near his home. That choice had nearly cost him his life. Logic suggested he shouldn't tempt Fate the same way twice. The next bomb might kill him.

CHAPTER 4

'Dirty' bombs? Jan was aghast. *They're using your uranium to wage a war?*

It had taken less than ten minutes to set up a mental conference between the major players on the three original member planets. Remarkable how effective the emergency code 'Hot One' was in rallying the troops, Jan thought to herself.

On Maxxift's orders. Ablakan shook his head sadly. *They knew we wouldn't let them use our asteroids for killing, so they just took them.*

U.N. Secretary-General Weejan Serapernan asked, *What about the holes they're making? Do they know they're doing that? And if so, surely they realize we'd find out sooner or later who was responsible and put a stop to it. Besides, you can't tell me there were radioactive rocks in all those other places that now have holes.*

Possibly they're doing it to misdirect our attention, buy them extra time, Trikon offered. *Even a few bombs might be all they need to win their war.*

If they're making atomic bombs, it won't take many, the U.S. President agreed.

Which brings up another point, Shownae said. *We could easily remove what they stole, but they'd probably retaliate by making more holes. And if we tried to stop them, it could escalate into all-out war. Not that they'd have a hope without 'porters of their own, but still. Interplanetary war is the last thing we want, and I suspect your governments feel the same.*

Maybe we could mediate between the two factions on Aq'Narl. If there's no war there, they won't need to make the bombs in the first place, Jan suggested hopefully.

Ablakan projected regret along with his answer. *It's too late for that. The war is not between factions; it's between the planetary ruling body and the people it rules. I could not maintain contact long enough to get the details without the Regent feeling my presence, but that much I do know.*

Ouch, Brenda winced. *'Come the revolution'.*

Administrator Wiltanus nodded. *They cannot fight a worldwide revolution* and *us at the same time. I agree that in general we must not interfere in the politics of other planets. But if we only remove what they have stolen, regardless of its consequences to the thieves, it sounds to me like natural justice will prevail. After all, we were seeking trade relations with a* species. *We did so through official channels – their government – but it was still the species we were looking to have relations with.*

Interesting distinction, the President agreed. *And a valid one, I think.*

Tweno said, *I recommend we three leaders call an emergency meeting with the rest of our 'ruling body' members on our respective planets, to discuss this suggestion. Shall we reconvene at this time tomorrow?*

The concensus was 'yes'.

* * *

Primary Tweno and Firsts Ablakan, Lisham and Konapi along with Tix adjourned to a small, well-appointed conference room at the palace. Kyollan had volunteered to 'man the fort' in their absence. Beverages and snacks were interspersed among the 'scribers and notes littering the table.

"What is the current number of holes?" Lisham asked. "I heard eighty-four."

"That we know of," Ablakan confirmed. "They are an annoyance, but at the moment, I don't think they pose any great threat. We just have to keep debris from being drawn into them, or plug them with something too big for them to 'swallow'."

"What about the Regent? Could he have 'porters we don't know about? Without any, they have no hope of winning, if they start something with us – which, frankly, they already have. They must realize that."

All eyes turned towards Ablakan, but by now he was used to it and no longer got flustered by the attention.

"We can only recognize a 'porter if we feel the 'signature' mental configuration we all use when 'porting. And that's assuming they would do it the same way, if they can do it at all." He shook his head regretfully. "We could not long maintain a global scan for 'porting. Besides, if they had the technology, wouldn't they just have 'ported the rocks from our asteroid field to their location, instead of going to the expense of sending ships?"

"That makes sense," Tweno agreed. "For the moment, then, let's assume they don't have 'porters, but would love to have. Who wouldn't, especially if they're engaged in a global war? They would be hard-pressed to kidnap one from our member planets and presumably, it would be relatively easy for us to just 'port him or her back. So what does that leave them?"

" 'Pathing a 'porter to learn how it's done," Tix said with aplomb. She seldom spoke during these brainstorming sessions, but when she did, her comments were usually perceptive if not always tactful.

"So why haven't they?" Ablakan prodded her, enjoying watching how her young mind worked.

"Who says they haven't?" she retorted.

"We'd have felt it."

"Would we?" Tix eyed him sharply. "As you pointed out about 'porting, maybe they don't do it the way we do."

"That's true," Ablakan conceded. He glanced at his protégé. "Could School tell if we've been scanned without our knowledge?"

"I suggest full scan. All 'porters," Tix stated firmly.

"Which would tell us if the Aq'Narl *have,* but not if they will tomorrow," Kyollan pointed out. "And how do you screen out an unknown method of 'pathing?"

Tweno shook his head. "You don't. So let's also assume if they haven't by now, considering what they're up against on their own planet, that they can't. We mustn't become paranoid."

There were general murmurs of agreement. It still disturbed Ablakan, but there were times when you just had to accept there were risks you couldn't protect against.

"Here's what I suggest," Tweno continued. "We remove all non-native uranium and every vestige of our asteroids from their world, including any bombs that may have been made with them. Then we 'port the entire asteroid field's worth of rocks far enough away that they can't get to them with their current technology, if they even knew where they were. And last, we search space within a 100 light-year radius of them, and remove any such material as well."

"And then?" Konapi eyed their Primary significantly.

"And then we hope his own people get him before he declares war on us," Tweno replied.

Lisham's eyebanks raised in surprise. "Surely we have more than enough 'porters, between our three worlds, to banish any invasion fleet he could send."

"True. But if nothing else, he could make life pretty tough, seeding those blasted holes all over our shipping lanes. Remember, not all our members have 'porters. And eventually, those holes will grow large enough to cause real problems."

Ablakan grinned as a thought struck him. "If we really want to sabotage their ships, all we have to do is 'port a few Schnookums on board."

"Especially if they value their legs," Tweno agreed. He turned back to Lisham. "We do seem to have a massive advantage. But if you study Earth's history, as I have, you would realize how quickly overconfidence can lead to disaster."

"So what do we do about the holers?" Konapi wanted to know.

Ablakan shrugged. "It would be a drain on our resources, but we could keep a mental watch on any ships that leave Aq'Narl heading towards allied space. If they're holers, we could just 'port them back to Aq'Narl. Eventually they should get the idea and give up on it."

Tweno nodded in satisfaction. "Ablakan, pass on our ideas through Jan and Shownae, although I suspect we'll find the others came up with much the same answers. Now, if we could only figure out what to do about the holes near Shalaii."

Ablakan went to bed with a sense of foreboding. As Tweno had predicted, their allies reached the same conclusions as they did. Aside from getting rid of those annoying holes, the Aq'Narl threat appeared neutralizable, if not truly resolvable at this time. Perhaps it was just an emotional backlash from their first brush with the spectre of war, Ablakan decided. Still, sleep took a long time to claim him that night.

* * *

As often happened after emotional turmoil, Ablakan awakened with a feeling of calm and equanimity. Tweno also seemed more relaxed, now that the decisions had been made.

"Any holers near our field?" the Primary asked.

Ablakan scanned a 10-light-year triangle outwards from the asteroid field, taking in the thieves' space hideout and the trajectory towards Aq'Narl.

"One ship about five hours from the field, heading towards it," he reported.

"Remove the temptation," Tweno directed.

The location chosen by the alliance as the new home of the 'hot rocks' was the center of a fiery nebula over 500 light-years from Aq'Narl. There were no stars in that region, and it was hoped the uranium-rich asteroids would give the fledgling proto-star the impetus it needed.

Ablakan made three 'trips', each time enclosing groupings of the rocks in his focus, then 'porting them close to the proto-star. Satisfied, he left Nature to take its course.

"Done. I'll let Jan and Shownae know we're ready at this end."

Tweno nodded silently. His facial muscles tensed much the way Ablakan could feel his own doing. For the first time in their history, the steps they were about to take could lead to war.

Pushing the hideous thought aside, Ablakan split his focus and simultaneously called Jan and Shownae. Both opened to him instantly, it being the appointed time.

Ready here, Jan reported. Her effort to project confidence didn't fool Ablakan, but he pretended not to notice.

And here, an equally nervous Shownae added.

Aq'Narl had been mentally divided into three regions of roughly equal land mass for the purpose of search and removal of the Shalaian asteroids and their elements. The three main 'porters would work in unison to move the rocks, and anything that had been made from them, to the asteroid field's new location.

The task turned out to be remarkably simple, for all three easily located the radioactive rocks and any items made with them. In all, seven bombs in varying stages of completion were found and removed. Two would have to be detonated.

What do you think? Jan asked, projecting an idea to the others.

Might work, Ablakan hazarded, though admittedly he was far from certain.

Ready when you are, Shownae added his agreement.

On my mark.

Mentally, Jan counted to three, then 'ported all the asteroids and partially-completed bombs into the proto-star. At the same moment, Ablakan and Shownae each sent a finished bomb onto the searing-hot outer rim of the core matter. They detonated with terrifying force, and a microsecond later, a full-fledged sun was born.

Ablakan let out a whoop of joy. *I'm a father!*

You have a sun, quipped Jan.

Boooo! Shownae laughed in their minds.

Ablakan was the first to sober. *And now we await an explosion of a different kind.*

You and me both. The thought leaked from Shownae as he took his mental leave. Ablakan barely caught it, but it was enough to confirm his earlier suspicions. Shownae was embroiled in a crisis of his own.

* * *

Everything considered, they had an incomprehensibly long wait. Jan felt an angry pounding in her mind almost four hours after the trio broke mental formation.

Here we go, she told herself, nodding to the U.S. President and the U.N. Secretary-General. She had 'ported to the White House in anticipation of the Aq'Narl's reaction, but up to now, there had been none. She could only hope her imaging was equal to the task of dealing with the outraged Regent.

Through the medium of his leading 'path, a spate of venomous sounds accosted her mental ears when she opened up to Maxxift. In his ire, he had obviously forgotten to switch to images. All Jan could do was wait it out. When a lull finally arrived in the tirade, she poured in surprise and query.

There was a moment's delay, then the images began to flow. Vicious, threatening images of death and destruction to the three member planets and their hapless inhabitants, overshadowed by the laughing visage of the Regent.

In response, Jan projected coldness and disapproval, followed by a repeat of the surprise and query images.

Do not pretend ignorance, Regent Maxxift told her in perfect English.

Jan almost fell off her chair in surprise. When had he learned English?

I had School implant it in me. My 'path took me there after I learned what the traitorous Shalaians had done – no doubt with your and the Orowans' blessings. But you shall all pay dearly, and very soon.

The transmission ended so abruptly Jan wasn't sure he had left.

"What did he say?" the President asked tensely.

"Threats of us paying for our treachery, images of the destruction of our three planets and him laughing. Much as you would expect." Jan said it with a nonchalance she didn't feel.

"Watch their minds, their ships, everything," the President ordered. "Let me know immediately of any development."

"I will." Her voice sounded small and scared, even to her, and Jan was only too glad to return to Eric's office, where Saunders and her colleagues anxiously awaited her return.

"How bad was it?" Tom's eyes searched hers fearfully.

"As expected, with one major surprise." She described the conversation, and the fact Maxxift now spoke English.

Saunders' eyes narrowed. "School?"

"School," Jan confirmed.

Jack looked shocked. "I thought they were our friends."

"If you don't need me right now, I'd like to pay them a little visit," Jan said.

"Go ahead. If they can't be trusted, better we know it now," Eric said.

Despite the crowd in the small office, Jan closed her eyes and located School.

You are confused, School observed when they opened up to her.

Yes. Why did you teach the Aq'Narl Regent English? Didn't you pick up from him what he's been doing?

We did, School said solemnly. *And in part that is why we agreed to teach him your language.*

Jan shook her head, not understanding.

Communication is necessary if war is to be averted. Imaging the way you do is too imprecise.

Jan let the gentle admonishment go, since School was making a valid point.

I think they're bent on revenge anyway. You wouldn't happen to know what they have in mind, would you? It didn't hurt to ask.

Yes, we know, as we know what you plan to do. But neither side has been or will be given any tactical information. We do not take sides, but if a mediator is desired, we offer our services in that capacity.

Jan could feel the benevolence of the multiplicity as the offer was made. Clearly, they wished peace to continue as much as she did.

I suppose you've seen many interplanetary conflicts over the eons, Jan remarked in sudden realization. To School, their present crisis must seem like kids squabbling in a sandbox.

A good analogy. School projected approval. *We may not interfere, but we can feel for all concerned. Even the most unconscionable deed is deemed justified in the eyes of the perpetrator. To use your terminology, no one sees themselves as the 'bad guy'.*

That gave Jan pause and fueled a growing suspicion. *You're not just putting this in a different light for me, are you? You're planting a seed, pointing out a way we might avoid all-out war.*

Perhaps. Come again whenever you wish. The mental door closed gently.

Despite School's noncommittal reply, Jan came away with a better understanding of the enigmatic cluster of beings. It must have shown on her face, for when she opened her eyes, Tom was looking hopeful.

"Bingo?"

"In a way – I think."

Saunders raised an eyebrow that meant both query and 'spill it'.

"School taught them English to keep communications open. School isn't telling either side anything about the other's plans. To them, we're like a bunch of squabbling children, and looking at it from their millions-of-years-old point of view, I suppose we are."

Jan leaned forward to emphasize what she was about to say, but she already had their full attention.

"I discovered something very interesting about School. What I've been taking for opinion or perspective is more than that. They're feeding us – and presumably others as well – subtle guidance, if we listen carefully to what they're saying." She recited School's dissertation on 'no bad guys' as a prime example.

"Hmm. Most interesting," Eric leaned back in his chair. "And maybe there is still time to avoid all-out war, if we use a 'no fault' approach."

"I'll call the President and the Secretary-General. If we're to try it, it'll have to be soon." Saunders reached for the phone. "And Jan, I want you to go through every conversation with them any of you have had to date; get out all the transcripts. I want to know what else School has been trying to tell us that we haven't twigged to."

Which was just what she had intended to do. "Do you need me for anything?" she asked Eric.

"Not at the moment. But don't go far."

The meeting broke up then, and Jan returned to her office to start digging through the records. They had known School for close to six years, and select people from each member planet had had dealings with them. There was a lot of ground to cover.

A split-focus call to Ablakan and Shownae served the dual purpose of apprising them of her conversation with Maxxift and School, and asking them to sift through their old transcripts of conversations with the multiplicity.

No, problem, Ablakan replied. *I keep all transcripts cross-referenced by subject, conversants and date. I'll go through them tonight when I get home.*

Thanks. Jan realized guiltily that her own records were strictly chronological. When she got some free time, she'd be wise to cross-reference them the way Ablakan had.

Cannot the secretaries do that? Ablakan asked, as usual reading her internal thoughts. *At least flag the conversations you're looking for?*

Good point. Jan still had a habit of trying to do everything herself.

Ours are also cross-referenced, Shownae said, adding to her embarrassment. *I will have the results for you by tomorrow.*

Thanks. I'll keep you posted.

Jan closed the connection, then sent out a similar call to the other member planets and those negotiating for membership who she knew had interacted with School. The various contacts took the better part of an hour, for she had to repeat the news about Aq'Narl to each one.

Finally, she leaned back with a sigh of relief. As often happened after lengthy sessions, her throat felt parched.

Tom strolled in just as she was reaching for the jug of juice she kept in the small fridge in her office.

"Any word yet?" Jan asked hopefully.

"No. The Big Boys are still debating it, I suppose." Tom rubbed his chin distractedly. "I hope they don't take too long. I have a feeling Maxxift will put whatever he has in mind in motion pretty quickly."

Jan nodded. "I got the same impression when he called. I tried to get a sense of what his plan is, but he didn't let anything leak out."

"That's too bad." Tom surveyed the relatively bare desk significantly. Obviously, he had expected to see her records piled on it by now.

"I just finished calling everyone, asking them to go through their records," Jan explained.

"Want a hand with ours?"

Jan smiled her thanks. "Thirsty?"

"A bit," Tom admitted, and helped himself to the jug before Jan could do the honors. He carried the sixteen binders of transcripts from the bookshelf and place them on the table. Jan and Tom were just starting to wade through them when Jack and Brenda walked in.

"Eric needs you," Jack told Jan. "Want us to go through these for you?"

"That would be great."

Jan hurried down the hall to Eric's office, infinitely relieved. She hated reviewing old records, but the task required someone who was used to School's often-multipurpose statements. After all these years, Tom, Jack and Brenda were imminently qualified.

"You called?"

Eric motioned her to her usual chair. "Just got word. You're to 'make nice' with Maxxift, try to stall his retaliation long enough for his subjects to unseat him."

Jan grimaced. "I don't like him either, but that's treachery."

Eric nodded slowly. "Not how we usually do things, I know. But for an entire world to turn on one man, he has to be all-around pretty bad."

"Which brings us back to what School said about nobody seeing themselves as a 'bad guy'. Perhaps I could suggest to him that he make concessions to his people."

Eric shrugged. "Play it as it comes. Just buy us some time for things to settle out one way or another on Aq'Narl."

"Okay."

Jan closed her eyes and put her call through to the Regent's prime 'path. She still didn't know his name; he had not seen fit to tell her.

There was a slight delay after the 'path opened to her. He was keeping his emotions carefully neutral. Then a warm wave of pleasure – or perhaps smugness was a better word for it – emanated from a second individual as he joined the link.

We bring you greetings from the new Administration on Aq'Narl.

New Administration? It hadn't taken them long to depose Maxxift, it seemed.

Yes, indeed. Our former ruler has escaped, but he shall be found, never fear. I understand from Oh'ra-mohynn here that your alliance removed the bombs he was about to use against us. Our people owe you and your colleagues a debt of gratitude.

Flawless English, Jan noted. She had to give the Aq'Narls credit. They certainly got things done quickly, and the easy way. And to think of the countless hours she and Ablakan spent giving English lessons, when they could have just sent the students to School!

I am happy for you and your people, Jan replied. *Perhaps in the near future, trade negotiations may become possible.* Exposure to gentler cultures might also make them reconsider their drastic response to disobedience in their young, Jan hoped.

Perhaps. Please extend our appreciation to your associates. Contact ended there.

"You're smiling," Eric pointed out.

"Maxxift is on the run. The new Administration is grateful to us all and is not discounting future trade relations. And their 'path's name is Oh'ra-mohynn."

"Well!" Eric smiled. "That *is* good news. I'll pass it along here. You let the member planets know." The extra creases on his brow had disappeared as if by magic.

"Gladly, but let me tell Tom and the gang first."

"Go," Eric nodded, already reaching for the phone.

Jan sprinted to her office, and stood in the doorway, grinning. Tom spotted her first.

"Well, look who ate the canary," he commented. "Let me guess. Maxxift is history?"

"On the lam," Jan amended. "The new Administration is grateful to us all and will consider membership. Looks like war has been averted."

"That's a relief," Brenda understated.

"No kidding!" Jack gave her a quick hug. "Told the others yet?"

"About to. And tell Richard when he's free, will you?" Someone had had to handle commerce while the others lent Jan a hand. The shaman had volunteered.

Jan plunked herself down on the closest empty chair and sent out a call to Ablakan and Shownae. When they were on-line, she told them the good news and asked them to relay it to the other planets. Averting wars made her right hungry. Her stomach growled confirmation.

Go eat, Ablakan laughed. *We'll take care of it.*

I love passing on good news, Shownae said with a smile, and they disconnected in unison.

Jan grinned happily. No war, they had created a new star and played an instrumental role in ridding a planet of a cruel despot. Not bad for a day's work. All that remained was to find some way of removing those blasted holes.

* * *

Just beyond the edge of Shalaian space, a faster-than-lightspeed one-person skiff came to a halt. To go any further might tip his hand.

Grimly, Maxxift placed the miniature torpedo into the launch tube and keyed in the coordinates and distance. They may have won the war, but he would have the last laugh.

The 'ready' light came on, and Maxxift gave the button a vicious jab, thus starting the projectile on its four-day journey.

"Eat this," he muttered in English.

Then he turned his craft around and set course for the one remaining fertile valley he had located some years before on a long-abandoned world half a light-year beyond the Shalaian system.

CHAPTER 5

Ablakan received an unexpected call late that afternoon.

"Wiki is hoping to speak with you, sir," the complex supervisor informed him.

Ablakan regarded the phone in surprise. Why had it rung through to Retreo instead of to him?

"Put her on."

"First Ablakan, how kind of you to take my call," the musical voice stated. "I just heard about our close call with – war, I think it's called? I wished to thank you personally for saving us from such a terrible fate."

"Actually, Jan and Shownae had as much to do with it as I did," Ablakan admitted. "Is it common knowledge already, or do you just have good sources?"

"Saymin and I had lunch, and he looked relieved. I already knew about the holes the Aq'Narls were planting. I guessed the rest correctly, and Saymin didn't deny it."

"I see." Ablakan was careful to keep his voice neutral. "Primary Tweno will be addressing the people tonight, to tell them about the holes and the good news that war has been averted."

"I won't tell anyone until then," Wiki assured him. "I'm good at guessing secrets, but also at keeping them."

"I would appreciate that. Is there anything else you were calling about?" Ablakan winced, realizing he could have worded it better.

"Not at present, no. You have been much too busy ensuring planetary safety to read my career history. Again, my thanks. Goodbye, sir."

"Goodbye."

Ablakan hung up and stood there, frowning at the hear-other. Fond though he was of Saymin, the valet was becoming a security risk. Yet he could hardly fire him for 'looking relieved'. Perhaps Juneli would have an idea how to ease him out. It was her job to handle staffing problems – not that there had been any to date.

The timemometer on the wall confirmed he should have left the office some time ago. Ablakan locked his door, made one quick stop, then 'ported himself to the Lair, as he called Shnookum and

Palette's quarters. He had named his second kitten 'Palette' because her helter-skelter color blotches reminded him of that human artist's tool.

The felines were curled up together in an intricate pattern of legs, heads and tails, sleeping soundly. Ablakan cleared his throat, and instantly they disentangled themselves and rushed to greet him, tails high. It didn't hurt that he had dishes of their favorite 'vittles' in each hand.

Palette took a moment to rub against Ablakan's leg before turning to her bowl, but Schnookums dove into hers with nary a look at him. Ablakan accordioned down to stroke their silken fur, crooning praises to them as they devoured their dinner. Soon they would be busy with personal grooming and a nap to sleep off the meal, so his presence wouldn't be missed for a while.

Ablakan made a mental note to return and play with them, then 'ported himself to the kitchen. A prominent note on the cook-keeper caught his eye, and he bent over to read it.

"Sir, we have made your favorites, at Juneli's request. She is keeping it hot for you in her quarters."

Ablakan blinked in surprise. How did she know he would work late and feel like celebrating? For the umpteenth time, he wondered how the tests could insist she wasn't telepathic. But she *was* precognitive, so maybe that explained it.

He 'ported himself outside her door and knocked gently. A smiling Juneli opened it.

"Perfect timing," she remarked, stepping aside.

Ablakan noticed that the table was set with gleaming cutlery and the ornamental Earth candles he had given her for her last birthday. Their flickering light cast an intimate glow on the steaming dishes.

"I'll just wash up. And thanks for this, June."

He hurriedly cleansed his hands and joined her at the table. Though they never stood on ceremony in private, Juneli insisted he be seated before she sat down, a throwback to their earliest times together.

"You never cease to amaze me," Ablakan smiled at her. "Just when I think I've got you figured, you pull something like this and I have to start all over again."

"Jan says always keep them guessing." A little smile played at the corners of her mouth, and her eyebanks were twinkling merrily in the candlelight.

Ablakan gave her hand an appreciative squeeze and dug in. They ate in comfortable silence for a time. The tensions of the past few days began to melt away. Finally, he leaned back with a happy sigh. "Have I told you how glad I am to have you here?"

"You have mentioned it a time or two," she smiled. "But it's always nice to hear just the same."

Ablakan waved a dessert utensil in her direction. "If I ever start taking you for granted, you have my permission to kick me."

"I'll keep that in mind." She wiped her mouth delicately. "But I think there is another who is already doing that."

"Taking me for granted, or kicking me?" Ablakan teased.

"The former." Her eyes met his levelly, with no trace of amusement.

"Saymin," Ablakan nodded, wondering how she knew.

"I asked Retreo to tell me if you received calls that weren't going through normal channels. He said Wiki called again, using your personal number. When I leave the office, I now route your line through Retreo."

Which explained why the complex supervisor had taken the call instead of Ablakan getting it.

"Good thinking. And yes, I was going to have a word with you about Saymin. Wiki thanked me for avoiding a war with Aq'Narl. And she also knew about the holes and that the Aq'Narl seeded them."

"Really." Juneli's eyebanks narrowed in displeasure. "So now he's become an informant?"

"Wiki guessed it and Saymin didn't deny it. Her words."

"We have what the humans call a 'leak'. Someday he may 'leak' something critical," she pointed out.

"I know. But I can't fire him for not denying something." He drummed his fingers on the table before reaching for a muchipans. "So what do we do with him?"

"Transfer him someplace less sensitive," Juneli suggested. "Perhaps with a small promotion, so he doesn't think it's a punishment."

72

"I can't reward bad behavior; it would set an improper precedent." Ablakan pursed his lips, thinking. "What if he received a better offer from some rich recluse?"

Juneli leaned forward hopefully. "You know someone who'd hire him?"

"Maybe. There are a few people who feel they owe me a favor. Perhaps I can persuade one of them to take him on." He looked at Juneli ingenuously. "He really is an excellent valet, you know. But frankly, I prefer to dress myself."

She started clearing the dishes and waved off Ablakan's attempts to help. "Do you want to make the calls yourself, or shall I?"

"I'd best do it," Ablakan decided. "First thing tomorrow."

"Jan sent a movie she thought you'd enjoy. I brought it home in case you wanted to watch it here." Juneli retrieved it from the side table and held it out to Ablakan. Trading forms of entertainment had become a major industry among most member planets. "Or you can take it back with you."

"Just let me tend to the kittens, then if you're not too tired, I'd like to watch it with you. What's it called?"

Juneli glanced down at the cassette. " 'The Abyss'. Science fiction, I believe."

"Good. I'll be back in a while. And thanks for dinner."

"I didn't cook it, just kept it warm for you," she called after him.

"I appreciated the company," he replied, and 'ported himself to the Lair.

* * *

As she had done on countless occasions, Juneli alternated between trying to contact Ablakan telepathically and attempting to teleport an item or herself within the room. An assistant was not mate material for a First. But if she could become a true telepath or teleporter, perhaps she would have a chance.

With love providing the impetus, Juneli focused her whole being on Ablakan's mind, willing him to hear her 'knock' and open up to her. She did not cease trying until he returned to watch the movie.

* * *

73

"Find anything interesting?" Jan asked hopefully, as Tom, Brenda and Jack popped into the kitchen just after six p.m. They had spent the afternoon pouring over the transcripts, searching out discussions with School.

"I think so," Jack replied. He glanced at his colleagues for confirmation. Both nodded.

"Something smells good," Tom remarked. "That wouldn't be lasagne, would it?"

"That it is. I felt bad having you guys slave over my ill-kept records, so I thought I'd try to appease your hunger as well as my guilt."

Tom snorted loudly. "As if you've had time to cross-reference your notes."

"Ablakan and Shownae did." Jan wasn't about to let herself off the hook that easily.

"More likely had their aides do it," Brenda pointed out. "But if it takes guilt to get some of your famous lasagne, go right ahead and feel guilty any old time you like."

"Thanks." Jan grinned wryly at the backhanded compliment.

The group gathered around the table, with Brenda's son, Billy unabashedly grabbing the first portion, and a hefty one at that. Jan was gratified to see that her culinary efforts were not going to waste. Precious little was left once everyone had filled their plates.

"So give me a hint," Jan asked between bites. "Was there a lot of things we overlooked?"

Tom nodded. "Rereading it, and looking specifically for hidden messages, I'd say School is a master of multiple meanings."

He reached for the thick folder of photocopied material he'd brought to the table, and began leafing through it. Many sentences, and sometimes whole paragraphs, had been highlighted.

"For instance," Tom's finger settled on one line. "Remember when they were talking to us about longevity?"

Jan waffled a hand. "Refresh my memory."

"Lessee." Tom's finger skimmed back up the page a ways. "Ah, here it is."

Your entire physical being interacts – through perspectives, reactions, emotions, etc. – with the outside world. That is why the body ages (decays, gets worn out). The idea of not interacting with your world would slow down the rate of decay, yes, but what purpose would that lifetime otherwise serve for you? Nothing to speak of. It is your interactions and perceptions, and responses to those interactions, that creates and validates a lifetime, regardless of what time frame is lived.

To do what you have in your mind – keep your body from aging – is as valid as any other dream or goal or decision. What it is, to you, is validation and victory over limiting beliefs. That is where the value comes in. What you do with your victories is up to you. It matters far less than the victories over perception and limitation.

For your body to live at peak health, efficiency and agelessness you need to remove time as an element where your body is concerned. This means removing the 'internal clock' sense and all the beliefs that go along with it. To do this, bring your mind to the foreground. Your mind, you are able to understand, is timeless, ageless, and though it can happily exist in a timespace world, it is not timespacial in origin and therefore is not bound by timespacial rules.

Your body is your mind in a visual form. Your body is as timespace-bound as you perceive it to be. If you accept it as a mind-form rather than a timespace form, then it, too, becomes timeless and ageless, and able to reflect and respond to any perceptions you choose to attach to it and its workings.

Now you have your answer. The 'work' is changing your perception and reattaching yourself to your physical manifestation through a mental belief rather than a physical belief. You will succeed, over time.

Jan whistled appreciatively. "I'd forgotten about that one."

"Yes, but did you get the double meaning at the end?" Tom fairly smirked at her.

"What double meaning?"

"Quote: 'You will succeed, over time.' "

Jan chuckled, as realization dawned. "Yes, take the comma out and it means something entirely different, doesn't it?"

"It's not only a one-line synopsis of the whole discourse, but a promise. For all we know, they're precognitive, like Juneli," Tom said.

"And sneaky," Brenda murmured.

"Your food is getting cold," Jan pointed out.

"So it is."

When Tom picked up his fork, Jan snatched the file, plopping it down proprietorily beside her plate. "Let's see what else you caught."

A half-hour later, Jan had to admit that they had been fed an awful lot of goodies on which neither she nor the rest had picked up, until now.

* * *

Negotiations had gone well with the allied planets. Dru Hepiak had been assured his planet would become the eighth member, with trade relations commencing upon receipt of Lowen's Supreme Commander, Taefek's signature on the precious documents in Dru's possession.

Shownae had offered to 'port Dru and his ship back to Lowen, to save Dru the time and cost of the long journey, but Dru had turned it down.

"There are several spacial holes along my route. I would like to see if there have been any changes in them, or if any more have been added."

Something on the monitor caught his attention. He was on the outskirts of Shalaian space, and the object was moving at a fair clip. The blip – likely some sort of space debris – was so small it would burn up in any atmosphere it hit, Dru decided. He checked its trajectory on his starchart. It would bypass Shalaii by a safe margin, anyway. He made a brief note of it in his log, then returned his attention to thoughts of home.

* * *

Slowly, things were returning to normal at Ablakan's complex. He privately admitted that the Aq'Narl situation had turned out better than they had had any right to hope for, but he certainly wasn't going to question their good fortune.

When he contacted the new Aq'Narl Administrator to extend his congratulations, his overtures were met with something akin to effusiveness.

On behalf of my people, I, Administrator Eshwyt, recognize your people in fellowship, Administrator declared with great formality. *We speak on equal terms.*

Ablakan took care to hide his amusement at the Administrator's elitism. An offer of friendship, however peculiarly worded, was still an offer.

We are pleased to have been of service to your people, Ablakan responded. *And we are hoping you may be able to assist us.*

Ablakan felt the other's surprise, but Eshwyt rallied quickly. *If we can.*

The small holes in space that your predecessor's freightships created could pose problems for small, slow-moving crafts. Have your scientists a means of closing them? Ablakan made sure his emotions suggested they were a minor nuisance at best.

Holes? There was no guile in the Administrator's surprise. *Please explain.*

Ablakan winced. If he didn't even know of them, likely he wouldn't know how to remove them, either. Painstakingly, Ablakan described the holers' actions and the subsequent punctures in what School described as space plasma.

Plasma? But space is . . . just space.

That is how we see it, too. But School has been around a very long time. Perhaps they see something there we can't identify with our equipment, Ablakan suggested.

Between us, I do not know what to make of this 'School'.

Ablakan chuckled indulgently. *I know what you mean. They're constantly surprising us, too.* Ablakan cleared his throat mentally. *If you could examine the holer mechanisms, perhaps they would suggest a method we could use to remove the holes.*

It will be attended to. Until we speak again.

Ablakan opened his eyes to find Juneli patiently awaiting his mental return.

"Financier Shoonat is waiting on line two." Her eyes told him the prognosis was good.

"Good morning, Shoonat." Ablakan smiled happily as he added, "I am told we may have good news for each other."

"Quite possibly, my First." Shoowana's jovial manner overrode the verbal genuflect. "My new valet is efficient, but far too surly for my tastes. He has been with me but a short time, and already we both know it will not work out. I hear yours is available? And more outgoing?"

"I've yet to see him out-of-sorts," Ablakan declared. "And he's been with me for seven years now."

There was a suspicious pause at the other end of the hear-other. "Forgive me, but if he's so good, why don't you want to keep him?"

"To be honest, I wasn't born into this kind of life. I prefer to dress myself. But when I do, it hurts his feelings and makes him feel that he isn't needed." Which was true, as far as it went.

"With all my aches and pains, I need the help," Shoonat said. "How much are you paying him, if I may be so bold?"

Ablakan told him, rounding the figure off on the high side.

"I could match that, maybe even raise it a bit, as the meals here are good, but probably not up to your Chef's standards."

"To be needed, I'm sure he'd forego a few pastries. It would be healthier for him to lose a little weight, anyway," Ablakan added.

"I eat slim. Can't afford to get fat and lazy, not with those human sharks out there trying to underbid me." Shoonat guffawed loudly to show he held no malice for the competitiveness of their trading partners.

"Shall I tell him you are interested, then?" Ablakan asked, trying not to sound too eager.

"Please do. I am indebted to you, sir."

And I to you, Ablakan thought to himself as he hung up with a smile.

Juneli grinned back. "All that's needed now is to convince Saymin. May I suggest you play up Shoonat's discomforts and how badly Saymin is needed there. That should get him."

Ablakan nodded. "That and the raise in pay."

* * *

The next three days were inordinately busy for Jan and her friends. She had been anticipating an enormous backlog of work when the threat of war had lifted. She had been pleasantly surprised that the trading community on each affected planet had held off during the crisis. Probably waiting to see what would happen, Jan mused. Now, however, they were making up for lost time, and the pressures on the 'paths and 'porters were greater than ever.

"I'm about ready to put in for some time off," Jan admitted to Eric at the end of the third gruelling day. "Maybe we'd better do another sweep, see if we can get more 'pathic recruits."

"It's just temporary. I remember it was the same when World War II ended. Business boomed something fierce, as everyone got started up again. At least here, there was no actual war, and the threat only lasted a day. It'll settle down by next week; you'll see."

"I hope so," Jan muttered. "I can't take too many more days like these."

"I know." Eric patted her arm sympathetically. "And you're right. It might be time to set the recruiting machine in motion again, especially now that Lowen's come on board. All indications are they'll make very energetic trading partners."

"I'd appreciate it," Jan told him, and meant it.

She was asleep by eight-thirty, and that was the night the most significant celestial event in Shalaian history took place.

* * *

Shownae was preparing a spartan dinner early that evening, when he realized he'd left a glowlamp on in the leisure room. No point in wasting power, he reasoned, as he reached to dial it off.

A metallic something appeared at the far end of the room, near the music console. Shownae consigned it to space with a panic 'port. It detonated an instant later, hurling shards of needle-like projectiles in all directions.

Shownae fell into the nearest recliner, badly shaken. Finally, he knew the nature of his enemy, and why he had been unable to feel the terrorist's approach.

As soon as his 'porting colleagues were up, Shownae resolved to tell them he now had a scan-proof rogue teleporter to contend with.

* * *

Juneli was restless that evening, pacing the floor of her luxurious suite in her boss' complex. Something was terribly wrong, but try as she might, she couldn't determine what it was.

Finally, she gave in to the overwhelming sensation of imminent danger and called Ablakan's private residence.

"I was just about to call you," Ablakan said. "There's something wrong, isn't there?"

"Yes. And as usual, I don't know what."

"As the humans say, 'your place or mine'?"

"I'll be right there," Juneli decided, and a moment later, she was, thanks to Ablakan.

"Start talking," Ablakan suggested. "It may trigger more details. Tell me what you're feeling and where; describe it any way you can."

"It's bad, but not conscious-bad, if you know what I mean," she began, sifting through her perceptions and their attendant feelings. "And it's coming. It's not here yet. But soon."

"Alright, let's try that human game Jan taught us. Is it a person, place or thing?"

"Not a person. It's a thing, and going someplace," Juneli said with more assurance.

"Is it here on Shalaii, or 'out there'?"

There was a pause, as she interpreted the sensations. "Out there. I think."

"Big as a planet? Or a moon? Or smaller?"

"Smaller. Much."

Suddenly, she saw it. A tiny, sharp-nosed object with a ball at one end. She gasped involuntarily, realizing what it must be.

"It's a bomb. A tiny bomb."

"Where is it, Juneli?" Ablakan's voice cut through her fears with its urgency.

"Near where the asteroid field used to be."

She felt Ablakan's focus join hers just as the object veered suddenly, ramming itself into the largest spacial hole.

Juneli cried out as the bomb detonated with unbelievable force. She clapped her hands over her ears and accordioned down into a ball, shaking uncontrollably.

Ablakan, who had surrounded the bomb with his focus a microsecond before it detonated, was flung halfway across the room by the force it exacted on his mental grasp of the object. He lay there, not moving, his breathing coming in short, ragged gasps.

Juneli managed to tear her focus free of the terrifyingly huge hole in their former asteroid field. Jan's term 'hell hole' suddenly felt all too appropriate.

And then she heard a low moan coming from the corner of the room and looked up to see Ablakan, his face a ghostly white, lying there catatonic, his pupils flickering frenetically. Juneli rushed to his side and accordioned down beside him.

"Ablakan!" she hollered. She shook him hard, trying with all her might to break his focus on the hole. She could tell that the toll it was exacting on his mind was horrendous, but still the lock remained. Throwing caution to the wind, she slapped his face, hard.

"Ablakan, get back here!" she screamed at the top of her lungs.

But it was no use; she couldn't reach him.

HELP! she shrieked in her mind, blasting out in all directions at once. *Someone help Ablakan!*

The flickering stopped, and his body went limp. As she watched, hardly daring to breathe herself, Ablakan's breaths slowed and became deeper and more regular. Juneli looked up to see young Tix smiling at her reassuringly.

"He will be alright now. I have disconnected him."

I thought I had, a surprised voice said in their minds, bearing the unmistakable mindprint of Jan.

Me, too, Shownae chuckled. *Was that really you, Juneli?*

She flushed. *I guess it was. I just got so desperate for someone to help him . . .*

Her voice trailed off in wonderment, as she realized not only what she had done, but that she was now hearing them as clearly as though they were standing in the room.

Congratulations, dear friend, Jan projected a monumental hug. *You've just become a telepath!*

Ablakan sat up, slowly shaking his head. "What happened?"

Juneli helped prop him up. He was having trouble keeping his balance. "Slowly, sir."

"I have little choice, it seems." Ablakan moved his head gingerly. "Do I remember right? Did someone detonate a bomb inside one of our holes?"

"I'm afraid so," Juneli said, feeling terrible guilt. Why hadn't she spotted the accursed thing earlier? "And it took the others with it and made it into one *big* hole."

"Very big," Tix confirmed. "It could swallow a moon with no trouble."

Jan's mental voice held a world of regret. *Eric was right about the danger of overconfidence. I'm so sorry, Ablakan. I should have taken the threat more seriously.*

I didn't either, Ablakn admitted. *But when I spoke to the Administrator, I didn't feel any treachery. I'm willing to bet it was Maxxift. They haven't caught him yet, you know.*

Well, if he's out there, armed with a bunch of those little devices, we're all in big trouble, Jan declared. *We'd better find him, and fast.*

Agreed. But I'll have to leave it to the rest of you for now. I can barely hold my head up." In fact, Juneli was gently supporting it.

We'll let you rest, Jan murmured, and the offworlders quietly disconnected.

"Would you 'port him to bed?" Juneli asked Tix, and a moment later Ablakan disappeared. Juneli opened her mouth to say something more, but Tix raised a hand.

"I know. I've already sent for the doctor. He's just gathering up his equipment, then I'll 'port him to Ablakan's room. Ready?"

"Yes," Juneli said, trying to keep up with Tix's quick change of subjects. Then she was standing beside her boss's bed.

"How is your head?" She could see that his pupils still weren't quite in focus.

"As the humans say, 'ouch!'."

"I'll get you a cold compress."

From behind her, a baritone voice said drolly, "I think we can come up with something a bit stronger."

Juneli gratefully stepped aside to let the doctor tend his patient. The examination took quite a while, and Juneli found herself reliving her role in the evening's drama. Had she really broadcast telepathically? She must have, for Jan, Shownae and Tix to have responded at the same moment. It reminded her of Tom's now-immortal statement: 'When the need is great, you somehow find a way'.

One of her fondest dreams had just come true; she was now a telepath. But as Juneli watched the pale young man laying on the bed, and thought of the terrifying menace so near their homeworld, she couldn't help but think that the cost had been too great.

CHAPTER 6

Jan, Shownae and Tix went into a mental huddle as soon as they were certain Ablakan was going to be alright. There was no time to lose.

We all felt Ablakan's experience of that bomb, right? Jan asked. Two voices confirmed that they had.

Okay, here's what I suggest: Let's each search our space, wherever there are holes, and work our way back towards each other's planet until we intersect. Then we can scan outward in, say, a five light-year line along the trajectory that bomb came in on.

Shownae nodded. *Detonate any bombs you find, but make sure they're nowhere near a hole.*

Right. And unless I miss my guess, we should find a bunch of them about the same place we'll find Maxxift.

What do we do with him, if we find him? Tix wanted to know.

Remembering Ablakan's close call with the hellish device, and the enormous black hole it had created in Shalaii's 'back 40', Jan's mental voice went hard. *Let Eshwyt know we found him, then 'port him and his damned bombs separately, right to Eshwyt's office.*

Shouldn't we check with our governments first? Shownae asked.

Go ahead if you want to, but I won't. Nobody *risks Ablakan's life and gets away with it.*

Shownae's mental tone firmed. *You're right, Jan. We have to send a message that we won't let anyone mess with us 'porters. Otherwise, in no time, it'll be open season on us all.*

Jan felt Shownae shudder. *Is something else wrong?* she asked him on a very private sliver of focus.

Yes, but it'll have to wait.

I don't think we should let Ablakan know what we're doing till it's done, Tix was saying.

Agreed, Jan said.

I agree as well, Shownae added, and each pulled out of the connection.

There began the most exhaustive sweep of that sector of the galaxy ever attempted to date. Two hours later, the exhausted trio reconvened to compare notes.

Nothing, Jan summed up their joint haul. *Not a darned thing! I can't believe it. Maxxift had holes made near each of our planets, presumably with this potential in mind. Why just imperil Shalaii? If I were him, I'd've done all his enemies at the same time, not give the others time to rally.*

Maybe he's not as bloodthirsty as you, Tix remarked with dry humor.

Shownae shook his head. *More likely, he holds Shalaii directly responsible for getting him deposed. But I do think he intends to pick us off, one by one, if we give him the chance.*

Which was probably true, Jan realized. Ablakan had been the last one to have contact with Maxxift. The former Regent probably thought Ablakan acted against him unilaterally.

Either way, he has to know we'll go after him. Having his mindprint, there's no place he can hide, Tix pointed out.

Well, he's eluded us so far. The question Jan couldn't figure out was, *how?* Where could he have gone, that they couldn't track his mindprint?

Unless he suicided, Shownae mused. *After getting his revenge. With almost every sentient planet in the galaxy looking for him, he was as good as dead anyway.*

It's starting to look that way, Jan admitted reluctantly. She knew it was unlike her to be spoiling for a fight, but Ablakan's endangerment had aroused her protective mother instinct. *I'm going to try again after I take a breather.*

I will, too, Tix agreed, and Shownae promised to do the same.

Jan split her appreciation two ways, then disconnected.

As usual, the whole household – except Billy, who slumbered peacefully on a nearby chair – was awaiting her mental return.

"That's got to be a new record," Tom said, his expression harried. "Where did you go for so long?"

Jan's face turned grim, remembering. "Someone – probably Maxxift – detonated a bomb inside one of the holes where Shalaii's old asteroid field used to be. It expanded to include all the other holes. And Ablakan's focus was attached at the time.

He's okay, though," she told them hastily, seeing the shocked looks on their faces.

"Jan, you've got to find Maxxift, right now!" Tom's eyes were wide with consternation. "Earth could be next, or Orowa."

"What do you think Shownae and Tix and I've been doing the last two hours?" Jan demanded, then winced in apology. She hadn't meant to snap at him. She continued in a gentler tone. "The only thing we can think of is he killed himself."

"He'd better have," Jack growled.

Jan gave him an uncharacteristically malevolent smile. "If he hasn't, and we find him, we're 'porting him and his little toys into the new Administrator's lap. Let them deal with him."

Brenda shivered convulsively. "Considering what they do to a disobedient child, I'd hate to be in his shoes."

"As I told the others, nobody messes with Ablakan," Jan said firmly. "But it does look like Maxxift saved us the trouble. I'm going for a nap, then I'll scan again. Shownae and Tix will do the same. If we still find nothing, we'll have to assume he's dead."

Late that night, after a brief mental conference, they officially closed the books on one Maxxift the Despicable, as they had privately dubbed him.

* * *

On the dead planet, in a subterranean chamber that had once held the coffin of an ancient chieftain, Maxxift lay in solitary stasis. He had set the timer to awaken him in two days, at which time he would put into effect the final phase of his revenge on Shalaii before turning his attention Earthward.

* * *

Shownae reluctantly 'ported his most prized possessions into storage and relocated to an abandoned shack surrounded by dense forest on the furthest continent from his home. He could not locate the mind which was stalking and endangering him, but just maybe he could pick up his own mindprint being used by his foe to search for him.

Hour upon hour, Shownae kept up his mental vigil. It was nearly morning before he felt it. The other's block came down during the moment of location. In that fleeting instant, Shownae felt the seething hatred and thirst for justice in the younger man's mind. Yes, justice!

Shownae was so bewildered, he barely managed to escape before the flimsy dwelling was reduced to kindling.

* * *

"How bad is it?" Tweno asked tensely the next morning. From Ablakan's angle, he could see the Primary jaw clenched against the prognosis he didn't want to hear, but knew he must. On Tunan and Enaxat, Ablakan knew Firsts Lisham and Konapi awaited the verdict with equal trepidation.

"Very," Dr. Weismer summed up the situation. "But not critical. Yet."

"Meaning it will become so?" Tweno asked.

"Yes. Bottom line, even if it doesn't increase in size and gravitational pull, its influence will pull your planet in within a month. Before that happens, of course, global disturbances will increase exponentially with the gravitational attraction. You can expect unprecedented earthquake activity, severe storms, even polar shifts." He looked from the Primary to Ablakan, as they took in what he was saying.

"I am sorry," he concluded slowly. "But I know of no way to arrest, or even slow this process."

Ablakan's throat felt like it had turned to dust. If NASA's top physicist could see no hope for their planet, Ablakan knew there was but one possibility, and it was a long shot at best.

Tweno was the first to recover. "Thank you, sir, for your honesty. I guess the rest is up to us. And our colleagues," he added, glancing significantly at Ablakan.

"Our staff and resources are at your disposal," Dr. Weismer assured him. "On Earth, your situation has been given top priority."

Tweno bowed acknowledgement. "Please extend our deepest appreciation to your leaders."

Dr. Weismer evidently recognized it as a dismissal, for he extended his hand. Tweno and Ablakan grasped it in turn, before Ablakan 'ported the scientist into NASA's decontamination chamber.

"One month, if we're lucky." Tweno shook his head in quiet despair.

Their eyes met, and in that brief moment they shared the joint burden of their planet's fate. The responsibility was almost more than Ablakan could bear. He felt his body begin to tremble as delayed reaction set in.

"I know what you're thinking," Ablakan whispered hoarsely. "But on my father's grave, I don't know if it can be done."

"Neither do I."

Tweno was silent for a time, gazing out the window at the golf course that had given them so much pleasure over the years. At that moment, Ablakan experienced such profound grief that his eyebanks filled with tears.

Tweno took a deep breath and shook himself. "This will get us nowhere. A month is a month. It will be enough, if it has to be." He turned toward Ablakan, resolute and unflinching. "No matter how this ends, we will both know we have done our best. And we are not alone; we have powerful friends."

"That we have," Ablakan agreed, rallying somewhat.

Tweno placed a firm hand on Ablakan's shoulder. "Right now, the last thing you need is more pressure on you. Until this crisis is over – one way or the other – consider me your high-level resource person, not your boss. I will prepare a global evacuation plan and oversee that end of things, should it prove impossible to save Shalaii." He gave Ablakan's shoulder a little shake for emphasis. "I know you will do your utmost to make my efforts unnecessary."

"You can count on that." Ablakan stood up straight, feeling despair give way to determination. They had done the impossible before. Why not again?

Tweno extracted his 'scriber from a fold in his uniform. "I'll draft up a statement, let you, Lisham and Konapi comment on it before I release it. There's no way we can keep this quiet, and we've got enough problems without riots and panic."

"That's for sure."

Ablakan felt guilty, leaving Tweno to take the brunt of the calls with which he was bound to be inundated, once the full extent of the problem became known.

"You *will* let your staff handle the calls, won't you?"

Tweno nodded. "I'll take only the high-level ones. And I'll need Kyollan working with me full-time on the evacuation end of things. Our trading partners will have to hold off till things are resolved, and I'll get Tix to handle planetary communications not destined for you or me."

"Tix will love you for that," Ablakan chuckled, surprised to find his sense of humor still intact.

Tweno nodded with a sigh. Brilliant and skilled, the one area of Tix' work ethic that remained underdeveloped was being a 'team player'.

"Let's stay in close contact," Tweno said, as he turned towards his office. "We haven't time to duplicate efforts."

"Agreed."

Ablakan watched their Primary leave, his steps strong and purposeful. Did Shalaians realize what a remarkable leader they had, Ablakan wondered. Probably no more than they realized a black hole was days away from destroying their planet. And Ablakan was supposed to prevent that. The hopelessness of the task returned to mock him. Not in this universe, his inner voice retorted.

Ablakan blinked, suddenly realizing the significance of the thought. If School was right, there *were* two universes involved, weren't there?

Ablakan 'ported to his office, anxious to run a half-formed idea past Juneli. He stopped in his tracks, appalled. Juneli was cleaning out her desk.

"June, where are you going?"

"Just next door," she smiled reassurance. "I made an 'executive decision' while you were gone."

Her eyebanks held conflicting emotions Ablakan which couldn't identify. She motioned to someone waiting in the adjoining office. Ablakan turned to see who it was and felt his face flame in embarrassment and pleasure.

"Good to see you again, First Ablakan." Wiki extending her hand in a humanlike gesture.

Taken off-guard, Ablakan grinned foolishly as they shook hands. He tried to cover the reaction by looking a query at Juneli. The latter shrugged.

"You needed the best, and my contacts tell me that's our Wiki."

Again, Ablakan was struck by the congruent emotions that emanated from Juneli. And the timing.

"When did you precog what the scientist was going to say?" Ablakan asked with sudden understanding.

"Just after you left for the palace." Juneli faced him then, her face transformed by the intensity of her feelings. "Ablakan, listen to me, please; it's important. You *must* forget about this office, Pantai, everything. Between Wiki and I, there's nothing we can't handle; I'll see to that. You just concentrate on saving Shalaii, if you can."

Ablakan glanced at Wiki, and was gratified to see her expression equally adamant.

"If we succeed, it will be in no small part thanks to you two," he told them, unspeakably relieved. "Pantai is in good hands."

"As is Shalaii," Wiki declared, awarding Ablakan a warm smile before turning with Juneli toward the work awaiting their attention.

* * *

Ablakan was surprised to receive a call put through by Lowen's telepath, Frundal.

I am so very sorry, Ablakan, a mortified Dru Hepiak cried, inadvertently projecting so much self-recrimination that Ablakan had to scramble to block his own empathic response. *I saw that horrid device, and took it for space debris. I could have stopped it, and I didn't. Please tell me I can help you somehow.*

It's not your fault. Ablakan carefully suppressed his own regret. *We also didn't realize what we were seeing, at first. Thank you for your offer; we may call on you soon.*

We will help in any way we can, Dru assured him.

Three hours later, Ablakan and Tix linked with the senior human and Orowan telepaths. Kyollan, Richard Ironhorse and Withish, Orowan's newest recruit, were handling the urgent workload on each of the three worlds until the conference call was over.

As a concession, Tix had negotiated being involved in the these high-level discussions, offering to work later hours if need be. Since she so often lent valuable insight, it had been an easy sell.

So what did School have to say? Jan asked knowingly.

Lots, but I'm not sure how much it helps us. Ablakan opened his eyebanks to consult his transcript of the conversation he'd had with School earlier that day. *I'll send you a copy, but here's the meat of it.*

The antimatter universe that is a sister, or companion, to yours is not a mirror universe. There is not an antimatter Shalaii on the other side. Of course, to those who know of it, or postulate of it on the other side, theirs is the matter universe, and yours is the antimatter universe. And yes, telepathic interaction is readily possible between beings in both – or any other – universe.

To use an Earth analogy, think of your two universes as huge fishtanks, with water being recycled between them to keep both refreshed. The 'water', though, has no germs it can carry from one to the next, no pollutants, for the 'door' between the two is the black hole, which crushes everything down and in a sense purifies it, so when it explodes into a star on the other side, it is not only 'pure' but benign.

In your companion universe, all the elements are polarity-backwards, and opposite chemical configurations; that is all. Other than that, everything is functionally similar between the two sides. Stars shine, planets revolve around suns, moons around planets, the same as here.

Somehow I expected something more bizarre. To Ablakan, Shownae sounded disappointed.

Having a gigantic hole in my back yard about to swallow my homeworld is quite bizarre enough for me, Ablakan declared. *I don't see many choices, and those I do see are pretty far-fetched.*

For example? Jan prompted.

Ablakan consulted his notes. *Such as maybe 'porting the hole itself somewhere else. If we could be sure it wouldn't cause a problem for someone in our sister universe.*

Which means finding at least one telepathic sentient on that side with the capabilities we have, Brenda pointed out. *That could take some doing."*

True, Ablakan agreed. *But if so, we'd have a way of finding out what would happen if we could feed one of those smaller holes enough to make it explode into a star on their side. Hopefully, it would collapse the hole on this side. That is, after we figure out what to do about the one menacing Shalaii.*

Wouldn't that mean we'd have to share a common 'wall' with the other universe? Jan wanted to know. *So far, it looks like this*

90

universe is a ball, with space objects, including black holes, willy-nilly throughout it. So where would the interfaces be, if black holes lead into another universe?

No fair! You've been studying, Brenda accused drolly.

I've been caught napping too often lately, Jan grimaced. *We can't afford that luxury any more.*

Ablakan finished scribbling down the question. *That's a good one to ask School. Obviously, we can't do that with this hole, nor can we plug it. There's only one other option I can think of to save Shalaii but it, too, would cause massive problems. Assuming it's even possible.*

You mean, move Shalaii into a different orbit? Tix frowned at him doubtfully.

Yes. Ablakan smiled at his protégé, pleased by her quick, analytical mind.

I don't see why it should, if you keep it the same distance from the sun, and at the same angle, speed of revolution, spin and so on, Jan disagreed. *After all, the sun shines the same from every angle.*

There's more than our sun to think about, Ablakan reminded her. *We have two other influences on our tides besides the moon to consider, and that could change the weather globally.*

Oh, that's right, Jan remembered. *But if it turns out we can't remove or move the hole or change Shalaii's orbit, that only leaves moving your entire solar system except for the hole. And that's preposterous. Isn't it?*

Outrageous, Shownae agreed. *But using every 'porter we've got, working as a team, could we pull it off?*

That's crazy, Tix snorted. *There's a limit to what we can move. I mean, think what you're saying.* A solar system?

Well, what's the biggest thing you've ever moved? Jan directed the question to Ablakan, but he could feel the others searching their own memories.

Certainly nothing as big as a planet. Maybe the size of a small moon, Ablakan replied uncertainly. He felt Jan's attitude turn reckless.

What about if I try it with a planet-size asteroid like the one near Vexika? Jan asked.

91

Careful, Jan, Brenda cautioned. *Remember what happened to that rogue 'porter three years ago who tried to move a truck the wrong way. Fair labotomized himself, as I recall.*

Anyone would've, doing it the way he did! Our way, there shouldn't be any size or distance restrictions. None I've found, anyway. It's just a matter of getting your focus around it all.

Before anyone could object further, Jan located the oversized asteroid, enclosed it with her focus and 'ported it near the sun they had helped birth a short time before.

See? Nothing to it.

Despite her bravado, Ablakan recognized the relief in her mental voice. Ablakan gently probed her mind, though he knew it wouldn't go undetected. He was relieved to find no diminution of Jan's mental clarity or strength. She was unquestionably tired, but perhaps she had been that way beforehand.

Impressive, Brenda acknowledged. *But what would happen if you tried to move a sun, especially if it was – or worse, still is – a black hole on the other side? What would moving it do, on this side and the other?*

Yeah, that's the real question, isn't it? Jan shook her head in frustration. *It always comes back to the same thing: We can't do anything till we have someone on the other side telling us what repercussions what we do here would have there.*

But remember what School said. Ablakan scanned his notes to find the passage he wanted. *'To those who know of it or postulate of it'* – meaning our universe – *'on the other side, theirs is the matter universe and yours is the antimatter universe'. That suggests to me School has contacts there. Maybe they could give us an introduction, or at least point us in the right direction.*

Do you want to do it, since you're far better at imaging that we are? Jan asked.

If Tweno approves it, yes. It will be my second time doing a 'first contact'.

Ablakan could feel Jan's emotions turn sheepish. *We* have *been hogging the first-contact limelight, haven't we?*

Actually, I was thinking we've been rather cowardly, letting you take all the risks, Ablakan told her. That realization did not sit well with him, but until now, he hadn't given it any thought.

I'll be glad to stand by you, if you'd like, Jan offered. *Remember, this isn't about bravery. You're Shalaii's best hope for survival. You can't afford to take unnecessary chances.*

There's that. But if the introductions or pointers are coming from School, it should be fairly safe. I doubt people there can hide things from School any more than we can.

Still, it couldn't hurt to have me along, Jan pressed. *Why don't you run it by Tweno, and I'll do the same with my bosses, see what they think?*

Alright, thanks. It *would* be reassuring to have her along, Ablakan knew. *Any other suggestions?*

There weren't, so after an exchange of farewells, the conference ended.

Immediately, Tix frowned up at him. "You're not seriously thinking of moving the whole solar system, are you?"

"Not unless all else fails. And I intend to get as much information as possible before trying anything at all."

Tix nodded and glanced at her timepiece. "I'd better be going." She immediately 'ported herself back to the palace.

Ablakan experienced a moment of pique. At her age he had been prohibited from 'porting himself off the island, and here she was, able to go anywhere she pleased. But then, at her age you hadn't been 'porting for six years as she has, he reminded himself. Besides, with his planet at risk, what was he doing feeling jealous of his protégé?

Banishing the unworthy thought, Ablakan buzzed Juneli and asked her to come into his office.

"How did it go?"

Ablakan synopsized the discussion, and watched her face turn pensive.

"Idea?" Ablakan prompted.

"Just an observation. We haven't heard back from Aq'Narl about the hole-maker technology. Since their former ruler caused this problem, they might let us examine the device ourselves, considering what we're up against."

"They might at that. I'll clear it with Tweno first, but I agree; we'd best act while they're feeling beholden to us. See you shortly."

Tweno looked up from his 'scriber as Ablakan arrived in the room.

"How did it go?" the Primary asked, unwittingly repeating Juneli's query.

"We've come up with a few desperate-sounding schemes, but I don't know if any of them are workable."

Ablakan outlined the ideas that had come out of their conference and the objections which had been raised.

"Jan seemed to have no trouble moving that asteroid," Ablakan noted. "So I'm guessing it's possible to move Shalaii. I don't know about moving the entire solar system minus the black hole. I admit, my mind boggles at the thought."

"Mine, too," Tweno agreed. "But I think you're right; your first stop should be Aq'Narl. Do you want me on-line with you, or would they be more receptive to you on your own?"

"I think me alone," Ablakan decided. "I doubt they're capable of compassion, but they may feel guilty, or at least responsible for our plight. But in case guilt isn't enough, it might be wise to offer something in return."

Between the member planets, that would constitute a staggering array of possibilities. But knowing the Aq'Narls, they would want technology. It had been what had drawn them to the bargaining table in the first place, and in part why they had been initially refused membership. Specifically, their singleminded quest for war machines, and their desire to use teleportation to catch their enemies by surprise, had made the veto unanimous. But that had been during Maxxift's regime. The new Administration might have a more benign agenda.

"Have you something in mind?" Tweno asked.

"I don't suppose they'd be interested in that super-grain Konapi's researchers developed on Enaxat last summer."

Tweno shook his head. "Not impressive enough. They'll hold out for us training one of their 'paths to 'port. Which we won't, of course."

"No, not with their history. What would you suggest?"

"I understand there's been a lot of activity on their sister planet."

"Where did you hear that?" Ablakan looked up, surprised.

94

"Juneli. Yesterday she told me she got a vision of them building rough houses on the planet and using crude implements she took to be mining equipment. If you scan the planet and find they're not mining anything radioactive, maybe we could trade advanced mining equipment for the holer technology."

"Now *that* they may go for." Ablakan recorded the reminder on his own 'scriber before asking, "How's it going from your end?"

Tweno grunted. "Slowly. Earth and Orowa between them could accommodate about ten million Shalaians, but that's without any of their belongings other than maybe one bag each. I wouldn't want to try to sell that to our people, even with the threat of extinction hanging over their heads."

Tweno was right, Ablakan realized. Trade had made their people wealthier and more comfortable than ever. They would not relinquish it easily.

"I understand Lowen is pretty crowded; they've been scouring their section of space for another planet they can colonize," Tweno continued. "Perhaps they've found one that would support life, but that they've rejected for one reason or another. Some place we could live until a better home is found. I was about to have Kyollan check with their Commander."

"They have explored space more than any other species we've encountered," Ablakan agreed. "That's a good thought, sir. I'll give you a progress report tonight, if there's nothing too pressing before then."

"Likewise. And I'll send the speech I'm working on to the Firsts this afternoon. I'll need a quick response, because I'm going global with it tonight. Rumors about the hole are already widespread. We can't delay."

"I will read it as soon as it arrives," Ablakan promised. "And 'path you my reply."

"Good."

Ablakan 'ported himself to his private kitchen for a quick snack before the next phase of his investigations. The last thing he needed was to have his stomach growl while he was negotiating with the Aq'Narls.

Automatically, his hand reached for the fresh muchipans his head chef always made for him, then he changed his mind. His body required nourishment, not tastebud gratification. He settled for a plate of appetizing leftovers and sat down to appease his hunger. He reached for the hear-other.

"I'll be up shortly. I just needed a bite," he told Juneli when she answered. "Anything new?"

"Nothing critical. We have a few questions that can wait."

That was a relief. Ablakan wolfed down the snack and returned to his office. His plush chair contoured silently to hold his spare frame in balanced comfort. He took a deep breath and closed his eyes. He felt his mind span the lightyears in an instant.

There was a short delay, then Aq'Narl's main 'path, Oh'ra-mohynn, opened up to Ablakan.

You are greeted, First Ablakan.

As always, the recognition was devoid of emotion, as the 'path waited for Ablakan to state his business.

We greet you as well, Ablakan replied. *I need to discuss a most urgent matter with your Administrator, if he is available.*

I will check.

The brief interlude seemed endless to Ablakan, considering how critical Eshwyt's cooperation could prove to Shalaii's future. At length, Ablakan felt the ruler's mental presence, and repeated his greeting.

We are open to you, in fellowship, Eshwyt stated. *My 'path tells me your business is urgent.*

Yes, Administrator. Last night the group of black holes near our planet was consolidated and expanded into one very large hole by the detonation of a minute, but very powerful bomb.

Ablakan described in detail the device which had so nearly taken his mind with it. He felt Eshwyt's reaction, as the Administrator recognized the torpedo to be undeniably of Aq'Narl origin.

We suspect your former ruler sent it as revenge. We have been unable to find him telepathically, which suggests to us that he may have suicided afterwards.

I expect you are right, the Administrator replied at length. *How much danger does this hole pose to your planet?*

Unless something can be done, Shalaii will be destroyed in approximately a month.

The Administrator made a clucking sound, which Ablakan interpreted as regret.

How can we help you?

The devices which were used to create those holes in the first place. If we could examine the technology, it might suggest a way of closing them.

I doubt there is anything that will close a black hole that is already large enough to destroy your planet, Eshwyt stated. *Perhaps the smaller ones. After receiving your earlier request, we searched carefully, but the technology has been lost.*

Lost? Ablakan had a sinking feeling he knew what the Administrator was about say.

Maxxift had those devices built in secret, I am told. Before we could drive him from power, he had a select group of his followers executed. I have learned that among them was everyone associated with the holer program, and the ships so outfitted were also destroyed. In effect, he took the technology with him.

So that was that. Eshwyt's mind was open, and as far as Ablakan could tell, clear of deception.

We regret your circumstances, the Administrator added. *Have you a secondary homeworld?*

Not as yet. We are hoping to find temporary lodging for our people before it is too late. You wouldn't know of such a planet, would you?

Unfortunately, no. Have you checked with School?

They know of none that are not already heavily colonized. If you learn of any, would you please let us know as soon as possible?

I will ask, Eshwyt promised solemnly. *And our scientists will consider your problem.*

Thank you.

They exchanged good wishes before disconnecting.

Juneli was standing close by. She looked at him hopefully.

"Good intentions, but nothing to offer," Ablakan sighed.

Her face fell as he synopsized the conversation. "You'd think they'd at least offer to put up some of our people temporarily, considering it's one of their own who put us in this predicament."

"Would *you* want to live in that society?"

Juneli considered the prospect, but not for long. "I think I'd rather take my chances with that hole out there."

"We'll find another place, if we have to," Ablakan assured her with more confidence than he felt.

"So now what?" she asked.

"Now we see what contacts School has on the other side."

"The way our luck has been running, they'll have none."

CHAPTER 7

None? Incredulity and disappointment merged painfully in Ablakan's question.

None still alive that you would want to meet, School amended. *Our contacts there are very limited.*

Ablakan's mind reeled momentarily, unable to accept yet another critical door closing on their chances.

We can tell you of those we know. At least if you find them mentally, you will know to avoid them, School offered.

Thank you.

It was a token gift – a consolation prize – but one which might in future prove useful. As Ablakan felt the information being transferred into his memory, a thought occurred to him. *If it was your planet instead of ours in this situation, what would you do?*

The response was singularly unreassuring. *Die, probably.*

You know what we plan to try, Ablakan persisted. *Have you ever heard of another species attempting anything similar, and if so, what was the result?*

You are the first. We are eager to see what will happen.

Does it matter to you whether we succeed or not? Or is it just of passing interest? Ablakan asked savagely, galled past the point of manners.

It matters, Ablakan. But we have no information that could help you.

He could feel their group sadness, and knew they spoke true.

I'm sorry, Ablakan sighed. *Please forgive my rudeness.*

We have heard much worse from other species facing disaster. We do not take offence.

Thank you. Ablakan hesitated a moment, wondering what else he could ask. *Your species amasses information. Does it also use that knowledge to formulate new ideas?*

Of course. School sounded surprised by the question. *That is what information is for.*

Have you applied your total knowledge to consider our situation?

Perhaps we can readdress it, School replied obliquely. *We will let you know if we discover any new possibilities.*

I'd be most grateful if you would. Thank you for your kindness. And patience, Ablakan added, feeling guilty for his outburst.

Focus on the problem, and do not be concerned about us, School advised, and withdrew from his mind.

The hear-other light was flashing when Ablakan opened his eyes. Juneli had turned the sound off so as not to disturb him. He picked up the receiver. It was a recorded message from Juneli, informing him Tweno's speech had arrived.

Ablakan rose from the chair to stretch muscles taut as much from stress as inactivity. He strode into the adjoining room, where Juneli and Wiki were conversing quietly as they assembled a large document.

Ablakan eyed it. "Hopefully that's not the speech."

"No. It's the final draft of the trade agreement with the Lowens," Wiki explained.

Wordlessly, Juneli handed him Tweno's proposed speech, her eyes searching his. Alakan shook his head sadly, and saw her face fall.

"I'll explain later," he promised, and returned to his office to read the script.

As usual Tweno had been thorough and honest. Ablakan made a couple grammatical changes and 'ported it back to their Primary. He would have liked to discuss with Tweno the discouraging results of his conversations with the Aq'Narls and School, but held off. It should wait until after the Primary's address to their people.

From long habit, he found himself wanting to talk to Jan. How many times, in the past, had she given him hope when things were at their bleakest? He put through the call, and it was instantly answered.

No wonder you're so down, Jan remarked sympathetically, when Ablakan related the contents of his discussions to date. *But we're ready here. All we need is a way to get our focus across into the other universe, and then Tom will see what he can pick up there. Did School just give you the name of those two species, or did you get a 'feel' of their mindprint? It might be something we can use for trailblazing into that universe.*

I don't know, Ablakan admitted. *I haven't accessed those memories yet. I'll do so now.*

Among the images and assorted data, he was pleased to feel School's mental experience of the contacts' minds. One, especially, was sharply defined, and he zeroed in on it, holding it open in his mind for Jan to experience.

Got it, she confirmed. *I'll let my bloodhound husband get a feel of it, then hopefully we can follow him in.*

I'll stand by.

Left to his own thoughts, Ablakan couldn't help but wonder if yet another disappointment lay in store for them. Even if they were successful in breaching the barrier between universes, how long before they found a suitably advanced and amicable species, then located a telepath among them with whom they could converse in images? How much longer still before that individual could reach someone in power willing to help them, if the ruler could be convince of their existence?

Too long, Ablakan realized, remembering his and Jan's quests to do so on their worlds. Which left – what?

Jan returned at that moment, with Tom mentally in tow.

What? she asked, hearing the tail-end of his last thought.

I was just thinking, even if we get lucky in finding someone, we don't have time to get from first contact to talking to the ruler. Look how long it took us.

But we didn't have School with us at the time, Jan replied smugly.

Ablakan shook his head in confusion, feeling like he'd missed part of the conversation. An integral part.

What do you mean?

School called just as I was fetching Tom. They'll let us ride across with them, so we see how to do it. Being a multiplicity, they can cover a much larger area faster than we can, and probably pick up on consciousnesses more strongly than us. They said they can usually locate planetary leaders in seconds, using a light global scan. They're standing by. Hang on.

Ablakan's heart did a flip-flop of relief. It would seem they really did care. He'd been given to understood that School rarely involved themselves in the fates of their contacts. Yet here they were playing a direct, even pivotal role.

A wave of gratitude welled up within Ablakan, as he felt their presence join the focus.

We have lived passively long enough, they told Ablakan, as he tried to express his appreciation. *You need our help, and we need some . . . excitement.*

Jan hooted with laughter. *If it's excitement you crave, you've gotten in with the right crowd.*

Ablakan felt School's humor change to determination. *The conversion is rapid. You must pay close attention. We go in now.*

Ablakan gasped at the sudden twist his focus underwent. It felt as though his mind was being turned inside out, to suddenly see as clearly as before, but . . . reversed somehow.

We are there, School announced with aplomb. *When we are ready, you will lead us back.*

I'm not sure I can, Ablakan said.

Me, neither. Jan sounded as confused by the process as he was.

It will become clearer as you align yourself with this universe, School assured them. *We will now search.*

Obediently, Ablakan, Jan and Tom quieted their minds to minimize interference. Without anything to hold their focus, it became increasingly difficult to keep errant thoughts from sliding in, but eventually they felt School's mental return.

There are no suitable species within five light-years of the universal border with Shalaii. Do you want us to search further afield?

Where are we now? Ablakan asked. *Are we close to Shalaii?*

Right across from it, yes. We thought that was where you wanted to start looking for advanced people.

It is, Ablakan agreed. *But our main concern is that our efforts to move or remove the hole, or to move Shalaii or our solar system, will not cause a problem for people on this side. But if there's no one in this sector, then what we do should be okay.*

We did not say there was no one here, just no species suitable for your first contact purposes, School pointed out.

Oh, Jan said, understanding. *Where are these people?*

Within a tenth of a light-year.

Too close, Ablakan acknowledged. *But why can't we contact them?*

They have not yet evolved to using tools or language. They would have no framework for understanding your mental presence or your questions.

Are you capable of seeing on both sides of the universal line at the same time? Ablakan asked, as an idea dawned on him.

For the first time, Ablakan felt consternation among the group egos.

Divide our focus? We have never done that. We think as one.

But could you do so, safely? Jan asked eagerly.

Doubt colored their response a dull grey. *We do not know what effect separating ourselves in opposing universes would have on us, or if we could rejoin after the experience.*

Ablakan shook his head. *We can't ask you to risk yourselves. We will find another way.*

Stand by.

Ablakan was surprised to feel a roiling confusion of thoughts and emotions interacting within the whole at unimaginable speed. So rapid was the exchange that he was unable to gain even an inkling of what was going on. He flashed a private question mark to Jan, who shrugged her ignorance.

It has been decided, School announced. *That we will attempt your most provocative experiment. Should we become separate multiplicities, we at least shall have a strong presence in both universes, and be able to gain and exchange far more knowledge than we can functioning only in one.*

You are certain you want to do this? Ablakan felt compelled to ask.

Yes, we have decided. The feelings they projected left no doubt in the matter.

Thank you, dear friends, Ablakan said, hoping they would feel the gratitude his words could never adequately convey. *The first thing we need to know is what that black hole near Shalaii looks like from this side. If it hasn't broken through yet, perhaps it can be moved without impacting this universe. Second, does Shalaii's sun have some sort of presence on this side that would keep us from moving it, if we have to try to relocate our solar system away from that black hole?*

School sounded somewhat distracted, as the grouped minds said, *We understand your needs. Now it is time for us to separate into two multiples. It has never been done before, and we cannot guarantee what will happen when we do. We recommend you disconnect from us, and the multiplicity that may remain here will reconnect with you when it is safe to do so.*

Understood, Jan and Ablakan replied at the same time. Both hastily broke the mental bond with the already-separating group.

They sure don't waste time when they decide to do something, do they? Jan remarked.

I'm just amazed that they're going to all this effort – and possible danger – on Shalaii's behalf. I get the feeling such active involvement is unprecedented for them. For which Ablakan was all the more grateful.

I had the same impression, Jan admitted. *Perhaps they just got tired of seeing species they have come to like dying out. Losing friends can't be any easier on them than it is on us, no matter how many times they've seen it.*

Perhaps. Ablakan suspected the idea of adventure (excitement, they had called it) had found a niche and taken root. *Whatever it was, they couldn't have started at a better time, from my point of view.*

I'll say!

She seemed about to add more when they became aware of contact from a much-depleted group presence. Smaller but just as powerful-feeling, Ablakan noted.

Was the division successful, healthwise? he asked solicitously.

Yes, we – and we – were successful.

Will you be able to continue to think as one, with separate exposures and experiences happening simultaneously on both sides? Ablakan could feel Jan's mind boggle at the idea, as he posed the question. Or was it his own he was feeling?

We-here and we-there assimilate and share almost immediately. It is not as rapid as before, but it is acceptable, School proclaimed. *And stimulating. But you had questions. Stand by.*

This time, the focus disconnected entirely, to scan the areas across from the black hole and Shalaii's sun. Perhaps, their halved membership did not lend itself to maintaining multiple focuses.

While I'm here, Tom said, startling Ablakan, as Tom had not uttered a mental word till now. *I'll just see if I can pick up on anything past the five light-years School searched.*

Good idea, Jan told him.

Ablakan stilled his thoughts, so as not to interfere, and felt Jan do the same. Ablakan focused on his heartrate to avoid slipping into reverie. Time seemed eternal, and he was beginning to feel his focus waver despite his best efforts, when Tom let out an elated grunt.

Found something. Remind me to run it by School afterwards.

As if you'd forget something like that, Jan smirked, just as they felt School-here rejoin the link.

We have done as you asked. The hole has punctured through to this side, and evidence suggests the aperture is growing, though no material has been expelled into this universe yet. We believe if your planet is pulled into the tunnel, its mass will be sufficient to create a sun on this side.

In which case, the exploding star would fry that emerging civilization, was Tom's assessment.

Yes, the event would destroy both worlds. However, even without your planet going in, over time the hole will become a sun in this universe. Either way, that species is doomed.

How long have they? Jan asked.

Indeterminate. Certainly not enough to evolve to encompass space travel.

Then we have to move or remove the black hole, Ablakan said.

School projected a strong negation. *We believe it is not possible to change something which has a shared presence in both universes. Unless another species on this side relocates them, eventually they will perish.*

Jan asked, rather timidly, *If you do find a kindly spacefaring species nearby, would you let them know about this?*

Yes, we would.

Thank you. Though it was by no means a done deal, the possibility made Ablakan feel a lot better. *What about our sun? Is it attached to anything on this side?*

There is nothing across from your sun except plasma, School confirmed.

Ablakan, Jan and Tom heaved a joint sigh of relief at the news. Moving the solar system had been the last option left open to them, unlikely as it seemed. But at least now they could consider it.

We have our work cut out for us, Ablakan admitted. *School, you have our eternal gratitude.*

We are pleased with the outcome, for us all. We find that you have not properly assimilated the route between universes. Stand by to have it implanted.

Moments later, Ablakan felt his uncertainty regarding the process give way to a vast and detailed knowing.

Before we leave, Tom mentally cleared his throat. *I scouted around a bit while we were waiting, and I think I've found a strong mental presence.*

Ablakan felt School's interest quicken, and they gleaned the experience from Tom's mind.

We may not make direct contact; they must approach us themselves. But we can check your impression.

They disconnected but returned almost at once. *Confirmed. They are strong consciousnesses, singular not grouped, and spread throughout the land masses on that planet.*

Maybe a species of telepaths, Tom ventured hopefully.

Our scan would suggest that possibility, School-here agreed. *We will enjoy your next visit.*

Which was a tactful way of saying goodbye, Ablakan thought. He projected his gratitude to School-here once more just as they withdrew from his mind.

Shall I? Ablakan suggested, and two minds gave him the go-ahead.

Confidently, Ablakan led the way, and this time the inside-out experience felt surprisingly natural. It was over in the wink of an eyebank, and then they were home.

Thank you, dear friends, for everything. I must report to Tweno.

And we to Saunders and company, Jan grinned. *I think you'd better start scouting around for a new address for your solar system. Perhaps someplace nearer Earth? Granted we are in the boonies out here, but there's not much traffic, and the view is nice.*

For the first time in what seemed like forever, Ablakan found himself laughing. *Wouldn't that be great? I can't think of nicer neighbors to have.*

Ablakan resurfaced in his office, blinking rapidly as a wave of disorientation washed over him. But then, it wasn't every day he went traipsing around an antimatter universe. Although nothing in their situation had tangibly changed, his heart felt lighter than air.

Flinging open the adjoining door, he beamed at the two wonderful ladies slaving at keeping Pantai functioning normally, and beckoned them over.

They exchanged looks of surprise and hope, and came to him. Impulsively, Ablakan enclosed them both in his arms, giving them a quick, heartfelt hug before releasing them.

"Good news?" Juneli asked with an impish grin.

"Yes, but I'll not tell you here." He extended a hand toward each. "I'll tell you over dinner. At the palace. Tweno doesn't know it yet, but he's buying!"

A moment later, Tweno lifted haggard eyebanks to behold three grinning faces.

* * *

"So we have to move our solar system, is that what you're saying?" Tweno was frowning more in confusion than disapproval.

They were enjoying a particularly festive meal hastily prepared by the kitchen staff in their honor.

"Yes. But the good news is, we can do so without fear of harming anything in the other universe. And wherever we choose to move our system, School-here can probably make sure we're not in someone else's presumed territory. Unless we want to be. Jan's offer is very tempting, though she'll have to run it by her leaders."

"They have been wonderful friends," Tweno agreed. "But remember what their President told me when we first met: Government leaders change, and those who may be friendly toward us may be replaced by others who are not."

"But that was before we became such great trading partners," Ablakan was quick to point out. "We've been in a stable friendship with Earth, Orowa and the others for many years now. And those years have seen quite a few changes in leadership."

Tweno nodded once. "But there's something else to consider. If I were them, I wouldn't be so eager to have a new neighbor whose planet was targeted for destruction. Maxxift might not be the only one who lost his job in their little revolution. Someone else may be out there, holding a grudge. If I were Earth, I wouldn't want to have us too close by, just in case our enemies try something else."

Ablakan grimaced, thinking that one over.

Tweno placed a conciliatory hand on Ablakan's shoulder. "Just concentrate on how to move us, and let me talk to Earth and Orowa. Between us ruler-types, we should be able to come up with a suitable location. Then you and your colleagues can make sure it doesn't hold any surprises before we actually move in."

"Fair enough," Ablakan agreed.

Tweno looked at his personal timemometer. "I must leave you now to prepare for my speech. I will add your news, if you don't mind. It will be good to have something positive to report, after such a horrifying disclosure."

"Yes, of course. But please don't make it sound too certain. We don't know yet if it can be done. You will continue with your evacuation plans, just in case, won't you?"

"Of course. Still, the possibility of relocation is heartening, and if it avoids panic and chaos among our people, it will have been worthwhile even if it later proves impossible." Tweno stood and adjusted his uniform, inclining his head towards the ladies. "It was delightful to have your company tonight."

"Thank you, Primary," Juneli and Wiki bowed in response.

Ablakan got up to leave. "One last thing, before you go: After your speech, you and I are bound to become Number One and Two on the media's most-newsworthy list. May I recommend added security for both our facilities and their workers?"

"I've already seen to it," Tweno nodded. "As well as for Konapi and Lisham. Do you three want to stick around for the speech?"

"Thanks, sir, but I'll catch it at the office. I'm expecting an update from Jan," Ablakan replied glibly.

Tweno snorted, as he turned to leave. "It's that damned cat, isn't it?"

Ablakan grinned sheepishly, having been caught in a white lie. "Cats plural, actually. I forgot to feed them. They'll be tearing the place apart by now."

Tweno chuckled and left.

"Shall we?" Ablakan held out a hand to his companions, who obediently grabbed hold.

" 'Expecting an update'," Juneli snorted as they arrived back in Wiki's office. "You should know better than to try to fool Tweno."

"One can always hope," Ablakan grinned, and 'ported himself to the kitchen, then into the Lair.

Immediately, he was set upon by a couple of hyperactive furballs. He barely had time to place their bowls on the floor before they pounced on the food as though they hadn't eaten in a week. Their water dish, he noted, was now upside down, and the puddle had been spread in all directions by what looked like a mile of shredded material suspiciously similar to the window coverings. He glanced at the window, and sure enough, one of the curtains was missing.

With an elaborate sigh, Ablakan picked up the remnants, speculating that Shalaii probably had a better chance surviving the black hole than he had of making it through the kittens' maturation period with his sanity intact. What the felines needed, he knew, was an outdoor place to play – one that was fully enclosed and climb-and-dig-proof. But that would have to wait until Shalaii's fate was decided, one way or the other.

Ablakan made a mental note to give his pets their playtime with him after they had sated their appetite. In the meantime, he 'ported himself to the library, where Juneli and Wiki were already glued to the player-box. Ablakan ease himself down on the seat beside them.

Tweno had just thanked everyone for tuning in. He was in full dress uniform, his mane gleaming in the lights above him, just out of sight of the cameras. He had chosen as his 'stage' the far side of the dining room with its wall-across windows offering as a backdrop the beautiful manicured golf course. He stood facing the cameras, as though ready to spring into some as-yet undisclosed action.

"By now you may have heard the rumor about deliberately-created small black holes in the asteroid field near Shalaii. Unfortunately, it is true. The former ruler of Aq'Narl was having special freighters he had commissioned mine radioactive ore from our asteroids to use in weapons against his own people. Tiny black holes formed wherever the holer technology, as we have named it, was used. Similar holes were also created in Earth and Orowan space. We do not know what purpose those were destined to serve.

On my orders, First Ablakan moved our remaining asteroids out of reach of the Aq'Narl freighters. He also confiscated all poached asteroids and anything which had been made from them, including bombs, and the bombs were destroyed. Shortly afterwards, we received word from Aq'Narl that their ruler had been deposed by the people, and that the new regime was most grateful to us.

We have since learned that, just before he escaped, their ousted ruler, Maxxift, ordered the execution of anyone who had knowledge of the holer technology. He also had every ship so equipped destroyed. That technology might have offered us a way to remove these tiny holes in space, but now we will have to learn how on our own. I wish that that was the biggest problem we face, but it isn't, by far."

Tweno took a deep breath, his expression turning grim. Ablakan knew he was doing this deliberately, to prepare his audience for the terrible announcement to come.

"Yesterday evening, First Ablakan and his assistant, Juneli, tried their best to stop a very powerful Aq'Narl needle-bomb from detonating inside one of the black holes where the asteroid field used to be. First Ablakan had just enclosed it in his focus, preparatory to removing it, when the bomb exploded. He would have been seriously injured, perhaps killed, had it not been for the heroic actions of Juneli, Tix, Jan and Shownae.

The explosion inside the tiny hole caused it to expand massively. Orowa and Earth's main links scoured the galaxy, searching for Maxxift, but they could not find his mindprint. They believe that, having exacted his revenge on us, he then suicided rather than face the consequences of his actions. This morning, Earth's foremost expert on black holes arrived to determine what impact the black hole, which now encompasses all the other holes in the former asteroid field, would have on Shalaii."

Tweno raised his head slightly, squaring his shoulders as though facing a terrible enemy.

"I will not lie to you good people; the prognosis is bleak. We may be forced to relocate to another planet – or perhaps several planets, in the short term. Although the danger to Shalaii is extreme, we still have approximately one month during which to evacuate, should that become necessary. I have assumed that task, with the wholehearted assistance of our allied worlds. They assure me that, no matter what happens, room will be made for every Shalaian until a suitable new home can be found for us.

But things may not be as bad as they seem. First Ablakan, in conjunction with our allied links, has been working tirelessly to find ways of removing the threat to Shalaii, or alternatively, to move our entire solar system out of harm's way. The ancient civilization known to us as 'School' has already gone to extraordinary lengths on our behalf, and should solar system relocation be decided, we have received overtures from Earth to move close by.

Never have we been faced with such a formidable task, but then again, never have we had so much power, talent and knowledge on our side. What your governors need of you, at this crucial time, is to be ready for possible relocation, but to carry on as usual until then. For if Ablakan and our allies are able, they will ensure that life on Shalaii returns to normal. Until then, we must prepare ourselves for the expected earthquakes, severe storms and other disturbances this singularity is bound to cause. The next little while will not be easy, but you have my word that we will keep you informed of every major development. Shalaians are a brave and resourceful people, and we will not insult your intelligence by keeping the truth from you.

I would ask one other thing: that you keep requests and queries of your Firsts and of me to a minimum, so that we may concentrate fully on resolving our current dilemma. In so doing, you will be contributing in no small way to our success, whichever form it takes.

Until my next report, I urge you to keep a positive outlook. We have not failed you in the past, and we are more determined than ever to serve your best interests now. On that you have our word."

Tweno inclined his head slightly and solemnly toward the camera, then stood tall and resolute as his image faded from the screen.

Wiki turned moist eyebanks toward Ablakan. "I don't know what we'd do without him. And you," she added, giving him a warm smile.

"We haven't done anything yet," he pointed out to cover his embarrassment at such unbridled hero-worship. "Which reminds me, I'd better tend to the cats."

Ablakan 'ported himself into the Lair relieved, for the moment, to be nothing more than a handy plaything to its hairy inhabitants. It occurred to him, as he fended off their aggressive mock attacks, that he might have to get used to being seen as larger-than-life. If he and his colleagues succeeded in relocating their entire solar system, Ablakan knew that monuments would inevitably be erected in his honor, and he would be perceived as a savior-of-sorts. The thought sat in his stomach like a lump of undigested muchipans.

CHAPTER 8

"Jan, what does it take to get it through your head? You're *not* to take unnecessary risks!" Saunders glowered at her underneath his black, bushy eyebrows, his voice much louder than the distance between them required.

"They *were* necessary – for Shalaii, at any rate," Jan insisted. "We didn't start out to go into the antimatter universe. But when School offered to take us, right then and there – and at some risk to themselves, I might add – what was I supposed to do? Say 'oh, wait a minute, I've got to check with my boss'? Anyway, School's been there before, and it didn't hurt them any."

"You just said 'at some risk to themselves'," Saunders pointed out.

"That was from splitting up their multiple selves into two parts, with one portion staying behind and the rest crossing over."

Saunders sighed in resignation. "Alright. But you're not to go there again without checking with me first."

Jan shook her head adamantly. "C'mon, boss. You know what Shalaii's up against. I need to use my own judgment if I'm going to be of any help. I can't check every little thing with you beforehand."

"Like that little number you pulled, moving that gargantuan asteroid, just to prove a point?" Saunders wagged a finger at her. "One of these days you'll try something that backfires, and there won't be anyone strong enough to pull your fat out of the fire."

Jan nodded slowly, realizing he was probably right. She had lead a charmed life until now, but if she kept pushing her luck it was bound to run out sooner or later.

"Alright, tell you what: From now on, before I try something new, I'll make sure I've got a back-up locked onto me, just in case."

"Your word?" Saunders' eyes held hers, unblinking.

"Promise."

Saunders nodded. "Alright. So how do you people propose to move that solar system?"

"That's where you come in," Jan smiled at him ingratiatingly. "All we'd need, for now, is a weightless vacuum room with at least one side glass, so we can see the models."

Saunders lifted an eyebrow. "Of the Shalaian solar system?"

Jan nodded, becoming more animated now that her initial request hadn't been shot down. "To scale, of course, with the correct distances, spins, et cetera. We'll need to practice each of us moving our part of it while remaining linked so we can move it as a unit without affecting angles, spin cycles or anything else that matters."

"Tall order," Saunders noted. "And I suppose you need it yesterday."

"Or as close to yesterday as possible."

"I'll get our people on it. And in the meantime, what will you be up to?"

Jan felt her cheeks pink a bit, as she realized for the first time what the next logical step would be. "Umm, well . . . We know we can move planets, but so far, no one has tried to move a sun."

"A sun." Saunders turned his back to her, staring out the window.

Jan thought she heard his teeth grind. Her own shoulders became lumps of lead, as the full magnitude of what she was proposing hit home.

"I could start with a little one," she said, trying not to gulp.

He turned to face her, then. "Do you *really* think that would make any difference?"

"No," she admitted in a small voice. She definitely wasn't looking forward to this particular experiment.

"Have you asked School if it's ever been attempted before?"

"They know of no attempts to even move a planet." The trouble with breaking new ground was that it was so . . . untested.

Saunders rubbed a weary hand across his brow. "Let me think about it."

Jan left the room, blinking in surprise. Until that moment, she hadn't realized how heavily Shalaii's crisis was weighing on Saunders. Although he was masterful at hiding it, NASA's head hauncho did indeed have a heart.

Tom had a large salad ready, and Jack was carving a roast when Jan 'ported into their kitchen a few minutes later.

"Hi, guys," she greeted them with a lightness of heart she didn't feel. "Smells good."

"Will be, too," Jack assured her.

114

"What did Saunders have to say?" Tom asked, effortlessly seeing past her facade.

"Chewed me out for jumping the fence, of course. Then he asked me what's next." She stopped, chewing her lip.

"What *is* next?" Jack wanted to know.

"He's going to make that model you mentioned, and in the meantime, I told him I wanted to try moving a sun."

"*What?*" Tom gaped at her, aghast. "I thought you 'porter types'd just be joining and move the solar system as one entity."

"Can't. There's just no way to get our minds around it all, even working as a group the way School does. I didn't want to admit it, but I stretched myself to the limit moving that asteroid. I almost didn't make it." She nodded confirmation, as she noted their shocked expressions.

"Oh, hon, you've got to be more careful." Tom's eyes were filled with worry.

"Yeah, that's what Saunders said, too. And I did promise I wouldn't try anything new without a back-up locked on."

"And you'll keep that promise, won't you?" Tom pressed.

"Yes."

"So what did he say when you told him you wanted to move a sun?" Jack asked it nonchalantly, but Jan noticed his knuckles were white on the carving knife.

"He said he'd let me know." Jan exhaled explosively in sudden exasperation. "Damn it, *someone*'s got to do it, and I'm the logical choice. They can't risk Ablakan, and we're the only two who could possibly manage the sun and the largest planet."

"I know. But we just worry about you, kid," Jack said.

Jan snorted, but felt her humor return. At 61, she could hardly be considered a kid, especially from someone in his forties.

"He didn't say anything about my little discovery in the other universe, did he?" Tom wondered aloud, as they sat down to eat.

"Sorry, love; it slipped my mind." Jan winced apologetically. "It might not be the best time to ask for more favors, anyway."

"Probably not." Tom dug into his dinner, but Jan could see he was disappointed.

"As soon as Shalaii is safe, we'll spring it on him while he's still elated by our success," Jan promised. "He'll be bound to approve 'first contact' then."

"Another devious female," Jack remarked, and at the same moment, Brenda arrived with Billy in tow.

"Who? Me?", she asked in feigned surprise.

"No, Jan," Jack said, rising to give her a quick kiss, and a hug for Billy. The youth had reached the age where hugs were tolerated, but kisses were not.

"You should have seen me," Billy enthused, pulling out his chair. "I swam eight laps in a row!"

"Pretty impressive," Jack agreed. "Better than I could do, I bet."

"And then Jimmy Somers did a belly-flop and . . ."

The balance of the dinner was spent listening to a play-by-play of Billy's afternoon at the pool, and the problem of black holes and moving suns was tabled for another day.

* * *

Shownae moved for the fourth time in two days. Between maintaining a constant vigil against the escalating attacks and preparing to move a planet, Shownae was becoming ragged with exhaustion. A person could only go so long without sleep.

Again he toyed with the idea of involving his 'porting colleagues, and again he dismissed it. Any distraction could further endanger their success in saving Shalaii. He would just have to work this one through by himself.

Think, Shownae ordered his tired mind. He had given up trying to devise a block of his own. He had nearly been killed the last time he tried, not noticing that he had been found by his enemy until it was almost too late. And no amount of soul-searching helped him identify what his foe considered him guilty of.

Shownae had only one advantage and no way to use it: He and his friends and colleagues had been locked down against unauthorized 'porting, just in case such an eventuality occurred. Presumably, the rogue 'porter hadn't and, if found, could be 'ported into confinement and sedated.

It was late, but Shownae didn't hesitate. His fellow 'porters must not be sidetracked from their duties, but there were others he could call upon.

"Trikon," he said when he reached the Co-Lead Spacefarer in the latter's private dwelling. "I need a fast-acting sedative to use

116

against a rogue teleporter who's after me. I haven't time to explain further. Can you get it?"

"I'll call the lab right away." Trikon hung up.

Shownae thanked his Fates for his friend's unquestioning trust, and 'pathed a call to Frundal on Lowen.

I'm sorry to call so late, but I have a big problem and I need your help and Dru Hepiak's, if you are willing, Shownae said. He dared not waste time on niceties in case his enemy was again seeking him out with lethal intentions.

I will find Dru. Please wait.

Shownae 'split-focus' the way Ablakan had taught him to do long ago, using the interlude to check for his own mind-print being used by the other. As far as he could tell, it was not in use. He gets to sleep whenever he wants, Shownae thought resentfully.

I am here, Shownae, Dru Hepiak spoke through Frundal. *May we read you, for speed? Frundal feels your urgency.*

Yes, please do. Shownae was quiet while they scanned the pertinent details.

You should not have waited so long, my friend, Dru admonished.

The listen-far chimed. *That must be Trikon,* Shownae said. He reached for the device without breaking contact with the Lowens.

"The night techno has it in her hand. Good Fates, Shownae. I'll want a full report in the morning." Trikon hung up without giving Shownae a chance to thank him. Instead, Shownae projected his gratitude into the techno's mind while simultaneously retrieving the syringe.

Next, he contacted the night head decontamination chamber operator on Orowa's moon, Shyr, to let him know Dru Hepiak was expected and would be spending an indeterminate amount of time in the lounge waiting room. Then he 'ported the Lowen into the chamber. When the chamber finished processing Dru, and he was seated in the waiting room, Shownae released a cautious sigh of relief.

Now both would scan for Shownae's mind-print being sought by the would-be assassin. When they found it, the crossing trajectories would provide the coordinates of his enemy.

Mercifully, it did not take long. Shownae locked onto the area surrounding and including those coordinates and 'ported them

117

beside him in the field in which he was standing. He hadn't dared do so within a building.

As he had hoped, the abrupt change of venue momentarily disoriented his foe. Shownae's blistering uppercut caught the young man unawares. The man dropped, his hand releasing the vicious-looking device he had been holding. Shownae threw it into space before plunging the needle deep into the man's arm. Then Shownae delivered him to the waiting techno.

Thank you, my friend, he projected to Dru.

Glad we could help, Dru said. He stepped back into the decontamination chamber. *Next time, don't wait so long.*

Shownae nodded solemnly. *You have my word, although I fervently hope there will not* be *a next time.*

After Dru had been returned home, Shownae took a moment to thank his Fates before 'porting to his current dwelling and consigning himself to sleep.

* * *

Early the next morning, a surprisingly rested Shownae sat in Trikon's office, distractedly drumming his fingertips on the table. Trikon had gone to find Moohri when the latter had failed to return his call. Shownae glanced at the door uncomprehendingly. It was not like Moohri to forget an important meeting, and Shownae had seen him in the building a short time ago. Where could he have gone?

Time dragged on as only empty waiting can, and at last Shownae could bear it no longer. Protocol be damned. He closed his eyes and cast his mind out to locate Moohri's familiar mindprint, then frowned as he felt the first tendrils of unease. Moohri was nowhere in the building.

Expanding the search parameters to include the entire city of Poshan, Shownae felt for the mind he had come to know almost as intimately as his own, and could find no corresponding mental signature. None at all.

Shownae felt his nostrils flare in dismay. This was not possible. To reassure himself, he checked on the now-open mind of his foe. He was still where he should be: restrained, sedated and awaiting questioning.

Reassured, Shownae cast about for Trikon, meaning to 'port him directly to the office and tell him the awful news. But again, ever-expanding searches produced no results. Both Lead Spacefarers had vanished.

In his heart Shownae knew they must be dead. Even if they were comatose, he should have been able to locate their minds. Shownae swallowed painfully, and gripped the back of the chair.

At that moment, Withish passed by the door. Shownae leaped forward to grab the startled junior 'path's arm and pull him into the room before closing the door and locking it.

"Shownae! What are you doing?" Withish stared at his boss as though Shownae had taken leave of his senses.

"I need you to do something for me, right now," Shownae told him, trying to calm the wild pounding of his heart.

Withish's face paled as he took in Shownae's mental state, but he said nothing, simply awaited instructions. Shownae's estimation of his assistant rose considerably in that moment.

"Moohri and Trikon have disappeared. I want you to mentally locate them."

Withish nodded, his expression grim. Then he shut his eyes and concentrated. For a long time, neither spoke. When at last Withish opened his eyes, a single tear fell from each of them.

"They are gone," he confirmed. "What is happening, Shownae?"

"I wish I knew. Unless . . ." Shownae lifted a finger to forestall further conversation, and sent his mind first to Earth, then Shalaii. It took quite a while, but eventually he knew beyond any doubt that the Spacefarers were not on either planet. Or if any part of them were, it was only their corporeal bodies. Certainly not the consciousnesses.

"Anything?" Withish asked in a small voice.

"Not on Earth or Shalaii."

"Could they have been *taken* somewhere else?" Withish ventured, then answered his own question. "No. They both have a 'porting lock on them."

The lock kept other 'porters from moving the person without their permission. And there was no way they could have been transported off-planet by ship in the short time since Trikon had left the room. Just to be on the safe side, Shownae searched a half light-year in every direction and found no trace of them.

"We need help," he decided. "Outside help."

Controlling his growing terror, Shownae sent out an urgent call to Jan and Ablakan. On both those planets it would be early dawn, he realized. He could only hope his friends would be alert enough to help him, should whatever had happened to his friends try to claim him, too.

Ablakan was the first to respond, quickly followed by Jan. Almost instantly, they became aware of Shownae's agitated state. The Orowans felt their minds being probed – acceptable in a crisis.

Permission? Jan asked tensely. There was no need to elaborate.

Shownae looked a query at Withish, then mentally nodded. An instant later, both he and Withish were in the decontamination chamber in Ames Research Centre. Jan arrived outside the room an instant later and placed a mental tracer on both Orowans as soon as they cleared decontamination.

Ablakan linked up again almost immediately. By mutual consent, they conversed telepathically, not knowing how much time they might have, should whatever happened to Moohri and Trikon overtake Shownae or Withish.

What about the other Orowan 'paths? Ablakan asked without preamble. *Can you locate them?*

Freo and Uulin are guest instructors at a 'pathic upgrade seminar on Lowen. They should be in session now. If anything was wrong, we would have heard. At least those two were safe, Shownae hoped.

Good. Stand by. I want to make sure all our 'paths are accounted for.

Shownae tracked Jan's mind as she quickly located her crew and placed a tracer on each of them, just to be sure. They were fast asleep, of course, and her minute intrusion did not awaken them.

Done, Jan announced unnecessarily.

My turn. Shownae cast his mind back to Orowa, and began systematically searching the Spacefarer complex, accounting for everyone who he knew should be there. For all he knew, the entire staff could have vanished. Jan and Ablakan remained attached, monitoring to ensure nothing untoward happened.

Satisfied at last, Shownae nodded. As far as he could determine, only Trikon and Moohri were missing. As if that was not bad enough.

Let me get Juneli, Ablakan said. *See if she precogs anything.*

He disappeared from their minds.

Does anyone seem disturbed, at Spacefarers? Jan asked. *Someone must have noticed by now that the three main players are missing.*

No, we go about our business, and often it is hours before we get back to our offices. We're supposed to let our assistants know where we are at all times, but we seldom do, Shownae admitted. It was a fatal mistake, he realized belatedly.

Who's next in line?

Wiltanus! Shownae exclaimed. He looked at Jan, stricken.

Jan stared back. *Wiltanus is your Administrator. I meant next in line downward.* She blinked, suddenly understanding. *You don't think –?*

Let me check.

It didn't take long. His face gave Jan the verdict.

Him, too? she asked in a hoarse whisper.

Yes. His second remains.

Jan's eyes widened in panic, and she broke off suddenly. Shownae didn't have to track her mind to know she was checking on her husband, her colleagues, her President and the U.N. Secretary-General.

She let out a long sigh. *Whatever's happening doesn't seem to be affecting humans. Yet,* she added, as an afterthought.

I checked on Tweno, Lisham, Konapi, Tix and Kyollan while you were busy. All asleep, Shownae contributed. *So far, it's only happening on Orowa.*

You've checked Shyr, of course.

All Orowan moons and satellites, yes. He regarded his friend, reluctant to voice the obvious next step. *I have to alert Wiltanus' second, and the managers of the four Spacefarer departments. A search must be made for –.* He gulped involuntarily. *– the bodies.*

We must know, Jan agreed. She placed a comforting hand on Shownae's arm, and the other on Withish.

Shownae glanced at the junior 'path, who was shaking with reaction.

We will find the answers. Do not fear. It sounded woefully unreassuring, even to Shownae.

Withish's lip curled bitterly. *In the meantime, we must hide, while people are dying. This is not a good way to fight.*

Shownae sympathized. It did not sit well with him either.

It is the only way, when you do not know who or what your enemy is. We are wiser to keep our bodies here while we investigate, till we know what we are up against.

Which suggests a plan of action, Jan noted. *If they've been murdered, you have conspirators in Wiltanus' complex and in Spacefarers. We should be able to pick up malevolence of that magnitude if we scan for it.*

Good idea. Shownae was greatly relieved to have something positive to do. *Withish, you check Spacefarers. I'll take Wiltanus' complex.*

And I'll keep a lock on Withish, Ablakan integrated his just-rejoined focus seamlessly into the plan.

I've got Shownae, Jan confirmed.

Without further ado, Shownae projected his mind into Wiltanus' complex, using an overscan cued to detect malice and murderous thoughts or feelings. Having used it so recently to try and identify his personal enemy, Shownae found it easy to do.

Only petty jealousies and various low-level vindictivenesses surfaced, but nothing of the magnitude he was seeking. Undaunted, he splayed out his focus in all directions, searching the entire city for such feelings surrounding Wiltanus. It pleased Shownae to find that virtually no one harbored ill will towards their ruler. The few who did were mentally unstable – which came as no great surprise – and none held a memory of kidnapping or murdering Wiltanus.

Clean, Shownae said.

Same with the Spacefarers, Withish confirmed. *I even checked the whole city. I don't understand. How could no one know?*

It's a mystery alright, Jan understated. *Did Juneli have anything to contribute?*

Nothing so far, Ablakan replied.

That's it, then. I have to alert the next-in-commands, Shownae said grimly.

"That won't be necessary," Trikon said from behind them.

They all whirled to gape at Trikon and Moohri, who smiled benignly at them as the Lead Spacefarers stepped out of the decontamination chamber.

"How did you get here?" Jan gasped in surprise. "And where have you been?"

Trikon said, "Wiltanus set it up with your colleague, Richard Ironhorse, and he sent us here on schedule."

"Sorry to worry you," Moohri said mildly. "But it had to be done."

A barrage of conflicting emotions and urges vied for expression in Shownae. For a moment, he wanted nothing better than to flatten both conspirators.

Moohri held up a staying hand, obviously interpreting the glare in Shownae's eyes. "Let us explain. Then, if you still want to hit us, feel free to do so. I know we've put you all through a lot." Trikon gave Jan an apologetic half-smile. "We hadn't expected him to call in reinforcements so soon."

"And that reinforcement includes Ablakan, so I suggest we continue this telepathically," Jan stated. "Coffee, anyone?" She gestured towards the sofa and chairs at the far side of the room. Nobody wanted any, but they all seated themselves on the furniture. The Orowans, with their distinctive anatomy, took a few extra seconds to get themselves comfortable on surfaces geared to human physiology.

So, exactly why did it 'have to be done'?, Shownae demanded. Resentment roiled within him, but he was determined to give them a fair hearing.

And where is Wiltanus? Withish asked.

Trikon faced Shownae. *In answer to your question, when we approached the Administrator with our idea, he said it would also answer one of his own concerns,* Trikon said.

Moohri was having trouble meeting Shownae's eyes. Shownae sensed Moohri's remorse at what they had put him through, and knew Moohri would always feel beholden for the assistance Shownae had given him all those months Moohri was marooned on the planetoid. Shownae's anger abated. Whatever their reasons for pulling this bizarre stunt, they must have felt it absolutely warranted.

Trikon adjusted his posture, trying to find a more comfortable position. *Remember last week, when Wiltanus wanted to talk to you? It took us forever to find you.*

He would *choose that time to call. I'd forgotten Dru Hepiak's gift at home, and he was leaving that day. I just popped home to get it, and noticed a spiggot leaking, so I fixed it.* Shownae grimaced apologetically. *I know; I should have called the office and let them know where I was.*

You're not the only one, Moohri assured him. *We all have been guilty of lax behavior. It worried Wiltanus, and rightly so.*

So where is *Wiltanus?* Withish asked again.

He went to Lowen with our 'paths, at their Supreme Commander's invitation, Moohri supplied. *They'll receive cross-training in telepathy, because the Lowens do it a different way than we do.*

Anyway, why we contacted Wiltanus in the first place is we wanted to test out a theory, and it wouldn't have been a fair test if we had let you 'pathic types know ahead of time. If we're right – and I think we are – Maxxift could still be very much alive, and still a danger to us all. We believe he's in a stasis chamber, with the timer set to awaken him at some future time. Perhaps very soon. He would only have to 'play dead' for a day or so to have us stop looking for him.

Jan was the first to recover. *Where did you get a stasis chamber? None of the member planets has that technology.*

Lowen does, Moohri said. *They loaned us a couple and taught us how to use them.* He swallowed, remembering. *Scariest thing I've done in a while.*

So there could be more of those murderous little bombs on their way here right now, Ablakan shuddered. His focus withdrew to, Shownae presumed, conduct a search of Shalaii's 'neighborhood' and probably outward in the direction from which the first needle-bomb had come.

Shownae felt Jan withdraw as well, and he projected his mind back to Orowa to check their own space.

Clean, so far, Ablakan announced.

Same with Earth.

And Orowa, Shownae confirmed. *Which may mean that, if Maxxift did hide out in a stasis chamber, he's not awake yet.*

Then we'd better find him fast, Ablakan said. His tone turned grateful. *You may have saved us all with your little experiment. Thank you both. And please extend our gratitude to Wiltanus as well.*

And from us, Jan added, giving the conspirators a quick hug. *That was a good call.*

Trikon turned a quizzical eye towards Shownae.

More than valid reasons. Shownae chuckled, as he added, *I may never forgive you, but I'm glad you did it.*

Me, too, Withish smiled, then sobered. *But where could he be? What's out in the direction that bomb came from?*

Nothing much. Just a dead planet. Ablakan let out a whoop. *What better hideout! I'll clear it with Tweno at once.*

Same here, with Saunders, Jan said.

Count us in, Shownae stated, after getting the nod from Trikon and Moohri.

The meeting over, Shownae and his countrymen took turns hugging Jan, then re-entered the decontamination room to be returned to Orowa.

"I'll see if Wiltanus is free," Shownae told the others, when they were cleared to leave their own chamber.

Apparently, Wiltanus had been expecting the call, for Sat Frundal put Shownae through immediately.

Administrator, your Lead Spacefarers are reporting success, Shownae said with deference.

So the experiment worked? Wiltanus asked, his mental voice carefully neutral.

Almost too well, Trikon said. *Shownae here had already searched your complex and the surrounding city, and the same with Spacefarers and our city. He'd checked that no one else was missing besides you and us, roped Withish in to help him, and mobilized Jan and Ablakan.*

Impressive! So stasis completely blocks mental tracking?

Completely, Shownae assured him, trying not to sound sour about it. *Jan and Ablakan are seeking permission to send troops to search the dead planet in the direction the bomb came from. We believe that's where Maxxift will be, if he is still in stasis. Would you permit an Orowan contingent to accompany them?*

125

Yes. Coordinate it with my office. I must get back to the meeting now. There was the slightest pause before he added. *You did well, Shownae. We are not as ill-prepared as I had feared.*

Thank you, Administrator. Shownae projected a bow before severing the connection.

Trikon headed for his office to contact Wiltanus' second, and Shownae 'ported himself to the cafeteria. Adrenalin had burned up his morning meal, leaving him famished. He hastily scanned the menu and made choices which would sustain him for as long as possible.

Knowing his colleagues, both Orowan and off-planet, it wouldn't take them long to organize a search party. He would be needed to 'port Orowan troops to the site and monitor them until they were ready to return. It felt good to be one of the hunters, for a change, instead of the prey.

CHAPTER 9

Ablakan waited anxiously while Tweno digested the latest developments and made his decision.

"We need all our peacemakers to keep the unstable from overreacting to our situation." He pursed his lips, eyebanks narrowing in concentration. "But we can send 20 palace guards, and the extra security I placed in each First's complexes, to search the dead planet. Our people seem to have taken my request to heart. The calls have dropped off sharply."

"With those being sent from Earth and Orowa, that should be plenty," Ablakan agreed. "He wouldn't have anyone guarding him, for the very reason he would be in stasis – because we'd pick up on their minds. If we do find Maxxift, it will be a nasty pleasure to send him back to his homeworld to face justice."

"Good. I will call Konapi and Lisham to have their extra security detail ready for 'porting. And speaking of 'nasty', you're sure there's nothing else nasty on its way here?"

"There wasn't as of when I looked," Ablakan temporized. "I've asked Juneli to remain as open as possible, as she was the first to pick up on it last time."

"Alright. I don't have a military mind, but if I were in his place, I wouldn't use the same tactic twice."

"Me, neither. I've been trying to put myself in his shoes, as the humans say, and predict what he might do."

"And?"

Ablakan sighed. "And I don't know. There doesn't seem to be much point in trying to move the solar system until we know he's no longer a threat. Which means, we have to catch him, and soon. That quake on Enaxat last night was pretty strong, I hear."

Tweno nodded sadly. "Thirteen killed, hundreds injured, and a lot of buildings collapsed. Our houses aren't built to withstand quakes of that magnitude; they happen – happen*ed* – so seldom." He reached out to grasp Ablakan's shoulder. "Find Maxxift. I don't want our cities in ruins because we dared not act for fear of further reprisals from that lunatic."

"I'll ask Kyollan to 'port our force to that planet and monitor them," Ablakan said briskly, and returned there himself.

Despite the early hour, Juneli sat in Wiki's chair, staring at nothing. Ablakan couldn't tell whether she was precogging or scanning for possible 'incomings'. Either way, he wasn't about to disturb her.

Wiki's back was towards him, but she must have sensed his arrival, for she turned and flashed him a sunny smile before returning to her task. She was composing something on the 'scriber. What, Ablakan couldn't tell from this distance. He was loathe to investigate, lest she think he was checking up on her.

He walked briskly down the hall to his office and set his hear-other for silent recording. Leaning back in his chair, he sent his mind towards the dead planet to search for a consciousness didn't expect to find.

A meticulous scan of the surface confirmed that there was no mental focus in use. But most livable planets would have caves and subterranean caverns, Ablakan surmised. He set his search parameters for depth, and again sought thoughts or feelings that would indicate a presence. As before, he found nothing.

Ablakan sent a call to Jan and Shownae. When both had responded, he told them what he had done, and why.

So did I, just a few minutes ago, Jan smiled. *I guess it's true that great minds think alike.*

Thanks! Shownae exclaimed drolly. *Like you two, I came up empty.*

So he's either in stasis there, and alone for obvious reasons, or was never there, or he's already left, Ablakan concluded.

And if he left, he's probably lugging that damned stasis chamber with him, Jan said. *You know, he could easily keep one step ahead of us, unless we have almost a round-the-clock scan going for his mindprint.*

Ablakan grinned, as a solution occurred to him. *That would be a perfect job for School, if they are willing to do it.*

Leaving us free to focus on how to move a solar system, Jan finished the thought. *I'll ask them, if you like. They already know his mindprint, so it should be no problem for them.*

Thanks. What did Saunders say about building a working model of our solar system? Ablakan asked hopefully.

He's got a team on it. I'll find out how they're doing, and ask Brenda to send our contingent to help look for that stasis chamber.

Again, thanks.

Ablakan reached for the hear-other and brought Tweno up-to-date on the latest developments, or lack of them.

"Since you left, I've been trying to think like Maxxift, but we don't know him well enough to even guess at how he thinks," Tweno said. "So instead, I started looking at our weaknesses. What would do us the most harm? And does he want to destroy us outright, or make us suffer as much as possible beforehand? My guess is the latter, especially based on what he has already done."

"Makes sense, if he's still alive, and I have a strong feeling he is." Ablakan wondered what the Primary was leading up to. "All we've done so far is found a way he *could* have fooled us and lived to tell of it. We don't know that he *has.*"

"I had a nice chat with Plaka this morning. He assures me that that temperament has an almost fanatical will to live. I think we can safely assume Maxxift is alive."

"How is Plaka?" Ablakan asked. He hadn't spoken to Tweno's litter-brother since the Analyzer introduced him to then-First Tweno seven years ago.

"His practice has flourished, and he is feeling very well." Tweno's voice held grudging respect as he said, "Didn't even grovel this time; just called me 'sir'."

"Glad to hear it." Ablakan owed a lot to the Analyzer, and made a mental note to visit him at the first opportunity. "But if Maxxift wants to hurt us before we die, he has already accomplished that, hasn't he?"

"Not really. He knows we are resourceful and have powerful friends. I'm guessing he would assume we can get our people off-planet before Shalaii is destroyed. Being dispossessed would be traumatic for them, but probably not sufficiently so to satisfy a mentality that I understand routinely inflicted torture on those who displeased him." Tweno took a deep breath. "No, I think we can expect something far worse. What, I haven't a clue. Has Juneli come up with anything?"

"She seemed to be in trance when I arrived. I'll check with her, if you want to hold."

"I'll wait."

Ablakan put the receiver down gently and hurried down the hall to where the ladies were working. Wiki was still at her 'scriber, but kept glancing at her supervisor. Juneli was blinking rapidly and frowning, apparently lost in thought.

Ablakan cleared his throat so as not to startle her. They both looked at him. Wiki made a little nod towards Juneli, letting Ablakan know something was amiss.

"June, Tweno's on the line. Would you come into my office?"

Wordlessly, Juneli complied. Once the door was closed, she pointed at the speaker-button and asked, "May I?"

"By all means."

Juneli pushed the button, and Ablakan sat back down in his chair. Juneli was seated across from him, near the hear-other.

"Juneli's here," Ablakan announced.

"Ablakan tells me you were in trance when he got in. Anything we should know about?" Tweno asked.

Juneli nodded once. "Yes, sir. Though I don't know what it means. I got a very fuzzy vision of several of those little black holes. But they were opening up *on Shalaii*, and pulling everything in from all around them. And they were growing at an unbelievable rate." She stopped then, her complexion a sickly ashen.

"When?" Ablakan asked in a strangled whisper. He cleared his throat, trying to loosen the constricted muscles.

"Not yet. But soon," she replied with grim certainty.

"Thank you, Juneli. Hopefully, you have given us enough time to avert it. But we need more information. Think back carefully," Tweno instructed. "Did those holes seem to just emerge from nothing? Or did something happen just before they appeared?"

Juneli squinted, as if trying to see something in the far distance. "There's a sort of 'popping' sound, like a bubble bursting." She straightened abruptly. "*Exactly* like a bubble bursting. It's something enclosed in a bubble, and when it bursts, something happens – I can't tell what – and then the hole appears."

"Good. That's useful information. Here's another one for you: Were those 'bubbles' planted in specific places, or did they travel through our atmosphere to land someplace?"

Ablakan had to hand it to Tweno. In the face of such a horrifying future, he was not only remaining outwardly self-possessed, but successfully keeping Juneli calm and focused. It took longer for her to determine the answer, but when she spoke, it was with confidence.

"Planted. Each will be in a spot where there is nothing nearby that would be too big for it until it has time to gorge itself and grow large. It *can't* be random."

"Alright. Feel backwards from what you're seeing. How will they come to be there?"

Juneli's eyebanks fluttered frenetically, as she tried to expand the envelope of her precognition to include those details. At length, she sighed and shook her head.

"I'm sorry, sir. I cannot see before."

"That's alright. What you saw will have to be enough. Again, our thanks."

"You're welcome. I'll keep trying." She got up, evidently recognizing it as a dismissal.

Ablakan reached for her hand and gave it a quick reassuring squeeze. Juneli smiled wanly, and left, closing the door behind her.

"We are alone," Ablakan said.

"Answer me one thing: When you searched for Maxxift out there, did you also search for him here?"

"Ohhhhh!" Ablakan felt chills shoot up his spine, as he realized his error. "No, I didn't."

"Don't blame yourself. Until this moment, I didn't think of it, either. But he'd almost have to be here now, wouldn't he?" Tweno's voice was far kinder than Ablakan felt he had a right to expect.

"So Maxxift launched that needle-bomb from the dead planet, put himself in stasis for a while, then somehow slipped onto Shalaii, to use the holer technology directly against our planet," Ablakan summed it up. There could be no other explanation for Juneli's vision. And a more diabolical plot he had never heard.

"I'll leave you now to find him before he can unleash those hell holes on us. If even one is created, and we don't find it almost immediately . . ." Tweno left the rest unspoken.

"I'll find him," Ablakan swore through clenched teeth.

Tweno's voice turned hard as the diamond from Earth which graced his finger. "And when you do, and have gotten rid of those 'bubbles', Ablakan, I want you to quickly learn from his mind all he knows about those holes, then 'port him into the sun. We cannot risk any more of his lethal plots."

Ablakan swallowed, hating what he knew must be. "Yes, sir."

"And get help on this one, quickly. Moments may count."

"I will." Ablakan pressed the button to end the conversation, took one deep, shaky breath, and split his focus.

It didn't take long for Jan and Shownae to respond.

Read me, please, Ablakan urged.

The familiar tickling sensation in his mind confirmed they were wasting no time in doing so. Nor did they hesitate, once they knew what needed to be done.

I'll take Enaxat, Jan said.

I've got Tunan, came from Shownae.

They disconnected as Ablakan sent his mind across Pantai. Time passed, but Ablakan was unaware of it. The universe had constricted to Maxxift's mindprint and his own searching focus. To his surprise, he found the echoing match disconcertingly close by.

I found him! Ablakan broadcast, and instantly felt his friends' focuses twinning with his.

Maxxift was squatting in the largest sandtrap on Tweno's golf course. In his hand, Ablakan could clearly see a 'bubble' – an irridescent clear globe perhaps half the size of a human child's marble, with a peculiar-looking device inside. Maxxift was digging a deep depression in the sand, apparently preparing to bury the globe.

Ablakan watched for a horrible moment, transfixed. Would the device activate on its own, or had Maxxift a means of detonating it?

On my mark, Jan whispered in their minds, as though Maxxift might overhear her. *One . . . two . . . three . . . NOW!*

As one, they blasted their focus into his mind, savagely assimilating every vestige of Maxxift's fiendish plan, as he screamed in pain and grasped his head with both hands. Unnoticed, the little globe fell into the hole.

Still shrieking in agony, the blackguard fell to the ground, gyrating in a vain attempt to rid his mind of their presence. His movements quickly covered the globe with sand. Almost immediately, there was a tiny 'pop' which went unnoticed in the frenzy occurring above it.

As he lay there, writhing under the onslaught of the 'paths' ferocious mental assault, Maxxift was unaware that the intended black hole was appearing right on schedule. It greedily sucked in the surrounding sand, growing exponentially as it gorged itself on sand and small rocks further down.

The globes! Jan cried, as several fell from the folds of Maxxift's gray tunic. Mentally, she enclosed her focus around every one she could find. But what to do with them? Ablakan could feel her casting about for inspiration.

The biggest empty space! he hollered in her mind, and a moment later, the globes disappeared.

When Ablakan returned his focus to their captive, Maxxift was struggling with renewed vigor, clutching at the sand, his eyes bugging out in unspeakable terror. It was then that Ablakan noticed that the hole was pulling Maxxift in, his body disappearing further into the darkness beneath with every passing instant.

Ablakan hastily detached his mind, unwilling to experience Maxxift's gruesome demise. Fittingly, Maxxift would be the first victim of his own treachery. And the last, if Ablakan could dispose of the hole in time.

Huge sections of Tweno's beloved golf course were flying into the gaping maw of the hole.

Stand back, Ablakan said, mentally dislodging the others from the connection.

Locking in a huge ring around the edifice and extending down as far as he dared, Ablakan threw the entirety of the mass enclosed by his focus into the same vicinity as Jan had jettisoned the undetonated globes.

Fearfully, Ablakan looked back at the crater he had left. Long moments passed, but no further activity could be seen. With a massive sigh, he opened up again to his compatriots.

Well done. Jan hugged him mentally. *But, boy, you should see the size of the hole we made in Nowheresville!* Then her tone became more serious. *I sure hope there was nothing on the antimatter side.*

Shownae's mental 'voice' had a touch of hysteria to it as he surveyed the golf course. *Now* that's *what I call a hazard!*

I'd better get some fill in it before someone else gets killed. The hole extended so far down, Ablakan fretted that the lava core of their planet would come bursting through at any moment.

Got a mountaintop you don't need? Jan quipped.

As a matter of fact, we do.

The recent earthquake had dislodged the whole side of a hill, and left a massive amount of rubble at the bottom. Moving it would save the Road Department a lot of work and solve Ablakan's problem at the same time.

The task didn't take long. Afterwards, Ablakan surveyed his efforts with a critical eye. Once the soil was enriched and seeded with suitable groundcover, the golf course would be as good as new.

He mentally accessed Tweno. *Sorry about the mess, sir,* he said. He could just make out his ruler standing at the window overlooking the golf course.

I know you hated that sandtrap, but wasn't that a bit excessive? Tweno asked with feigned disapproval.

I've never been one for half-measures, Ablakan admitted.

Too true! May we now assume the danger from Maxxift and his infernal devices is over?

Ablakan heave a gusty sigh of relief. *Yes, sir.*

And you're certain he acted alone?

Absolutely; his mind confirmed it. For which Ablakan was infinitely grateful. It had been much too close a call as it was. *We all owe our lives to Jan and Shownae, you know, and most especially to Juneli.*

That assistant of yours deserves a big promotion.

How about setting up something like a Shalaian Precog Center, with her in charge? Then we can see if we've any other precogs, same as we did with the telepaths, Ablakan suggested. Then his mood flattened. *Assuming Shalaii continues to exist.*

Even if the planet doesn't, at least we can make sure our people do. How is the model solar system coming?

I don't know. I'll just get something to eat, then I'll call Jan back.

Tweno let out a bark of laughter. *Looks like not all the black holes are gone. I'd forgotten about your stomach. Have your assistants join you, and we shall have a celebratory banquet of whatever the chefs can put together between now and evening meal.*

Thank you, Ablakan said sheepishly, as his stomach growled melodiously.

With a humorous snort, Tweno hung up, leaving Ablakan to appease his hunger.

* * *

Shownae entered the room where the young man who had so singlemindedly hunted him was being held. The prisoner looked up from his chair, eyes slightly out of focus but blazing with hatrid.

Shownae pulled up a chair facing him, and gazed at the man sadly. "So you are Aridi, son of Chancellor Bendaar. You hold me responsible for his heart attack, don't you?"

"You shocked him into it, you murderer! I swear by the Fates, I will kill you."

Shownae sighed. "You will never know how badly I feel about that, because you are right: I will never know for sure whether my attempt to save his life actually cost it. I think of it every day."

"As do I."

Shownae leaned forward on his seat. "But put yourself in my place. If you realized that a wonderful person like your father was about to die, what would you do? Just stand by and let it happen? Or try to prevent it somehow? I only picked up on it moments beforehand." Shownae felt his eyes fill with tears of frustration. He lowered his head to hide them. "Maybe I did the wrong thing, Aridi, or maybe it was already too late to save your father. I wish with all my heart I knew which, but I don't. And neither do you."

A strangled sound made Shownae look up. Aridi's head was in his hands. He began sobbing – great heaving gasps of grief and impotent rage. Shownae knew the feelings only too well. He stayed with the man, silently accepting the vitriolic abuse the other hurled at him. It was nothing he hadn't called himself a thousand times before.

When at last Aridi became silent, Shownae risked a gentle probe. To his immense relief, only sorrow and regret remained; the anger and hatred that had consumed Aridi for so long had finally been purged. And now Shownae had a decision to make.

He knew that the emotional storm had long since burned the sedative out of Aridi's system. Another dose would have to be administered at once if Aridi was to remain a chemical prisoner. The techno guarding him must have realized it as well, for he opened a drawer and withdrew a syringe. At the sound, Aridi lifted his head.

Shownae raised a hand to stop the techno, then turned to Aridi. "Is that necessary?"

The prisoner looked at Shownae, a multitude of emotions flashing across his face. "I don't know," he admitted at last.

Shownae nodded. That was as honest an answer as could be expected. He motioned for the techno to put the syringe away. "Release him, please. If he feels he must kill me, I direct that he not be charged, so long as no one else is harmed or killed." Turning back to the astonished young man, Shownae raised his hands in a shrug. "That is as fair as I know how to be. But if you choose against murder, we could sure use another teleporter. Either way, you know where – or at least how – to find me."

With that, Shownae got up and left the room.

* * *

"Geez!" Tom whined. "She helps save a planetful of people, and she thinks that entitles her to dinner out. Women!"

"I know. They're so unreasonable," Jack commiserated, rolling his eyes expressively.

"I'm staying out of this," Brenda laughed, making a pushing motion with both hands.

"Well, I'm not!" Billy smiled. "Let's go for pizza."

"I second the motion." Jan ruffled the youngster's longish hair. "After I report in."

Fortunately, Eric was still at the office, so she hit the high points and promised to give a more detailed report the next day.

"Would you pass it up the ladder for me? I've been invited out to dinner. At my request," honesty forced her to admit.

Eric grunted. "Well, you earned it this time. I'll handle things at this end."

"Thanks, boss."

This time? Jan started to hang up, not certain she should have thanked him, when she remembered something else.

"Any word on how that solar system model is coming? Ablakan said Shalaii had a pretty severe earthquake. Killed and injured a lot of people, and fairly levelled a city." Which was an exaggeration, but the next one could easily do so, as they increased in strength.

"It'll be a few days yet," Eric replied. "But Saunders did get word back from the President about the other matter. I'm sorry, Jan, but it's nix on you moving a sun."

Jan frowned into the phone. "Eric, I *have* to. We can't risk Ablakan; you know that. And I'm not being egotistical when I say, I don't think there's anyone else strong enough yet to do it. If it can be done at all."

"Precisely. There isn't any *one*. But a multiplicity might be able to do it safely."

"School?" Jan asked in surprise. The thought hadn't even occurred to her.

"It can't hurt to ask."

"I don't know," Jan hesitated. "Don't forget, they've just halved their membership already. If you took away half a committee, you wouldn't expect them to do nearly as much work. And it would take time to reorganize themselves to work as a team."

Eric sighed. "Yes, I expect you're right. But I still want you to ask. Saunders believes they're best suited for the job. After all, they've been around for eons. That's got to count for something."

"Alright. But they've risked a lot on our behalf already."

"After Shalaii's solar system is relocated, we'll find some way to make it up to them," Eric said, though Jan couldn't see what Earth could possibly offer that School would value. Stationary beings would have little use for – things.

Jan hung up and turned towards the others with a pensive expression.

"Let me guess," Tom said quietly. "You don't get to play with a sun."

"They want School to do it. As if they haven't done enough already. Anyway, School said they'd never heard of anyone even

137

attempting it, so they have no more experience in that area than I have." She blinked, remembering the planetoid she relocated. "Less, actually."

Jan realized her resentment was only partly to do with taking advantage of School. It felt like a slight against her abilities, almost a non-confidence motion. And, she privately admitted, she felt cheated of a chance to show off.

"Well, the model isn't ready yet anyway," Brenda pointed out. "Why don't we forget about suns and black holes and all things celestial, and just have a divine evening?"

"So let's go!" Billy took Jan's hand, tugging.

"Guiseppi's?" Jan looked an inquiry at her family. When that establishment had received the thumb's up from all concerned, Jan 'ported them to the restaurant and they joined the cue awaiting a table.

* * *

Ablakan, Juneli and Wiki were enjoying Tweno's hospitality when Juneli froze, utensil halfway to her mouth. Instantly, all eyebanks turned towards her.

It didn't last long, but whatever she had foreseen was enough to leach all the color from her cheeks.

"Problem," she said, rising unsteadily. She gave Ablakan a look he had come to recognize as imminent danger.

"Excuse us." Ablakan 'ported himself, Tweno and Juneli to the Primary's office.

"Tonight, our moon's orbit will be stretched greatly. On the next pass, the black hole will have it." Her eyebanks told Ablakan she fully understood the cataclysmic effect it would have on Shalaii.

"How long before it begins?" Tweno asked tensely.

"It has already." Juneli swivelled her head to regard Ablakan, eyebanks hopeful. "Is there any way to stop it from happening?"

"Not without repercussions," Ablakan replied.

"You're thinking of having the moon skip that part of its orbit, aren't you?" Juneli realized.

"It's that or give it an orbit at right-angles to the one it has, and I think that would create more problems on Shalaii than skipping a portion of its regular orbit. But I'll need technical expertise for this one."

138

"Primary, there is an urgent call for you," a breathless minion paused at the door to Tweno's office. "It is the Director of the Pantai Observatory."

"Perfect timing," Juneli murmured.

Ablakan said, "That's the one that was moved to the top of Troyell, to make room for my complex, isn't it?"

"Yes." Tweno nodded to the minion. "Put her through." As soon as the instrument rang, he depressed the button.

"Director Briadt, we were just about to call you. I presume you are concerned about the moon's orbit?"

"Yes, Primary. It has been vastly distorted, and our calculations confirm it will be drawn into the spacial hole on its next pass."

"We have independent confirmation of that as well." Tweno gave Juneli a quick smile. "First Ablakan is standing by. Are you in the main observation dome?"

"Yes, sir." Briadt sounded immeasurably relieved.

"He will join you there."

Ablakan raised a hand in goodbye and 'ported himself into Briadt's presence. It was Ablakan's first visit to the Observatory. Under happier circumstances, he would have taken the guided tour. But what he needed right now was a crash course in the moon's orbit, speed and revolution.

Briadt wasted no time getting started. "Thank you for coming," she said, her smallish pinched features made homelier by the worry etched into the lines on her face. She was almost as tall as Ablakan, but perhaps half-again his girth, which made her undersized head look even more incongruous.

Now she indicated tables and charts spread out on the immense surface before them, and began to feed Ablakan the data he needed as quickly as possible. It didn't take long for Ablakan to realize he was hopelessly out of his league.

"Wait," he begged, rubbing his forehead. "I can't get it this way. I need to *see* in my mind what the moon should be doing."

"Rayham, come here," Briadt ordered, and a gray-maned technician of indeterminate age hurried over. "First Ablakan needs to access your knowledge about the moon."

"You mean, in my mind?" Obviously, this did not sit well with him.

"All you'll feel is a slight tickle," Ablakan assured him. "But I must hurry if I am to be of help here."

Rayham gulped, and nodded once, then screwed his face up as he closed his eyebanks. Despite the man's inadvertent effort to shield his mind, Ablakan was able to get an unhindered experience of how the moon had historically moved.

"Right. I'll need to concentrate now," Ablakan stated.

"Everyone be quiet!" Briadt bellowed, and the soft murmur of voices from the others in the large dome subsided.

Ablakan resisted the temptation to shake his head. His ears were ringing from the unnecessary volume of her command. He gave her a look of mild annoyance before shutting his eyebanks.

The moon was already an eighth again out from where it should have been, and increasing that distance as it revolved around Shalaii. It would soon be at its closest point to the black hole. Pulling on Rayham's mental image, Ablakan was about to 'port the moon to the early-morning location in its orbit when he heard an ominous rumble.

Before he could react, the observatory floor tipped and rocked, knocking Ablakan off his feet. All around him, people screamed, heavy objects toppled, and the glass roof shattered, showering them all with shards. Ablakan found himself being rolled and bounced helplessly as the massive, deafening earthquake gained momentum. Unable to orient himself to his surroundings, even teleporting was denied him.

An agonizing cry pierced the roaring in his ears, and he tried to pinpoint its source. Something enormous smashed a chair a handsbreath from his legs, and Ablakan hastily tried to roll his body out of its path. But the upheaving floor would not let him move any appreciable distance. In the dust and debris flying all around him, Ablakan never saw the other end of the supporting beam as it came crashing down. In a blinding flash, Ablakan's consciousness disappeared into its own personal black hole.

CHAPTER 10

ABLAKAN! Juneli shrieked in horror, as her mind filled with his motionless body pinned underneath the massive beam. The horrendous shaking in the palace had ceased, at least for the moment. Everywhere there was broken glass, and innumerable objects were strewn haphazardly across the floor of Tweno's office. As far as she could tell, the palace structure had taken the quake in its stride, a tribute to its ancient architects. But her telepathic vision showed the observatory in shambles.

As she had done once before when Ablakan had been injured, Juneli sent out a mental all-points appeal for help. And again, a multitude of telepathic focuses answered the call. Each mind registered shock at the state they found him in.

I'll get him, Jan told the others tensely. Juneli felt Jan search for, and locate in Juneli's mind, coordinates of the nearest medical facility, then of another and another.

They're all badly damaged, she reported, a note of panic in her mental voice. *Where is Tunan's best hospital?*

Juneli visualized the location and a moment later, Jan found the matching structure.

It's intact! An instant later, Jan closed the link.

It took a great effort not to follow her, but Juneli knew Ablakan couldn't be in better hands. And right now, every 'path would be needed for the mammoth clean-up job ahead of them. Briefly, the specter of the moon, badly off course, swam into mental view, but Juneli knew there was nothing she could do about it. Right now, time could mean lives needlessly lost.

As the other 'porters silently withdrew from her mind to help rescue trapped victims, Juneli was stunned to feel the entry in her mind of a group consciousness. She tried to block, then realized it must be School.

We will help you, Juneli, the multiplicity told her.

Help how? she wondered. She felt her mind expanding for a time, then the feeling stopped.

Now you can help directly, she was told, and then they were gone.

A wild hope blossomed, to be replaced almost immediately by a vast knowing. Across the light-years, in the direction of their disappearance, Juneli sent her overwhelming gratitude, then turned her focus toward the shattered observatory. A moment later, she stood on its crazily tilted floor, and knew she had just become a teleporter.

* * *

"Dr. Weismer," Tweno tapped his 'scriber with a tapered digit. "Are you sure about these figures?"

NASA's resident expert on black holes nodded glumly. "Yes, sir. That singularity has grown a lot faster than anticipated, despite your efforts to minimize space debris being drawn into it. What that means is, you don't have the time we thought you'd have."

"How long?" It had been a hellish night for everyone, and Tweno knew he must look as haggard as he felt.

"Eight days, if you're lucky." The scientist coughed diffidently. "I took the liberty of diverting every available resource to finishing your model solar system. I'm afraid if you're going to save your planet, you will have to act quickly. My colleagues confirm that Shalaii's crust is destabilizing under the tremendous pull being exerted by the singularity. The next few days will make what you've just been through pale in comparison."

"Thank you for the warning." Tweno struggled to quell the panic welling up inside of him. "Please let me know the instant the model is ready."

"Count on it, sir." He nodded towards Tix, who carefully 'ported him back into NASA's decontamination chamber.

"What's the latest on Ablakan?" Tweno asked.

"They are keeping him sedated, sir. He has several broken ribs and a broken arm, as well as a concussion," Kyollan reported. "His doctors assured me he will recover fully, given time."

Tweno shook his head. "We don't *have* time. Why are they sedating him?"

"To keep him from teleporting," Kyollan said drily. "He wanted to participate in the rescues, and 'porting would have put too much strain on his concussed brain. They couldn't talk him out of it, so they sedated him."

"Take me there."

No sooner were the words out of his mouth than Tweno found himself standing beside Ablakan's bed. His protégé's eyebanks

142

were closed, but pain lines were clearly visible on his too-pale face. Tweno's heart went out to him, and the Primary placed his hand on Ablakan's.

"I'm here, dear friend. You will be alright."

Ablakan's eyebanks flickered slightly, and he turned his head to regard his leader. Tweno winced at the conflict he could see raging within the young man.

"Make them let me help," he whispered hoarsely. "We don't have much time left."

"I know," Tweno nodded. "But you will have to sit this one out. You'll do us no good by risking yourself any more than you already have." He forced a little smile to cross his face. "School taught Juneli to 'port, and I believe they will help us to move our system away from that accursed hole."

"Hell hole." Ablakan grimaced. "I wouldn't wish it on our worst enemy."

"Our worst enemy inflicted it on us," Tweno reminded him. "But I promise you, Ablakan, we will not let him win. The humans assured me the model will be ready shortly."

Ablakan struggled to sit up in his bed.

"Keep still. You have broken ribs," Tweno gently pressed him back down. Weak as he was, Ablakan was unable to offer more than token resistance.

"I am needed," Ablakan insisted between gritted teeth. "You know that. Let me help. I promise I will be careful."

Tweno shook his head. "Jan will move the moon tonight. And every 'porter we know is on call to handle casualties if we have more earthquakes."

"We will," Ablakan muttered bitterly.

"So I understand. But we are ready for them."

Ablakan shook his head. "At this rate, there won't be much left of Shalaii to save."

"Then we will rebuild. But now, you are to rest and heal. In a day or two, the model should be ready. If you want to have any hope of playing a part in moving Shalaii, you will listen to your Primary and *rest!*"

A ghost of a smile pulled at the corners of Ablakan's mouth, and he inclined his head. "Yes, sir."

Tweno squeezed Ablakan's arm. "We need you, Ablakan. But we need you *well*. I will check on you tomorrow."

"Thanks, Dad."

With a bark of laughter, Tweno joined Kyollan, who was waiting outside the room.

"Your office?"

Tweno pursed his lips, thinking. "No. Juneli's."

As he had expected, Wiki was there by herself.

"How is he?" she blurted out, when she spotted Tweno.

"Stubborn and impertinent. Which means he will be alright."

Wiki's face became radiant with relief. If I were a couple decades younger, Tweno thought, then shook his head. He hadn't time for pointless musings.

"Do you feel capable of handling things on your own for a while? We're going to need Juneli."

"I believe so, Primary. Would I be able to reach her if something urgent came up?"

"Unless she is tranced or 'porting, yes."

"Thank you. In that case, I should manage alright," Wiki said.

"I'm sure you will," Tweno smiled, and Kyollan, waiting in the background as always, 'ported him back to his office.

* * *

It was early dawn when Jan wearily crawled into bed. She had seen more shattered bodies and buildings than she had ever imagined possible. Every hospital on Tunan and Enaxat were filled to capacity, and emergency shelters had hastily been erected in the dead of the night to protect the million-plus Shalaians rendered homeless by the giant Pantai quake.

What depressed Jan more than anything was the certainty that more were on the way, and far worse yet than this one had been. How can we keep up this pace and still be able to move a solar system? she wondered dully. Her head throbbed from too many hours of concentration. Near the end, she had had to check herself to ensure she had indeed 'ported people and debris where she had intended.

"Turn over, love," Tom told her. Too tired to argue, Jan complied, and was immediately glad she had. Gentle fingers massaged her knotted shoulder and neck muscles, expertly working their way down her back.

"Oh, I needed that," she breathed.

"Shh. Just rest. We'll talk later."

Tom continued his labor of love, and Jan felt herself slide into reverie. She didn't even notice the blankets being pulled up over her, as blessed sleep snuck up to claim her tired mind and body.

* * *

The chime awakened Tweno, and he forced himself to climb smartly out of bed. Four hours was all the sleeptime he could afford. So much had to be accomplished so quickly. He was in his office in record time.

'Scriber in hand, Tweno finalized his blueprint for emergency evacuation. If their planet could be saved, they would return. But he was not about to risk any more lives unnecessarily. To that end, Tweno was prepared to be ruthless. If people's opinion of him fell too far to salvage, he would step aside. But not until every Shalaian had been moved to safety.

Tweno reached for the hear-other to put through a priority call to the private residences of Firsts Lisham and Konapi. He hesitated a moment, considering. On Pantai, Ablakan had no 'second', having opted instead for a team approach lead by Juneli. He hated awakening her after the mammoth rescue effort in which she had just participated, but time would prove more ruthless than he could ever be.

He rang her suite. The hear-other sounded four times before a fuzzy voice he barely recognized as Juneli's answered.

"Sorry to awaken you, but I need you to mobilize the evacuation of Pantai. I'm about to call Lisham and Konapi."

"Yes, sir," Juneli smothered a yawn. "Can you give me a moment to throw water on my face?"

"Two. But no more."

"On my way," Juneli chuckled, and the receiver clicked shut.

Tweno called the two other Firsts, to give them an equal chance to become alert, then took advantage of the pause to wolf down a makeshift meal before convening the meeting.

"My apologies for the early hour, but you all know what we're up against. As of now, your first priority is to get your people ready for transport off-planet. As soon as it is a reasonable hour, I will contact the leaders of the member planets, and begin evacuation. They have assured me temporary shelter and supplies will be made available until a permanent home can be found for us. I intend to take them up on that. We cannot – I *will not* – risk any more lives."

"I'll get the word out," Konapi agreed in a clipped tone that told Tweno better than anything how seriously Enaxat's First was taking the directive. The quake that had hit his continent had done more than enough damage to make the point. And now two of Pantai's major cities were also in ruins.

"We'll be ready, too," Lisham said. "When do we start moving them out?"

"If the leaders can arrange it, we could start today." Wishful thinking, probably, Tweno thought. Shalaii's allies had been counting on a lot more lead time, same as Tweno had. But that black hole just couldn't wait to swallow Shalaii.

"Stay where I can reach you," Tweno said, hanging up just as Juneli appeared in his office. For the minimal sleep she had had, she looked remarkably alert.

"We need to have all the 'porters on standby," Tweno said. "And that includes Tix."

"She'll love you for that," Juneli grinned. Tix was not a morning person.

"Too bad." No doubt Tix would make her displeasure known, but despite her grumbling, Tweno knew they could always count on her to pull her weight – what little of it there was. "Wiki will take care of things not evacuation-related."

"She's a gem, that one," Juneli admitted. "Every bit as capable as her reputation."

"That's my impression, too. Now, here's what I want you to do."

It took some time for Tweno to map out his evacuation strategy for Pantai, but Juneli quickly showed that she had a good grasp of the logistics. By the time she left, it was late enough to contact most of the allied planetary leaders.

The U.S. President promptly took Tweno's call, put through by Kyollan. Tweno got the feeling the man had been expecting it.

Dr. Saunders of NASA advised us yesterday of Dr. Weismer's findings. The U.N. Assembly has been on standby ever since, in anticipation of your request.

You don't know how glad I am to hear that, Tweno breathed. *How many people can your resources accommodate?*

Globally, for the short term, about 10 million. They would be divided among a number of sites.

That is most generous. How soon can we start transporting? That, of course, was the crucial question. With the minimal number of decontamination chambers on each planet, it would be a very time-consuming job. And Tweno knew they had precious little time left.

You can start sending them over, 6100 at a time, as soon as the U.N. gives the word. Probably this afternoon. Our people have been working overtime since the hole was discovered. I am pleased to say, there are now 122 decontam chambers on Earth available for your use. I will have Jan send you the coordinates of each one. And all of our 'porters are standing by to help in the evacuation. There was understandable pride in the President's voice.

Someday soon, I hope we can express our appreciation properly, Tweno told him with heartfelt gratitude.

Jan must have been close by, for no sooner had he hung up than a thin leaflet appeared on Tweno's desk. As promised, it contained the location of the chambers, each able to process 50 people at a time, working at capacity.

Administrator Wiltanus of Orowa promised to shelter seven million Shalaians. In anticipation of the need, they had been able to construct and get operational 58 chambers, thus handling 2900 people at a sitting.

Since Earth and Orowa were Shalaii's oldest and closest allies, it was too much to hope that the other planets in the alliance would be equally prepared and generous, but food and lodging for 17 million Shalaians was already a wonderful start.

For the first time, Tweno was glad their little planet held relatively few people. The remaining four member worlds would only have to shelter another 15 million for the evacuation to be complete. That averaged less than four million refugees per planet. Tweno hadn't counted School in the equation, since that world would not support oxygen-breathing biological life. Precisely what type of being School was had never fully been determined.

Tweno spent the balance of the morning contacting the leaders of the other planets. By noon, he leaned back in his chair, tired but happy. Even starting mid-afternoon and working the universe's known 'porters in rotating shifts, Shalaii would be abandoned in three days.

An ominous rumble from deep within Shalaii's crust underlined the need for haste. Tweno picked up the hear-other, still warm from being clutched in his hand all morning, and punched in the code for Maintenance.

"We will be starting evacuation this afternoon," Tweno told the senior caretaker. "I will need someone to stay behind with me until the evacuation is complete. The part of the building housing the decontamination chamber, and the emergency power to run it, must be protected at all cost."

"I will see to it personally," the caretaker promised.

"Thank you. I will remain till our people are safely off-planet. You, and your colleagues maintaining and running those chambers across Shalaii, will be 'ported out with me last."

"Understood, sir."

Next Tweno called Juneli, Lisham and Konapi to give them the good news about the evacuation, and to have them make similar arrangements with the other chamber runners and maintainers across the planet as he had for the palace's decontam chamber.

"Juneli, I have copies of where to find each chamber on every world except, of course, School's. Please distribute these lists for me."

By way of answer, they disappeared from his desk, save one copy for the palace's use.

Tweno smiled at her alacrity. "Thanks. I'll call you as soon as we get the go-ahead from anywhere."

He had no sooner hung up than Jan spoke in his mind *We're ready when you are – all of our 'porters, that is.*

My deepest appreciation, Tweno told her before disconnecting.

He was just reaching for the hear-other when Ablakan appeared in front of him, balancing unsteadily. The young man raised a hand to forestall Tweno's objection.

"Other than the ribs and my arm, I'm alright. I want to help." Ablakan's jaw was set in firm lines, and he held his ruler's eyes.

148

"Okay. But if I see you tiring, you're going to stop even if I have to sedate you myself." Tweno glowered at him with as much ferocity as he could manage.

"Understood. Would you bring me up-to-date?"

That done, Ablakan picked up the list with his healthy arm, ran off two copies for Kyollan and Tix, and 'ported himself and the precious original to his office.

Juneli beamed the instant she saw him, then caught herself and gave him an accusatory frown. "Why aren't you in the hospital?"

"They needed the beds for sick people. Let's get to work. Have you been coordinating?"

"I was just about to start," Juneli confirmed. "But you know the ropes better than I do."

"Not much better," Ablakan smiled at her, then extended it to include Wiki, who had just come into the room at the sound of voices.

It took over an hour to designate who would use which machines, and to mobilize people to be moved off-planet. The first couple of million Shalaians to be 'ported were easy to locate. They had already been made homeless by the recent quakes, and were assembled in prefabricated shelters not dissimilar to human warehouses. Most of them had nothing more than the clothes on their backs. They eagerly cooperated in the evacuation process.

It would not be so easy to move those whose homes were still intact, Ablakan knew, and they would want to bring precious belongings with them – a practice that could not be permitted, given the shortage of space in the temporary quarters they would be inhabiting.

By mid-afternoon, the homeless from the two previous quakes had been transported to Earth and Orowa. All morning, every means of communication save telepathy had been urging people to show up at designated locations, ready for transport. Panoramas of the devastation caused by the quakes were interspersed with instructions and muster locations, and emergency vehicles went down every street, repeating the directives over loudspeakers. Volunteers drove the infirm and those lacking transportation.

During that time, Pantai suffered another quake, though not nearly as large as the previous one. Still, it served to reinforce the urgency, convincing many who had been holding back.

On each continent, the same process was in motion. By early evening, every planet had announced its readiness to receive refugees. Throughout the long night, 'porters from each planet worked in four-hour shifts, keeping all available chambers working at capacity. A steady stream of people arrived, went through the decontamination process, then were ushered into waiting rooms, from whence they were 'ported to emergency camps.

Thousands of volunteers and relief organization workers, government and military personnel situated them, seeing to their basic needs and identifying those who might require medical attention. One 'porter spent an entire shift transporting hospital patients, staff and necessary medical equipment from Shalaii to hospitals on the other worlds.

* * *

At the end of her third shift, an exhausted Jan 'ported herself home.

"I need food, a shower and 10 hours sleep crammed into three," she told the lone occupant of the kitchen.

Tom stared at her in dismay. "I know it's got to be done, but how can you and the others keep up this pace for three days?"

"When the need is great . . ." Jan intoned weakly. "What scares me is that, right after we finish, we have to somehow move that solar system. I don't think we'll be in any shape to do it, and Shalaii itself is fast running out of time. There were two big quakes in the last eight hours." She shuddered, as memory of the devastation returned afresh. "Thank goodness we had pretty well evacuated those areas."

Tom nodded. "Y'know, the ones I feel sorriest for are the animals. They must be in shock by what's happening."

Jan gave him a haunted look. "I know."

"I feel so damned useless. I'd do anything to be able to help."

Jan patted his arm, understanding how hard it was for him to be idle in the face of such need. "I know, love," She tried to think of something heartening to add, but she was just too dog-tired to think. "I've *got* to shower."

"Okay, Stinky. And I'll prepare your dinner. That, at least, I can do."

"It's what I need the most. Second-most," Jan amended, kissing him soundly, before heading for the shower. Despite her resolve to be quick about it, she found herself repeatedly dozing off under the warm cascade. Good thing I didn't opt for the jacuzzi, she thought.

The aroma of Tom's homemade Chinese food wafted through the crack under the bathroom door, and Jan inhaled appreciatively. She hurried through the balance of the drying process, then donned her pj's before making a beeline for the dining room. What she saw made her eyes gleam and her mouth water.

"You must have been cooking all evening," she remarked.

"Most of it. If I can't participate directly, at least I can fuel the participators."

Jan shamelessly began shoveling large quantities of the various dishes onto her plate, smiling her gratitude while she ate. Now that her stomach was getting what it so dearly wanted, her need for sleep reasserting itself in no uncertain terms.

"How's it going?"

"We're remaining on schedule," Jan told him between forkfuls. "Oh, and Ablakan booked himself out of the hospital. He shouldn't be 'porting yet, but you know him."

"Indeed I do," Tom smiled. Then his expression sobered. "I heard there were more quakes on Pantai."

"Yes, two while I was working. We were lucky to have pretty well cleared those areas before they were hit. Just the outlying farming communities were left, and the people there had been warned to stay clear of buildings and trees until we could evacuate them."

"Much damage?" Tom looked as though he already knew the answer.

"The cities are pretty well write-offs," Jan grimaced. "Even if we can save the planet, it'll be a long time before there'll be sufficient housing for her people. And then, we have to keep remembering to move the moon so it doesn't get pulled into that hole."

"I'd forgotten about that," Tom admitted. "Good thing you guys didn't. Finished?" He indicated her half-empty plate. She was eating slowly now, almost mechanically.

Jan looked down at her plate, which wasn't quite in focus. "I think so. I've got to sleep."

"I'll take care of the dishes." Tom came around to help her to her feet.

Part of her resented the treatment, but she soon realized how unsteady she was. She let Tom shepherd her to their bedroom, where he pulled back the blankets and waited for her to crawl in. He tucked the blankets around her and kissed the tip of her nose.

"Sweet dreams, love," he murmured.

Tom clicked off the phone on his night table and turned off the light.

"You can get two-and-a-half hours unbroken sleep," he spoke into the gloom. "I'll awaken you a half-hour before you're due to go on again."

"Thanks," came the muffled reply.

When he got back to the dining room to clean up, Jack and Brenda were there, helping themselves to leftovers. Brenda's condition was a carbon-copy of how Jan had looked.

Tom regarded Brenda, puzzled. "Weren't you due back same time as Jan?"

"I was nearly done with a sector," she explained, shoveling food into her mouth. "Wanted to finish."

Jack flashed Tom a worried look. Tom shrugged his shoulders surreptitiously. If the 'porters were in this shape after putting in two shifts, how were they going to make it through the other two-and-a-half days?

Brenda had showered between shifts, so as soon as her hunger had been assuaged, Jack ushered her off to their bedroom. He returned shortly, shaking his head.

"There's no way they can keep up this pace, let alone move that solar system afterwards," Jack concluded. "Just no way."

"What I'd like to know is, having assimilated the 'how-to' of 'porting from so many people, why School won't help."

Jack shrugged. "Maybe they can't. Maybe thinking as multiples keeps them from being able to 'port things. I don't know."

"Well, I'd sure like to ask them," Tom grumbled.

"I'm sure they would if they could." Jack turned to leave. "I'm gonna get some shuteye. I suggest you get some, too. It'll be a long three days."

"G'night."

Tom watched Jack disappear towards his and Brenda's wing of the rancher-style house. Tom stood there, reliving a long-forgotten event. Seven years before, Jan's empathy had trapped her briefly in the nightmare of Moohri's unconscious mind, shortly after his ship crashed on the planetoid. Watching her sit there, shocky and weeping, Tom had acted out of desperation, trying with all his might to get a message through to Ablakan that his help was needed. And it had worked. Only that one time, but it had worked. When the need was great.

Now, another need at least as great existed. Tom thought about what he wanted to do, and wondered if there was any way to pull it off. He had only 'met' School once, the contact a gift from Jan. It was not an experience he would soon forget, having his mind laid open like that. But in exchange, he had mentally received star charts of the entire universe known to School from their contacts with other species over the eons.

Gulping back his reticence, Tom held the memory of his contact with School firmly in mind and projected his thoughts in the direction of the multiplicity. *Please, please answer,* he begged mentally, opening his mind as much as he could.

Silence mocked his efforts. He was no telepath, and he knew it. How did he expect to make contact with a group consciousness so far away? And yet, he was able to get a feel of solar systems that held consciousness. So why shouldn't he be able to do the reverse?

Conflicted as his thoughts were, he was about to give up, to try again later, when he felt a curious tickling sensation in his mind.

We greet you, Tom, a chorus told him. *And we congratulate you on your achievement. Do you wish us to read your needs?*

Uh, yes, please. This was not something Tom had ever wanted to experience again, but this wasn't the time to be squeamish. Immediately, he felt his mind expanding endlessly, but just for a moment.

Jack's comment is correct, they told him. *We cannot teleport as a multiple focus.*

Can you dissociate and function singularly?

Tom could feel an amiable roiling within the multiplicity. Might this be their version of conversation among themselves?

We do not believe so. It would not be possible to exclude knowing the thoughts of each other.

But you separated into two groups, Tom pointed out. *And showed that although you can share thoughts, you can also work separately.*

That is only because we mentally exist in separate universes.

Have you ever tried working separately? Tom pressed.

Once, millions of your years ago, there was a need. We failed, was the discouraging response.

But you have evolved a great deal in that time. You didn't know then about teleportation, is that right?

There was a brief pause, and another spate of conversation between the group. *What you say is true. We shall attempt it again, but we offer no promises.*

Trying is all we can ask. Thank you.

As he felt the connection break, he stumbled back against the counter, spent. How did Jan do it, hour after hour? All he wanted to do was crawl into bed and sleep for a week, but that was the last thing he could afford. He was the 'home team', caring for Billy, making meals, keeping the house running smoothly while Jack saw to the needs of the 'porters on the job.

* * *

Mid-morning, a bleary-eyed Ablakan arrived at his complex's decontamination chamber to relieve an equally-exhausted Kyollan. Each 'porter was managing anywhere up to ten chambers spanning two planets simultaneously. This was possible due to the time it took for the decontamination process to cycle through.

Ablakan smiled tiredly at Kyollan, then accessed Kyollan's memory of the past couple of hours – just an overview – to know what had been done, and to be able to take over seamlessly from where Kyollan had left off. No sooner had he finished than Kyollan 'ported himself back to the palace to rest.

A mental 'knock' heralded the arrival of a 'pathic visitor. Ablakan opened his mind, then froze in surprise. It wasn't anyone he knew. Or rather, he corrected himself, it was only a tiny part of someone he knew.

154

We – I – greet you, Ablakan. I am a voice of School. At Tom's suggestion, we tried again to work separately, and this time, we were successful. You are to return to your bed. There are 173 of us who will take over from the 'porters who have been involved in the evacuation so far.

Ablakan was startled to realize his eyebanks were leaking in unspeakable relief. *Thank you, dear friends. I cannot tell you how grateful I am – we all are – for your help.*

Sleep well, and worry not. The mind gave him a gentle mental push, then disappeared.

Ablakan stayed just long enough to 'see' the first group of 50 Shalaians disappear from the staging area before 'porting himself to Tweno's office. One look at his ruler's haggard countenance was enough.

"It's off to bed for you, too," he told a surprised Tweno. "School has split themselves into individuals and we now have 173 'porters to relieve us."

Tweno gave him a tired smile. "That's the best news I've heard all week. But I'll stay till the job is finished."

Ablakan shook his head firmly. "They've got it well in hand. There's nothing more any of us can do right now. We'll be needed later, when decisions have to be made." Ablakan frowned at Tweno, noting the set cast to his face. "Look, sir, you said until this crisis is over, that you're our resource person, not our ruler. We need our resource person alert, not half dead from fatigue and worry. I will go to bed, *and not set the timemometer,* as soon as I inform Lisham and Konapi, if you'll agree to do the same. Do we have a deal?"

Tweno raised a hand in capitulation. "It's hard to let go the reins, even when you know you must."

"I know the feeling. But doing otherwise would suggest we don't trust School to do the job right."

"You're sure they can?" Tweno asked him bluntly.

"Yes."

"Alright, then, I will sleep. Until the next damned quake hits, anyway."

"Rest well." Ablakan 'ported himself back to his office, then remembered the cats. He was about to pay them a visit when Wiki emerged from the adjoining room. Even tired as she was, she looked beautiful.

"Is it true School is taking over the 'porting?"

"Yes, I'm glad to say. Why don't you get some sleep? I'll do the same as soon as I've taken care of the cats."

"Already done," she announced, looking smug. "I fed and watered them, and played with them a while."

Ablakan regarded her in surprise. "When did you find the time?"

"Business has shut down. Everyone's going off-planet, remember?" She wagged a finger at him. "You need sleep."

"So do you," Ablakan noted. "I'll see you later."

With that, he 'ported to his bedroom, removed his shoes and crawled into bed, fully clothed. He didn't even remember pulling the blankets over himself.

CHAPTER 11

So far they had been lucky, Ablakan realized, if you could call it that. The storms and tsunamis Dr. Weismer had predicted had not materialized. Till now, that is.

It was the second day of the evacuation, and a storm of unprecedented ferocity was lashing Pantai and the island capital. Ablakan watched the collosal waves hurl themselves against the shore and wondered how the palace, not far inland, was holding up to the wind.

The frequent quakes had been unable to cause more than minor damage to his own complex, it being new and state-of-the-art. Still, it creaked ominously as the hurricane-force winds howled around it. And the complex wasn't out in the open the way the palace was.

For the second time that day, Ablakan 'ported himself to Tweno's office.

"Let me move you all to my place," he pleaded. "Just as a precaution. There's plenty of room."

"We're running on a skeleton staff already, and I need them here to make sure the chamber remains operational."

"One of us can do that remotely. Just leave a maintenance person there to keep an eye on things."

Tweno shook his head firmly. "I promised I would remain as long as they did. I will keep my word."

Ablakan frowned. He knew the palace was running on emergency power as it was.

"We can manage with one less chamber. Shut things down and let me get you out of there." Ablakan could feel perspiration beading on his forehead.

"We don't know for sure how much time we have, and I won't risk any lives by closing this chamber," Tweno growled. "I appreciate your concern, Ablakan, but we both have to do what will give our people and Shalaii the best chance of survival. Now stop worrying about me and get back to figuring out how you and your colleagues will move us away from that accursed hole."

"Alright, but at least stay near an exit door. You're the best ruler we've ever had; everyone says so. I don't want to lose you."

"You won't," Tweno promised. "Now get back to work!"

"Stubborn old man!" Ablakan muttered under his breath, but returned to his office without the Primary.

All morning, he, Jan, Shownae, Tix and Kyollan had practiced with the model solar system. Jan had finally convinced her President to let her try to move Shalaii's sun.

Ablakan shuddered, remembering her first try with a relatively 'cold' dying sun 230 light-years from Earth. There were no planets associated with the star, only groupings of ejected stellar material. It had taken Jan several minutes to work up the courage to surround it with her focus.

"Remember, consciousness cannot be affected by anything in time-space," Ablakan had reminded her. "At least, according to School."

Jan had nodded, gulping. Then she had squared her shoulders and, chin jutting out belligerently, she had wrapped her focus around the sun and 'ported it a short distance away.

"There! Nothing to it," she had said, grinning at them.

But within seconds, her body had begun to shake uncontrollably, as reaction set in. Her friends were shocked to see her skin turn an unrealistic shade of red, right before their eyes. A panic call was made to Ames' resident physician.

"Beliefs," he announced after examining her. "She believed it was too hot to handle, and so her body reacted as though it was. In essence, she has a psychic sunburn."

By then, Jan was feeling better, if somewhat sheepish.

"Just wear some psychic sunscreen next time," the doctor commented drolly, and wrote her a prescription for something to alleviate the psychosomatic symptoms. But at least they now knew it was possible to move a sun.

Ablakan grimaced, his eyebanks glancing at Shalaii's star shining so reassuringly above them. It was thousands of times larger than the one on which Jan had practiced, and unimaginably hotter. Would Jan be able to move such a massive body? Could she dismiss from her mind its deadly heat? In her place, Ablakan doubted that he could.

Juneli poked her head through the doorway. "Any luck?"

"None. He won't budge till the evacuation is complete."

Juneli sighed. "At least I can keep a lock on him without his knowing it. If I feel he's in imminent danger, I'll yank him out of there, like it or not."

Ablakan grinned at her. "In that case, I'll release *my* lock on him."

Juneli returned the smile. "I should have known you would have one. But you're needed on Earth. Jan says they're ready to practice with the model solar system again."

"Okay. Don't forget: If this building fails, get out immediately. We can't afford to lose you."

"I know," she sighed. "We're indispensable."

"At the moment, yes. I have your word?" Ablakan was taking no chances on her sometimes misplaced sense of loyalty.

"I promise," Juneli told him with obvious reluctance.

"Thanks."

Shortly afterwards, Ablakan stood in Ames' chamber, along with 49 of his countryfolk. His eyebanks immediately sought out Jan. Ablakan was relieved to see the redness was hardly noticeable. They exchanged warm smiles while the decontamination procedure cycled through. Then he joined Jan and the other 'porters waiting to move the model solar system.

"How are you feeling?"

"Fine now, thanks." Jan's eyes held his. "How are *you*?"

"My ribs are sore, of course, and I can't use this arm," he automatically glanced down at the cast and sling. "But overall I feel better, thanks."

"Good."

As Jan turned her attention to the others, Ablakan watched her speculatively. Was her good humor the result of rest and a happier outlook, or was she in a reckless mood again? He had a sinking feeling it might be the latter.

"I've been wondering what we can do to thank School, after this is all over with," Jan said as they were walking towards the sealed room that held the model. "What do you give someone who lacks everything, but wouldn't know what to do with it if they had it?"

"We've been wondering the same thing. They already have everything from us they wanted – namely, our memories. I suppose we could try to convince all our specialists in the various fields to let School tap theirs."

"Good idea," Shownae put in, for by then Jan and Ablakan had joined the others outside the room which held the model. "I'll run it by Administrator Wiltanus."

They turned to gaze through the heavy-gauge picture window from which they could watch a miniaturized representation of Shalaii's solar system moving in 'real time'. Conversation stopped as each took charge of 'their' celestial body.

"Ready?" Jan asked. Unanimous nods confirmed they were. "On my mark. One . . . two . . . three . . . *NOW!*"

As they had before, each team member merged with the others lightly, while holding onto their portion of the solar system. They 'ported the unit as a whole to the predesignated location in the room, then gingerly released their item.

"How does it look?" Jan asked.

The technician monitoring the various spins, trajectories and orbits did not respond immediately. They could only wait while he interpreted the continuous readouts. When he sighed, they knew they had failed again.

"Between you, you're only off by 0.01 percent," he told them. "Tix, yours was wavering just a touch. That might account for it. I'll reset."

He pressed a button, and carefully as Ablakan could watch the system, he could see no change. But the technician's grunt of satisfaction told him the readouts were again as they should be.

"Ready?" This time Jan directed her query at the technician. He nodded once.

On her mark, they redid the exercise. This time, Tix was able to hold hers steady during the transition, but again the technician shook his head.

"Now Shownae's is off, but just by 0.0046."

"How accurate do we have to be?" Brenda asked.

"You must understand that even a small variation like that could make a significant difference over time. 0.0046 in this little model would translate to hundreds or thousands of miles with the real thing. I can run the data and give you an exact count, if you'd like."

"No, thanks," Jan held her hands out to emphasize it. "But what if, with the real solar system, we were 0.0046 off? Would *that* make any appreciable difference?"

"Yes. It would just take a while to become apparent." The technician rubbed his chin reflectively. "As I understand it, the problem here is that you've been trying to keep the bodies moving as they normally would during the brief time it takes you to 'port them to their new location. Is that right?"

Ablakan blinked at him in surprise. "Isn't that what we're supposed to do?"

"Not necessarily. As long as *none* of the bodies are moving for that moment, it won't make a difference. Your solar system's movement would be offset by that one moment forever. But it would be like time froze, then carried on as usual. The important thing is that they all stop the same length of time before resuming." The technician looked from one to the other of them. "Do you understand?"

"Yes. That *would* make it a lot easier," Jan nodded. "But we'd have to hold our piece motionless at the exact same time for all of us."

The technician cleared his throat. "Not really. As long as the *time* you hold it motionless is the same for all of you, it doesn't matter when it occurs prior to the system resuming its movements."

Shownae grimaced. "How do we make sure it's identical? I for one cannot cut it that fine. 0.0046 may be easy for computers to pick up, but not for me."

"I don't think any of us can," Jan said. "What if we just do the best we can, then fine-tune the solar system later, if it's needed?"

The technician shrugged. "You do have that option. But it means that, over the coming eons, so long as the solar system continues to function, there will always have to be a 'porter able to make adjustments as and when required, unless at some point he or she can get that precise a calibration."

In the ensuing silence, Ablakan, like the other members of the team, considered their options. Tix was the first to reach a conclusion.

"I don't see why this should be such a big problem. We don't have to worry about whether our hearts will continue to beat or we keep breathing, when we 'port ourselves somewhere. As long as we each take the same time to 'port, we should be okay."

"Now that's something I hadn't considered," Ablakan smiled at Tix, inclining his head slightly in tribute to her observation.

Jan nodded. "Makes sense to me. Let's try it as a group 'port, like we did before, but this time not trying to keep the movements going."

Obediently, Ablakan held 'Shalaii' lightly in his focus, allowing it to continue its movements unhindered. Once the merge with the others was complete, Jan led the 'mark' and they moved the system as one.

"How'd we do?" she asked the technician breathlessly.

Ablakan was feeling a bit lightheaded from the unaccustomed extra concentration needed to be so time-precise. But he barely noticed it, as he watched the technician correlate the figures.

"Closer, but not by much," was the disappointing response.

"Damn!" Jan muttered. "I was sure we had it that time."

Ablakan tried to look on the bright side. "However close we get, it's going to be better than having that hole devour Shalaii. Why don't we just do the best we can, and fine-tune later, if we have to?"

There was a noticeable pall on the group as they bid each other goodbye and returned to their various planets.

* * *

Can I interrupt briefly? Ablakan almost whispered the query, not wanting to pull anyone's focus away at a critical juncture.

You are not interrupting. Many of us are at rest, a much-diminished chorus of School replied. Despite the arduous task of transporting that many people off a planet in physical turmoil, they seemed in their usual good spirits.

I'm free until we're ready to try to move the solar system. I'd like to take a couple of shifts, Ablakan told them. *And again, we cannot thank you enough for what you are doing.*

Actually, it is refreshing to work independently for a time. Unless you are truly eager to have a shift, we suggest you rest. We will be finished tomorrow, and then you and your friends can move the solar system. Has the practice gone well? they asked. Ablakan couldn't tell if it was out of curiosity or merely a polite inquiry.

162

Not too bad, I guess. We've been unable to coordinate fully. Our best practice still held almost a 0.0064 error factor on the tiny model. I don't know how we'll do with the real thing, but hopefully we can correct any discrepancy afterwards.

Oddly, School seemed impressed. *That is a remarkable achievement for individuals with so little experience as a multiplicity.*

Ablakan had the impression they were about to say more, but changed their collective minds. Still, the praise bolstered his flagging spirits.

Please call me if I can take a shift, he said by way of goodbye.

Ablakan's focus returned to the present. The storm above Pantai had spent much of its fury, and aside from occasional hefty gusts of wind, it was no worse than any other storm for that time of year. Even the seas had abated appreciably.

Ablakan's complex had been one of the first to be evacuated; he had seen to it himself. Surprisingly, Saymin, who had been scheduled to start his new job shortly after the crisis began, had remained on staff, stoutly refusing to leave until he was certain Ablakan would be alright. Only he, the head chef and Jusire, the maintenance chief stayed behind with Ablakan, Juneli and Wiki. Had worse come to worse, Ablakan reflected wryly, he would have gone out suitably attired and with a full stomach. But now the danger was too imminent to ignore.

Spreading his focus to include the complex in its entirety, Ablakan projected a mental request into each resident's mind to meet in his office. When they arrived, he motioned them to be seated. They looked at him expectantly.

"I've called you together to thank you for your loyalty, but now it's time you to go someplace safe. And I have just the place. Jan has asked me to beg you, Wiki, to stay with them. Something about needing an extra sitter to keep Billy out of mischief. Think you can handle it? I hear he's a handful and spoiled rotten. Saymin and Chef, they have a small cottage nearby they'd like you to move into."

"And I suppose you'll be staying here," Juneli said pointedly.

"Till the evacuation is over, yes. Someone has to keep an eye on our Primary. You know how stubborn he is."

"And you're not?" This time it was Wiki on the attack. "I'm staying unless you go, too."

As though it had been rehearsed, each of them made the same vow. Ablakan looked at the mutineers with a mixture of pride and frustration.

"Look, don't think I don't appreciate what you're trying to do. But so long as you're here, I have to keep a mental lock on each of you, and keep monitoring to make sure you're safe. That's draining, folks." He held up a hand as several voices raised in objection. "Say what you will, if you were in my place, you'd do the same; you know you would. But there comes a time when, through no fault of your own, your 'help' becomes a liability. That time is now. We've had four quakes today alone. Fortunately, none of them were severe enough to bring down the building, but we may not be so lucky the next time. The fewer people I have to account for, the better."

His audience stared at him in reluctant understanding, and he took full advantage of it.

"Juneli, if you're willing, I'd like you to remain here with Jusire, to make sure the decontam chamber stays operational. If the complex starts to crumble, get everyone out – and that includes you. I'll do the same for Tweno and his crew. The rest of you can best help by being where we won't have to worry about you. Please pack one bag of what you really need, and be ready to be 'ported in half an hour. Juneli, will you transport them?"

"Certainly."

"And the cats?"

"Wouldn't forget them." The whimsical little smile pulling at the corners of Juneli's mouth made Ablakan wonder whether she was truly fond of them, or just glad to be rid of their peskiness for a time. "Who's going to take care of them for you?"

"Jan," he replied, then chuckled as he caught Juneli's look of doubtful surprise. "I agree; it contravenes the good neighbor policy."

Juneli nodded soberly. "You might cause an interstellar incident, unleashing those two on her."

"I know," he grinned. "I'll owe Jan massively for this one." Which reminded him. "I'd better check how the evacuation is going."

The resting portion of School assured him that they were on schedule, and would be finished about mid-day tomorrow. This meant Ablakan and his colleagues could try to move the solar system that afternoon. His stomach did a flip-flop at the thought, and he resolutely pushed the thought away. No use worrying about something ahead of time; it just made it seem that much harder.

His stomach lurched again, but this time he recognized the insistent demand for nourishment. The pantry held a variety of items, any of which would have sufficed, but the complex was already running on emergency power. It wouldn't do to strain it further.

As Ablakan passed the window, he was startled to see Pantai in darkness. In the gathering gloom, it had the eerie ambience of a doomed world. Involuntarily, Ablakan shuddered and looked away. Even the sight of muchipans didn't lift his spirits, and he sat down with a cold bowl of chilcona. His throat constricted spasmodically, as though unwilling to accept the offering.

With a sigh, Ablakan pushed it away. For the first time since the crisis began, he allowed the doubts to voice themselves. And they did so, with a vengeance.

'Move a solar system?', they mocked sarcastically. 'Why not a galaxy? Your puny efforts are but the desperate squirming of the doomed. And you would allow your best friend in this universe to risk her life moving your sun, and for what? Just to save your planet? There are billions of other worlds out there, but there's only one 'Jan'. Call it off, before it's too late,' they whispered urgently. 'Don't let her die because you wouldn't let go of what was already lost.'

Ablakan hissed in alarm, jumping at a soft touch on his shoulder.

"Sorry. Having second thoughts?" Juneli asked, accordioning down on a chair beside him.

Wordlessly, Ablakan nodded and took a long, uneven breath. "I was just thinking about tomorrow. How can I risk Jan's life, even to save Shalaii? How can I put a life above a thing, even if that 'thing' is home?"

"You can't," Juneli replied. "Only Jan can make that decision. And she has. All you can do now is talk her out of doing it, if that is what you wish."

"It is," he replied, suddenly resolute. "If we do this at all, *I* will try to move our sun. Jan can move Shalaii."

Juneli's eyebanks enlarged in alarm. "Don't. Please, Ablakan. You haven't even practiced yet, like Jan has." She gripped his arm, her nails digging in painfully. "I love Shalaii as much as you do, but it's not worth your life. *Nothing* is worth that."

"I have to try," he said hoarsely. "I owe our homeworld that much, at the very least." Immediately, he felt his limbs begin to tremble, as the horror of what he was proposing coursed through his nervous system.

"No, you don't!" Juneli hissed savagely, her pupils piercing through the gloom. "Listen to me! You don't owe anyone anything. Don't you dare throw your life away! We need you too much. *I* need you too much." Abruptly, the moisture that had been welling up in her eyebanks spilled over in a cascade of revelation. She looked at him, trembling. "I love you."

For what felt like an eternity, Ablakan just stared at her, uncomprehending. "You do?"

"Yes, damn it, I do! How can you be such a great telempath, and not know that?" She was angry now. "I've loved you from the moment we met."

"Why didn't you say something?" This was all happening too fast. Ablakan felt like he was being hit broadside to get his attention, and all it was doing was confusing him more.

Juneli snorted in derision. "I was a lowly attendant. I had no right to such feelings, and even less right to voice them." She shook her head sadly. "Maybe I shouldn't have said anything at all."

Ablakan took her hands then, noticing for the first time the tenderness in her eyebanks, the sensuousness of the person he had always considered a dear friend and confidante.

"I'm glad you did, June," he murmured lamely. "But right now, with all this chaos, I honestly can't tell you how I feel." He winced as he saw her face fall. "I love you, too. I just don't know what form that love takes."

166

"Bad timing," she said, her mouth twisted in self-deprecation. "Just promise me you won't try to move our sun. Please, Ablakan."

"I'm sorry," he whispered.

Juneli nodded as though she had been expected it. "In that case, I'd better let you get some rest." She turned away and left the room.

For a long time, Ablakan sat there, staring in the direction of her departure. Now he knew how Shalaii must feel, with unfamiliar forces pulling at her, tearing at the very fabric of her being. An emotional war raged within him, with fear, love and despair vying for top billing. At length, his thoughts is tatters, Ablakan 'ported himself to bed and the blessed relief that only the amnesia of sleep could provide.

CHAPTER 12

For the umpteenth time, Jan shook her head in annoyance. She had spent the better part of the afternoon wrestling with her fears. The mental image of Shalaii's sun, awesome in its enormity and ferocious heat, mocked her plans to move it. Every time she tried to do a mental 'dry run', she had to stop, overwhelmed by even the thought of capturing that seething mass with her focus.

"It's only a *thing*," she admonished herself aloud, glaring fiercely at her reflection in the bathroom mirror. "Weight, size, *heat* doesn't matter. If you can get your focus around it, you can move it. Period."

As with the times before, disbelief stared back at her, calling her bluff. With a groan of defeat, Jan turned away.

I need help, that's all there is to it, she decided. But who could she turn to? Even School had admitted no one they encountered had ever tried to move a planet, let alone a sun. Still, they were the closest she had to a resource.

Jan plunked herself down on the toilet seat cover, mildly amused at her choice of 'throne' from which to potentially make history – or at least, the preparations for making history. She sent out her call to the resting portion of School, then leaned back against the cold toilet water box to await their reply.

We greet you, Jan, several voices chimed in perfect unison. *And we understand your confusion. We also have wondered how it might be possible to move so large a sun.*

Jan's heart sank at the admission, but she doggedly pressed on with her questions. Sometimes, you don't know what you know till you hear yourself say it, she thought.

We always know what we know, School declared, taking her errant thought as communication. *Still, it may help you. Please proceed.*

You told us once that our focus, our consciousness, doesn't originate in time-space and so can't be affected by anything in a time-space. That is what you said, wasn't it?

Indeed, School assured her. *But you can anticipate and so experience any effects or reactions you want from the interaction. In your case, because your thoughts and feelings are imprecise, it would be a result of belief rather than desire.*

How much damage could I do to myself, if I tried to move that sun and my belief that it's too hot to handle gets in the way?

You could kill yourself, was the sobering reply. *We would not recommend you proceed until you have disposed of your belief that you cannot succeed.*

Which was pretty much the conclusion Jan had come to on her own. *How do I remove the belief?*

There was the customary short delay, as School discussed her options among themselves. *We would like to attempt an experiment with you. We have not done this before, so we cannot guarantee how, or if, it will affect you. May we proceed?*

Jan felt her pulse quicken in alarm. *What kind of experiment?*

We propose to merge your mind with ours. Temporarily, of course. It would let you understand from our understanding. We believe this would help you greatly, if it does not cause harm to your unique mental configuration.

Jan gulped. Sometimes School could be *too* candid. But if it might help her survive moving that sun, it was worth the risk.

Good. Await us a bit, School said, effortlessly reading her tepid agreement.

She sat there, shivering in anticipation, but mercifully she didn't have long to wait. She felt her mind being engulfed by another, far larger mind, but one with a multitude of aspects to it. Hers felt like a drop in the ocean, and she struggled to keep tabs on it.

Do not worry for your selfhood. We have ascertained that you will remain singular after this is complete. The words seemed to be coming from her, and yet she knew she had not thought them.

Abruptly, her focus filled with the specter of Shalaii's sun, magnificent in its fiery massiveness. As she watched, her expanded focus effortlessly wrapped itself around the object, closing in on all sides.

From what seemed like a billion miles away, Jan felt her body inhale sharply, then the sensation was cut off, as a sense of calm descended upon her. She watched in morbid fascination as the joint mind-focus touched the 'surface' of the seething, roiling ball, then continued inexorably towards the core. As they reached the nucleus, Jan had a fleeting glimpse of her body resting quietly below her, unaffected by the unimaginable heat of the sun.

You see? she said in 'her' mind. *Nothing your mind does can affect your body unless you tell it that it will, through beliefs and expectations. We will rest here a while. Feel free to explore.*

Explore the sun? The unprecedented opportunity tickled her curiosity. Tom would be heartbroken if she didn't bring back some juicy observations on the subject. Timidly, Jan took the helm of the mass focus, directing it up and down through the layers of action and reaction, noting the relative temperatures without exposing her mental body to them. She had never noticed it before, but a sun was undoubtedly one of the most beautiful and efficient structures in nature.

Scooting up a promontory, Jan experienced the exhilaration of its precipitous flight from deep within the star, out through the corona to bullet far out into space. Next, she parked 'her' focus amidst a seething cauldron of reaction. To her it felt like the effervescence of a hot tub with the jets on full speed. Below her, she felt her body's mouth curl into a delighted grin of wonderment.

Now we will return you to your self, 'she' said, and a moment later, the separation took place.

"Ouch!" Jan exclaimed. She felt so incredibly small compared to the vastness of the focus she had enjoyed a moment before. It was almost painful, readjusting to think as a single mind.

I never realized what a sacrifice you were making, breaking yourself into single focuses to help us teleport, Jan remarked, deeply moved. *You are truly remarkable beings.*

We are what we are, they replied simply. *We believe you can now move Shalaii's sun safely. The experiment was a success.*

I'll say! I could have stayed there all day. What a rush! Jan found herself grinning foolishly, and wanting to return to the sun to play.

You will be doing so as a singular being, remember, School said. *But singular or multiple, consciousness – focus – has the same abilities and impunity.*

We are immensely in your debt. Her words failed miserably to describe her gratitude to them for their timely and continued help. For the first time, Jan realized how truly advanced these beings were, and yet here they were, going to extraordinary lengths to help creatures they must see as hopelessly inferior.

170

Not inferior. School produced a humanesque chuckle. *Before we met you, we were unaware of teleportation. You and your friends are very young, evolutionarily, but with enormous potential. What we do for you now, you may one day do for other fledgling species.*

If we survive that long.

You will. Of that we are certain.

On that note, School disconnected, leaving Jan with much to think about. But first she needed to find another roost. Her butt hurt from the hard surface on which she had been sitting for so long.

As Jan walked towards the kitchen, she realized her stomach was empty, which reinforced the impression that she had been 'away' a considerable time. The kitchen clock confirmed it: 4:23 . Tom, Jack and Brenda would be home soon, and she hadn't done a thing about dinner. Thank goodness Billy was staying at his buddy's for the night.

A quick foray through the fridge produced scanty results. But then, she always welcomed an excuse – any excuse – to order in. Jan reached for the phone and dialed the number she knew by heart. Within two minutes, she had arranged for a large order of seafood to be delivered within the hour. Billy didn't like even the smell of seafood, so this would be a rare treat for the others, all of whom loved it.

Tom was the first through the door, a short time later. His eyes searched hers as he bent to greet her with a warm kiss. "How was your day?" Somehow, he managed to fit a multitude of meanings in the innocuous query.

"Remarkable," she summed it up, returning the kiss with gusto. "I'll give you the details when the others arrive."

Tom wrinkled his nose at her. "How about just the high points, then? Hubby's prerogative."

"Nope. I'll serve it to all of you at once, along with the seafood I just ordered."

"Then it's good news?"

"Indeed it is."

"How about a hint?" he wheedled, drawing her to him and smiling into her eyes in the way that had so often broken her resolve.

"Alright, but just one." She saw satisfaction flit across his face. "I had a personal *and* scientific breakthrough."

Tom leaned towards her in his eagerness for more details. "Scientific or science fictional?"

"Uh-uh. You'll have to wait for the others. Let's just say, I got my moment in the sun." Jan turned away, grinning smugly at her pun.

Fortunately for Tom, the others arrived soon after. The kitchen became far more crowded, as Brenda 'ported in with Jack in tow.

"Ah, here they are," Tom exclaimed. "Now, what was this gigantic achievement of yours?"

"Achievement?" Brenda's eyes lit up as she turned towards Jan expectantly.

"Gigantic? Our little Jan?" Jack teased.

"Little, am I?" Jan glared at him. "Just for that, you'll have to wait till the seafood arrives."

"*Now* look what you've done!" Tom groaned. "And after I had her all softened up to spill the beans."

Brenda passed a weary hand across her eyes. "I admit, I could sure use some good news for a change."

"Yeah, I guess we all could," Jan relented, and described in great detail her mental joining with School and her romp through Shalaii's sun.

"Oh, what I wouldn't give to have been there with you." Tom's eyes were full of longing. "How come you get all the fun?"

"Because I also take most of the risks," Jan pointed out. She immediately regretted the thoughtless comment. "I just mean, thrill-seekers like me get to take the good with the uh . . . scary," she finished lamely.

"But you're sure you can move that sun?" Tom was watching her very closely.

"After merging with School, I have no qualms about it at all. If they say my focus can't be harmed unless I give in to fear, then I believe them. It would seem that old saw is true after all – you know, the one about there being nothing to fear but fear itself."

"In that case, you're about to make history. Again," Brenda smiled, giving Jan a quick hug. "Don't you get tired of all the fame and glory?"

"Do you?" Jan teased.

"Not me! I live for it," Brenda admitted.

"Me, too. Maybe I should have ordered ham."

* * *

As they were sitting down to dinner, Shownae was preparing for bed. He had been uncharacteristically quiet all afternoon, which prompted Moohri to ask if anything was wrong.

"Just fretting about tomorrow," he admitted. "I'm worried about Jan."

Moohri nodded, his eyes clouding over. "I wish there was some way we could help her, something we could do."

"Maybe there is!" Shownae straightened up, as an idea occurred to him. "What if we moved Shalaii into a stable orbit around *our* sun? As long as Shalaii gets the right amount of heat and light, it shouldn't matter what sun it's around, should it?"

"No, it shouldn't," Moohri agreed slowly. "Why didn't we think of that before?"

"First thing tomorrow, I'm calling Jan and Ablakan. School was right when they said 'there's never only one way'. And I, for one, would welcome having Shalaii in our solar system."

"As would I. But before you call them, give me a chance to run it past Trikon and Wiltanus. Then we can give the others the good news."

Shownae spent the evening thinking it through. The more he considered it, the better it sounded to him. And he knew exactly where Shalaii would fit best among the orbits of his solar system. With Aridi having come on board to handle other high-priority 'porting requests, Shownae and his team could now devote their full attention to Shalaii and her people.

* * *

Ablakan awakened with a dual sense of anticipation and foreboding. This was the day everything would change. Overhead, the brighter stars were still visible in the lightening pre-dawn sky. For the longest time, he stood at his bedroom window, drinking in the sight, as though that could somehow emblazon it in his mind for all time. After today, he would never witness it again. Other stars, other constellations would take their place above Shalaii, or would already be in place above whatever distant world would become 'home' to his people. But never these. A yawning void opened in Ablakan's stomach that he knew no amount of food would never fill.

A void not unlike the one Juneli had revealed to him the night before. Having so recently reached the Age of Arrival, and with all that had occurred since then, Ablakan had given little thought to the prospect of finding a mate. Perhaps, in part, because Saymin had so aggressively labored to that end; it was hard to say. But Juneli?

He stroked his chin, unconsciously mimicking Tweno's habit. Juneli had been and always would be his dear friend and confidante. Over the years, she had been a constant source of wise counsel, unquestioning loyalty, consideration and compassion. And, on occasion, devastatingly objective critiques. She was one of the three most beloved people in Ablakan's life, rating right alongside Tweno and Jan. But love?

He stared out at the stars, but his mental vision was filled with memories of her. Juneli patiently tutoring him in protocol. Juneli teasing him out of a fretful mood. Juneli . . . Her face, with its kaleidoscopic range of expressions, the softness, gentleness, sometimes fire in her eyebanks. And always, behind it all, there had been love. How could he never have recognized it, never have known?

"Juneli." He whispered the name aloud to himself, and felt the echoing comfort that it evoked deep within him. Could that be love?

The stillness of the room, and his introspective thoughts, were shattered by an ominous rumble from deep within the earth. Almost automatically, he 'ported himself and the two remaining occupants of the complex out onto the grounds, to wait out the shaker. This had become so commonplace that Juneli did not immediately awaken. Jusire smiled his thanks to Ablakan. At least this time, there had not been anyone in the chamber awaiting clearance, as had happened the time before.

"It's just a small one, I think," Ablakan said encouragingly.

"Yes, sir."

The operator seemed to take it in his stride, and neither of them spoke again for a long minute, as they felt the earth rattle beneath their feet. Juneli sat up abruptly, looking startled.

"Just a small one," Ablakan repeated.

174

Juneli relaxed visibly and glanced at the brightening skies. "Time I get up anyway. It's going to be a busy day."

Ablakan nodded. History would be made this day. Whether it would be a day of glorious achievement or heartbreaking defeat remained to be seen.

"When you're up to it, would you cast your mind forward a bit, maybe see how things turn out?"

"I'll try." Juneli shook her head doubtfully. "But usually it's just critical things I pick up on." Her voice trailed away for a moment, her eyebanks pensive. "Which should easily encompass today's events. I'll see what I can do."

"Thanks." The shaking had ceased, and Ablakan could feel no further complaints from the stressed planetary crust. Over the last few days, he had become somewhat attuned to Shalaii's activities, at least locally.

"That's it for now," he said, inclining his head towards the ground. "Stand by." A moment later, all three were where they had been before he removed them and himself from the complex.

By midday today, Shalaii should be devoid of his species, at which time he would 'port himself to Earth to join the others preparing to move his solar system. He shook his head in amazement. Over the eons, many species must have faced the destruction of their world. Had any of them ever had the option he and his friends would be trying? If so, he would have given a lot to know how it had turned out.

Ablakan's stomach growled plaintively, and he grimaced, remembering the aborted attempt the night before to fuel his internal furnace. He'd better stoke it up; he would need his full attention to be on the task ahead of them.

The day-old muchipans would still be delicious, he knew, but his body was demanding serious nourishment. Ablakan carefully prepared a meal based on nutrition rather than taste, then consumed it down to the last bite. He was just clearing the dishes when he felt a 'knock' in his mind.

Greetings, Ablakan, Shownae smiled, as Ablakan opened his mental door. *I thought you'd be up.*

Big day, Ablakan agreed. *Big scary day.*

That it is. But we may have a way to make it less so.

175

Something in Shownae smug manner made Ablakan's heart leap with hope. *I'm all ears, as the humans say.*

I'm delighted to tell you that we – and that includes Wiltanus – would be honored to have Shalaii join our solar system. That way, you would only have to move one planet and its moon. Our sun's emanations are compatibly similar to yours, so it should make no difference to Shalaii. Here's where we suggest putting your planet.

Ablakan's mind filled with a view of the Orowan solar system with Shalaii added to it.

What a wonderful, generous offer! And you're right; it would be the safest route. I was going to try to move our sun myself. I just couldn't let Jan risk it. But now —

Now, *there will be virtually no risk*, Shownae concluded happily. *And I can't think of anyone I'd rather have as a neighbor.*

Ablakan felt his mental voice turn husky, as he said, *I hope someday I can thank you adequately, but I don't see how.*

You already did, seven years ago, when you worked so hard to rescue Moohri, Shownae reminded him. *I'll call Jan in a while, let her know she's off the hook. Would you care to ride along?*

Sure would! Ablakan relished any excuse to chat with Jan. It would be a joy to hear her response to good news, for a change.

In half an hour, say?

I'll await your call. It had been years since Ablakan thought of time in Shalaian terms. Shalaii, like most member planets, had adopted human time measurements along with English, for ease of communication between them.

Shownae disconnected, after projecting a heartfelt mental handshake which Ablakan returned with gusto.

Ablakan was still smiling as he 'ported himself to his office, but one glance out the window wiped it off his face. To the east, thunder clouds were amassing, roiling like a video played in quicktime. The air around the complex had become ominously still, as though nature was holding its breath in apprehension.

He had only witnessed this phenomenon once before, in a newscast from a region of Tunan that had been devastated shortly afterwards. The sight of it sent shivers down Ablakan's spine. And it was coming straight towards the complex.

Look east! he transmitted to Juneli urgently. *'Port whatever you value most to the palace, and be ready to go there yourself when I give the word. I'll take care of Jusire.*

He checked the chamber. Mercifully, it was at the moment empty.

Jusire, shut down the chamber, gather your most precious belongings and get ready to leave. The complex is about to be destroyed.

Next, he broadcast in all directions a general alert that his chamber was out of commission for the duration. It was the fastest way to ensure whoever of School was using that chamber would stop doing so and reroute refugees elsewhere.

Finally, he 'ported himself about, sending things too precious to lose to his old quarters in the palace. A quick check confirmed that Tweno was awake and in his office.

I've 'ported valuables over, he told Tweno briskly and without preamble. *Look east.*

He felt the Primary's mind tighten in consternation at the ominous sight.

Shut down the chamber and move your people here, Tweno ordered.

Respectively, we have and we will. See you soon.

Another hasty look out the window showed him exactly what he had expected to see. An enormous funnel was barrelling down on them, but much faster than he had anticipated.

Think of your valuables, he telepathically yelled to the operator.

Though somewhat rattled, the technician complied, and Ablakan unceremoniously threw the items in with his own stuff. They could sort them out later. A quick glance into Juneli's mind confirmed she was doing the same with her treasures.

Ablakan 'ported himself from room to room, choosing only irreplaceable items, all the while monitoring the tornado's progress. Even Tunan's worst paled in comparison to this one. He still had two rooms to go when he decided to pull the plug.

NOW! he ordered crisply to Juneli, and felt that mind relocate instantly, along with a few last items. Jusire was still snatching up articles when Ablakan sent him and every non-furniture object in the room to the palace.

The funnel was nearly upon him as Ablakan, with one last sorrow-filled look at his beloved complex, 'ported himself to Tweno's office.

Tweno covered his relief by retorting, "That was cutting it a bit close, don't you think?"

"Probably. But I couldn't very well leave my trophy behind, could I?" Ablakan clutched the prized item to his chest. "It's not every day I beat you at golf." Especially in a tournament, Ablakan thought smugly.

"Fortunately, no, it isn't," Tweno agreed, his shoulders relaxing now that the danger was over.

Their banter stopped, though, as they looked out the window. Juneli joined them, and together they watched the savage whirlwind tear the complex apart, wing by wing.

Ablakan felt tears sting his eyebanks, and almost at the same moment, Juneli took his hand. The tactile contact comforted him only marginally.

"We will rebuild, better than before," Tweno assured him, as the twister continued westward to vent its fury harmlessly out at sea. In its wake lay the wreckage of what had just moments before been their home.

"Thanks, sir." Perhaps one day he would look back on these times philosophically, but right now, it just added to the burden Ablakan already carried, as he thought of all the destruction, all the upheaval and despair Maxxift had caused his world and those he loved. For the first time, Ablakan allowed himself to feel satisfaction that the despot's demise had been a grisly affair. Maxxift had deserved every anguished, horrible moment of it.

"Don't give in to hate," Juneli whispered close to his ear, and Ablakan realized he was scowling. "Concentrate on the future. We will be alright."

Ablakan gazed at her uncertainly. Had that been reassurance, or the result of a precog? "Did you pick up something?"

"No," she shook her head in quiet denial. "Just that I have confidence in you and Jan and the others, that you'll save Shalaii."

Ablakan nodded mutely and turned away from the disheartening scene. A glance at his personal timemometer reminded him of Shownae's imminent call. He had almost forgotten to tell Tweno and Juneli about the Orowans' suggestion.

"I got a call from Shownae this morning," he said. "Wiltanus is offering us an excellent orbit around their sun. That way, we wouldn't have to risk moving ours." He projected the modified Orowan solar system for them to see. "They verified their sun's emanations are compatible with our needs."

For the first time in what felt like forever, Ablakan saw Tweno smile with pleasure. "What friends we have! I never even thought of that."

"Me neither," Ablakan admitted. "And yet it's such an obvious solution."

"Have you talked to Jan about it?" Juneli asked. "She must be worrying about moving our sun."

"I'm to tag along when Shownae calls her, which should be any minute."

As though he had been listening to their conversation, Shownae signalled Ablakan to join him.

"Here he is now." Ablakan plunked himself down on a handy chair and sent his focus to Earth. He 'parked' it beside Shownae and Jan's.

Good morning, Jan greeted them happily. *I was just about to call you two. I have some good news.*

So have we, Shownae remarked. *But you go first.*

Okay. I confess I was pretty worried about moving your sun, Ablakan. In fact, I was downright terrified. So I called School. What they did is merge my focus with theirs. Talk about a strange experience! They took me into your sun, all the way to the core, and then they just 'parked' there to let me get used to it. If you'll pardon the pun, it was a gas!

Ablakan 'read' her experience in surprise. *And you didn't even get a sunburn?*

Nope. No reaction whatsoever. I'm ready to move your sun, whenever you say the word.

That's wonderful, Ablakan exclaimed.

What's your *good news?* Jan asked.

Actually, it's Shownae's and Wiltanus'.

Shownae pretended to pout. *Your breakthrough took the wind out of my news' sails,* he said.

Ablakan chuckled privately to himself. Shownae loved to show off his knowledge of idiomatic English every chance he could.

What news? Jan demanded.

What's different about this picture?, Shownae asked, smugly projecting into Jan's mind the modified Orowan solar system.

Wow! Really?

Wiltanus called me himself, to sanction it, Shownae confirmed.

I'd better talk to Tweno, Ablakan said, adding with heartfelt candor, *But thank you both. Either solution would be excellent.* He detached his focus and turned towards the Primary and Juneli, both of whom were watching him closely.

"What did Jan think of the idea?" Tweno asked.

"She was delighted, of course," Ablakan replied. "But she had some developments of her own." He described her experience with School, concluding, "So the question is, which solution would be best for Shalaii *and* Orowa?"

Tweno's eyebanks had enlarged in surprise at the news. Now he turned them upward in thought. Ablakan and Juneli waited in respectful silence.

At length he asked, "Is Jan *certain* she can move our sun safely – safe for her and the solar system?"

"She says she can, and I believe it," Ablakan said.

"Alright, then. Would you get Lisham and Konapi? This must be a joint decision."

"Right away," Ablakan said, and split his focus to send the same message to both minds. Presently, he nodded. "They're ready for transport."

"I'll go sort out our belongings," Juneli said, and departed, leaving Tweno and Ablakan to attend to the affairs of state.

Once Konapi and Lisham were in the room, they got right down to business.

"We need to discuss this afternoon's relocation," Tweno began.

"Are we still on schedule?" Lisham asked.

"Not quite." Tweno pointed out the window towards where Ablakan's complex had been.

Lisham blanched and turned sorrowful eyebanks toward Ablakan.

Konapi stared mutely at the spot for several seconds, visibly shaken. "Was anyone injured?" he asked.

"Fortunately, no. And we were able to save most of the important things." Ablakan said, trying to put the feeling of loss behind him. "But with that chamber out of commission, the completion time will be set back, though not by much, I hope."

"When did it happen?" Kisham asked.

"Just a few minutes ago," Tweno said. "But I had you brought here to discuss what happens after the evacuation is complete. Thanks to Orowa, we now have two very viable options for relocation." He described them to the other Firsts.

"Quite the choice," Konapi nodded, equally impressed. "If we go with moving our solar system, has a place been decided upon?"

"Yes." Tweno turned the star chart, prominently displayed on his desk, towards them and pointed to the red circle that had been drawn on it. "It isn't near any of the holes the Aq'Narl made, or any other obstacle. There are no suns within 100 light-years, and it is roughly in line and halfway between Earth and Orowa. That'll make it easier for member planets like the Lowens, who still use conventional methods to visit our worlds. They can visit all three in the same voyage."

"Good idea," Konapi nodded.

"The way I see it, the decision about whether to take the Orowans up on their offer is whether it would be a benefit or a detriment to us and the Orowans. Give it some thought, and we'll meet here again in two hours." Tweno looked at each First, and all nodded their agreement.

Both Lisham's and Konapi's eyes had the slightly-out-of-focus expression which told Ablakan they were already thinking it over, so Ablakan 'ported them home after a brief farewell.

"What is your opinion?" Tweno asked him, when they were alone.

Ablakan grimaced. "I haven't had time to consider it yet. What's your take on it?"

Tweno's hand did a flip-flop. "I can see pros and cons to both. So much depends on future interplanetary relations. Right now, we're all the best of friends. But what if Wiltanus or I am replaced by a warmonger or a zenophobe? What if your replacements, over time, aren't as chummy as you bunch are? Shalaii and Orowa might find themselves much too close for comfort, even though teleportation has made distance an illusory factor."

Ablakan nodded. "Like mates who fall out of grace with each other. Proximity just makes things worse, makes it go sour faster."

"Exactly. If our solar system can be moved safely for all concerned, I think we'd be doing both ourselves and Orowa a favor by having our own space. Still, I'm willing to entertain arguments to the contrary."

"I'll give it some thought. See you later. And thanks for letting us move back."

"A pleasure always," Tweno assured him. "Regardless of the reason."

Ablakan found Juneli and Jusire separating into piles the items which had been sent over.

"Need a hand?"

Juneli straightened up and flashed him a quick smile. "Thanks, but I think we've got it under control. How are the deliberations going?"

"We're all to make our suggestions in just under two hours. By then the evacuation should be almost done."

Juneli opened her mouth to say something, then changed her mind. "Why don't you get some rest while you think about it?" she said instead. "Your day started pretty early."

"That it did." Ablakan 'ported himself to his old bedroom. It was exactly as he had left it, and with a sigh of relief, Ablakan crawled in, after setting his timemometer to awaken him in an hour-and-a-half. He would think better after refreshing himself a bit.

"Ablakan!"

Someone was shaking him, a mere moment later, or so it felt. Reluctantly, Ablakan pried his sleep-heavy eyelids open, to peer into Juneli's frightened eyebanks. That brought him up in a hurry.

"What's wrong?"

"Something. I don't know what. Something big," she said, her body tense with foreboding.

Ablakan jumped out of bed, glad he had had the presence of mind to remain fully clad in case another earthquake hit as he slept.

"Give me what you can," he said.

Juneli's eyes looked into the distance, unseeing.

"The moon!" she hissed suddenly.

Ablakan had a brief glimpse of the satellite careening crazily away from Shalaii, out in the direction of the singularity. In all the hubbub, Ablakan had forgotten to move it as its orbit passed closest to the black hole. He grabbed Juneli's arm, to stop her from trying to snatch it. If both did so, the moon would be destroyed.

Determinedly, he wrapped his focus around the accelerating object, feeling the tremendous pull the hole was having on the moon and his focus. For a split second, he thought he was too late. Then he felt Juneli add her focus to his, strengthing his grip on the moon, and he was able to move it back into its orbit, far enough from the hole to be safe.

"Thanks, June," he gave her a quick hug. "I almost lost it there." He passed a trembling hand across his eyebanks. "How could I have forgotten?"

"I did, too. But this is the last time we'll have to worry about it, if all goes well."

At that moment, the timemometer alarm went off, and they both jumped, then broke into slightly hysterical giggles. Ablakan rested his forehead against hers.

"When this is all over, I'm going to sleep for a week, like that human fable, Rip Van Wrinkle."

"Winkle," Juneli corrected, still chuckling. "And I think it was a lot longer. But I know what you mean. Do you realize it's only been a couple of weeks since this whole mess began?"

"Feels like forever," he admitted. "I've a good mind to suggest we ask the Aq'Narl to pay restitution."

Juneli snorted derisively. "As if they would!"

"I know, but we should anyway, just to bring home to them how much their freedom has cost Shalaii and her allies. Next time any of them have a grudge against us, they may take it into account before they retaliate."

"Couldn't hurt," she agreed. "Do you want to go back to sleep?"

"Not really," Ablakan replied, an unprecedented idea coming to mind. He took her hands in his and pulled her close.

Juneli's eyebanks enlarged in surprise and hope.

Gently, almost timidly, Ablakan kissed her, feeling the responding pressure as her lips pressed sensuously against his. A hunger like he had never experienced welled up inside of him, and he pulled away, shocked.

"Was it so bad?" Juneli asked, her eyebanks holding his searchingly.

"No, it – it was wonderful. It's just . . ." Ablakan gulped spasmodically. "I felt . . ."

"Felt what?" she prompted.

"Something not right. Not now," Ablakan replied in a low voice, blushing furiously. He felt like a child who had been caught stealing fruit.

Juneli patted his arm understandingly. "You're right. Not *now*." She left quietly, the emphasis on her final word promising there would be a next time.

Ablakan sat down on the bed, shaken. It was the first time he had ever experienced such intense feelings. Could that be love? Or was he just looking for a refuge from recent events?

Carefully, he allowed himself to re-experience the fullness of that first kiss, and once again, sexual urges threatened to overwhelm him. Ablakan hastily tabled the matter for future resolution, instead turning his attention to the more immediate problem of where to put Shalaii.

Tweno had made a valid point, that they should not count on relations remaining as friendly as they were now between Orowa and Shalaii. But if it did, non-teleporting member species would find it useful to have two of their biggest trading partners so close together. Also, Shalaii and Orowa could more easily protect their worlds against potential marauders or invaders than they could apart. As Tweno had pointed out, either way, there were pros and cons.

Ablakan spent the remaining time before Lisham and Konapi were to be 'ported back to the palace packing breakables for the potentially rocky journey to their new location. Usually, there was no discernible movement in teleportation, but if they opted to move their whole solar system simultaneously yet individually, it might be a different story. As he packed, he continued to ponder the advisability of joining Orowa's solar system.

He still hadn't come to a firm conclusion by the time the meeting was due to begin. By the time he reached Tweno's office, he had received confirmation from Lisham and Konapi, and 'ported the Firsts over.

Tweno solemnly shook hands with each of them, to underline the importance of the imminent decision.

"What are your suggestions?" he asked.

Konapi cleared his throat. "Either would be more than acceptable, but I recommend we keep our solar system together. In a way, the other planets, and our sun, are part of our identity as Shalaians. I think our self-image would never be quite the same, if we became a satellite of another solar system. It would serve as a constant reminder that we have lost our rightful place in the universe. We would always feel like a refugee, or worse – an orphan."

Tweno kept his expression carefully neutral. "What about you, Lisham?"

"My recommendation is the same as Konapi's, but for a different reason." He bent over to tap the red circle on the star chart. "Here we would be independent, yet in the midst of the largest concentration of powerful, allied sentients we know of. If as a group we had to defend ourselves against a superior force or technology, we would be facing the enemy like a skirmish line, unless they came at us angle-on the line. In another orbit of Orowa's sun, we could well be on the other side of it at the time, which might make a concerted defence more difficult. Also, I'm not sure adding another planet to their solar sysem wouldn't disrupt our tidal forces – or theirs, for that matter."

"Ablakan?" Tweno prompted.

"I also suggest we remain on our own, mostly to minimize problems if in future Shalaii and Orowa aren't on as good terms."

Tweno nodded. "I as well lean towards staying on our own. It's good to see we're all in agreement. How is the evacuation coming?"

"Tunan's is finished. School told Tix, who told me." Lisham reported. His was the smaller continent, and also the least populated.

"There were only eight chambersful of people to be moved off Enaxat when I left," said Konapi. "How about Pantai?"

"I haven't gotten an update yet," Ablakan told him. "I should hear pretty soon, I expect."

"As soon as you do, let me know and the chamber operators can be 'ported out with us. We are expected on Earth, aren't we?" Tweno asked.

"Yes, sir. And us 'porter types will merge for the relocation as soon as we have the 'all clear' from School. I understand they'll do a mental search to ensure no one got missed." Once again, Ablakan felt beholden to School for their herculean efforts during the crisis. "Do you want to tell Wiltanus and Shownae our decision, or shall I?"

"I will. Would you get them for me?"

Shownae tracked down Wiltanus easily enough, and soon the 'conference call' was ready to proceed.

Shownae told me your complex was destroyed, Ablakan. Please accept my condolences, Wiltanus began. *Have you considered our proposal?*

Indeed we have, sir. It was most generous of you, and we shall always be grateful to you and your people for your kindness during these trying times. Tweno mentally bowed his head an inch in appreciation. *However, Jan is now convinced she can move our sun safely, and we have decided to keep our solar system intact, if we can. I believe it would be best for all concerned, for I cannot guarantee that my replacement, or Ablakan's for that matter, will always make good neighbors.*

It was Wiltanus' turn to incline his head slightly. *Yes, we had considered that as well. Even now, with all the benefits we have derived from our mutual trade and friendship, there are those who oppose our close relations. Perhaps one day, they will rise to power.*

I'm glad we are in agreement, Tweno said with obvious relief. *But your offer will go down in our history books, so that Shalaians will never forget your generosity. I will see to it personally.*

We are honored. I wish you success in your move, and will eagerly await news of its completion.

With your permission, I will call you myself, when it is over, Tweno offered.

Thank you. Wiltanus severed the link, and Tweno did likewise.

See you on Earth, Ablakan smiled to Shownae. *It shouldn't be long. The evacuation is almost complete.*

I'm relieved to hear that. Bye for now.

They disconnected at the same time.

"If you have no further need of me, perhaps Ablakan would transport me back to my complex." Lisham directed the question to Tweno, with a respectful nod to Ablakan. "I vowed to remain there till the chamber operator is no longer needed."

"Certainly," Tweno said.

Lisham turned towards Ablakan expectantly, but the young First held up a staying hand.

"Incoming message," he explained, preoccupied with opening his mental door to his visitor.

Greetings, Ablakan, the unmistakable merged voices of School began. *We have removed all of your species save the – we believe you call them 'skeleton crews' – in your three locations. We will now retire and let you move your solar system.*

School, if it were possible to hug you all, we surely would! Ablakan beamed. *I just cannot thank you enough for all you've done.*

It was exhilarating for us, too, School told him. *We enjoyed the experience of using our minds individually and in such a unique way. It has added immeasurably to our options for self-expression.*

I'm delighted to hear that. Would you like to monitor our move? That also could prove valuable for them, perhaps.

Yes, indeed, School chorused enthusiastically. *But rest assured, we will be careful not to interfere with your focus.*

Till we speak again, Ablakan bowed deeply to express his profound appreciation, then disconnected and smiled at his ruler and counterparts. "That was School. We and our skeleton crews are the last on the planet. If you're ready, I'll alert the others and 'port us all to Earth."

Each consented, so Ablakan sent out a cryptic message globally, waited a couple minutes to ensure everyone was ready for transport, then 'ported all remaining personnel into Ames' decontamination chamber. School must have notified Jan as well, for she, along with Saunders and Rhodes, were there to greet them when they emerged.

What surprised Ablakan most was to see the U.S. President and the U.N. Secretary-General step forward to greet them. Evidently, they had been on standby, awaiting news that the evacuation was finished.

Secretary-General Serapernan thrust out his hand as Tweno exited the chamber.

"So good to see you again, sir," he beamed.

"It has been too long," Tweno agreed.

The President extended his hand as soon as Tweno's was free, saying, "It's a relief to know you and your people are safe. I tell you, I was sweating bullets worrying that our estimations regarding that damned hole might be off."

Tweno's face broke into a sheepish grin. "Forgive me, but so was I."

They all shared a laugh at that. Ablakan was wrapped in a mutual embrace with Jan and only half-heard the exchange, but the unmistakable relief on the leaders' faces said more than their words could convey.

"After this is all over, you and I are going to have a good, long visit," Jan told him firmly, framed by smiles.

"Count on it!" After this, he would *need* a vacation, and there was noplace he would rather be than visiting Jan.

Hand in hand, they walked purposefully towards the room that held the model solar system.

"The others are already gathered," she told him as they rounded the last corner. "So we can begin at once, if you like."

"If the 'dry run' with the model is a good one, let's do the real thing right after."

"My thinking exactly," Jan agreed.

The next couple of minutes were occupied with hugs and hand clasps. Besides Tweno and Juneli, Ablakan considered these people his real family. How fitting that they collectively would give Shalaii one last chance to survive.

CHAPTER 13

The technician took his place at the monitors, resetting a number of readouts before nodding towards the waiting 'porters.

As prearranged, Jan led off, capturing the model sun with her focus.

"Ready," she confirmed.

Ablakan held Shalaii and her moon loosely enough that their movements would not yet be affected. On either side of him, Tix, Kyollan and Shownae snagged their respective planets. As before, they extended their focus to lightly encompass each other, so that they could move the model as synchronously as possible.

"On my mark," Jan said. "Three . . . two . . . one . . . *NOW!*"

Despite the time lag since their last rehearsal, Ablakan felt the coordinated movements come together as one. Instantly, all eyes turned toward the technician, who was busily interpreting the readouts.

It seemed to take him longer than usual to make his determination, or perhaps it just seemed that way to Ablakan.

"You're off by a very respectable 0.0012 percent. If you can keep that kind of coordination for the real thing, you should be home free." The technician smiled at his little pun, then turned back to reset the instruments. "Did you want another go at it first?"

Ablakan shook his head, and was pleased to see his friends doing the same. "Wish us well," he told the technician before turning to Jan. "Care to do the honors? I don't know where you're set up."

He immediately found himself in a glass-domed dark room. To his right, someone gasped in amazement. Wherever they were, it was nighttime. The cloudless skies provided a magnificent view of the starfield above that section of, presumably, Earth.

"Appropriate, no?" Jan said smugly. "Jack's idea."

"Perfect," Ablakan agreed. Just *seeing* space definitely made mentally traveling in it feel more natural. Effortlessly, he located Shalaii, spinning so perilously close to the singularity.

"Here's where we'd like the system to go." He projected an image of the new location into the minds of each participant.

"Excellent choice," Shownae remarked.

"A natural," Jan agreed. "Okay, here we go."

Ablakan had the brief sensation of her shoulder tensing slightly where it brushed against his arm, as she stretched her focus to encompass the giant sun.

"Got it," she announced, with understandable pride.

Shalaii seemed to hold her breath, as Ablakan lovingly enclosed his homeworld and her moon with his focus.

"I have Shalaii," he stated, and one by one, his associates confirmed 'their' planet was also ready for transport.

There was just a hint of tremor in Jan's voice as she started the countdown. Ablakan felt his body constrict in anticipation, his pulse quickening in his veins.

". . . one . . . *NOW!*"

Unlike with the model, Ablakan had the disorienting sensation of himself being relocated, but he doggedly held onto his planet, ensuring he 'released' Shalaii at the precise instant the others released their solar objects.

His heart pounded painfully against his ribcage, as he carefully checked his homeworld for signs of undue stress or even rupture. There would be quakes and other disruptions, he knew, as the crust readjusted itself, now that the terrible strain on it had been removed. That was unavoidable. Ablakan jumped his focus from location to location across Shalaii, but so far as he could determine, she had survived intact the abrupt removal of the singularity's influence upon her. High above, her moon revolved in unperturbed ease.

Jan! Ablakan's mind reached out through the darkness, as his hand grasped hers.

"I'm fine," Jan told him mentally. "Though I wouldn't want to make a habit of it."

A quick check reassured Ablakan that his sun was where it should be, as were each of the planets in its system.

"We did it?" He asked, in hushed incredulity. "We really did it?"

Abruptly, the lights went on, and suddenly everyone was laughing and crying in an orgy of relief and joy, hugging and clapping one another on the back. The door burst open, and the room became very crowded indeed with jubilant well-wishers, among them the U.S. President, U.N. Secretary-General, Drs.

Saunders and Rhodes, and Tweno. Evidently, Richard Ironhorse, who had not taken part in the exercise, had monitored the move and 'ported the dignitaries over the moment it was a *fait accompli.*

"*WE DID IT!*" Ablakan cried, as Tweno came towards him with eyebanks silently begging for confirmation. They clasped each other's arm ecstatically, Tweno taking care with Ablakan's still-casted forearm.

Then out of the crowd, Juneli stepped forward, her face aglow with pride and love. How had he not recognized it, seeing her every day as he had for so many years? A moment later, he had no time for retrospective thoughts, as she came into his waiting arms. Ablakan hugged her blissfully, only releasing her with great reluctance as the crowd closed in on them.

Ablakan found himself overwhelmed by merry-making on the outside at the same time as an exultant School congratulated and praised their achievement inside his mind. In an effort to reach everyone at the same time, he broadcast his gratitude in all directions.

School, he added. *Whoever and whatever you are, better friends we have never had!*

Nor we, they chorused. *We leave you now to a well-earned celebration.*

With that, they were gone. Which was just as well, considering half a city seemed to have crowded into the room, everyone hooting and yelping in unbridled glee. At the height of the pandemonium, Drs. Saunders and Rhodes rounded up the President, Secretary-General and each of the 'porters, and they snaked their way through the crowd towards the rear exit.

"Whew! Those Aussie technos sure know how to party when they let their hair down," Rhodes remarked. He smiled broadly to show he meant no disrespect.

"Is that where we are?" Tix asked. "Australia?"

"Yup. Next stop, Ames?" Jan regarded the dignitaries with raised eyebrows.

Saunders used eye contact to check with the others, and they all agreed, so he gave Jan the nod.

Their arrival sparked a second round of excitement and jubilation, though not quite as uninhibitedly as the Australians had shown. The 'porters stayed just long enough to be polite, then excused themselves.

"What we have here is literally a media event of galactic proportions," Rhodes remarked, as he led the way down the corridor that led to several conference rooms. "I'll stall the reporters as long as I can."

No doubt, there would be endless functions and interviews to attend in wake of the history-making events, Ablakan realized.

"I would appreciate that," Tweno confirmed. "We need to inform our people on each planet of recent events. They should hear it firsthand, from me."

"Of course. This way, please." Rhodes motioned the others into the larger conference room, and Ablakan and Tweno to the adjacent one. As Ablakan was closing the door, he heard Rhodes tell the security detail that they were not to be disturbed unless it was urgent.

Tweno turned to Ablakan at once. "Can you put me through to all our people at once?"

"On one planet at a time, yes," Ablakan replied.

"Good enough. How do you want to work it?"

"Why don't I feed your mental voice through my focus? That way, I can broadcast it directly into every Shalaian mind here."

Tweno regarded Ablakan doubtfully. "What do I do?"

"Just think of what you want to say, and I'll do the rest. Let me know when you're ready."

Tweno's brow furrowed in concentration, then he nodded.

The mental gymastics over, Ablakan pointed to Tweno to let him know he was 'on'.

Fellow Shalaians, I bring you wonderful news. Thanks to our own teleporters and their able associates on Earth and Orowa, our solar system has been moved intact to a new location roughly in line with, and halfway between, Earth and Orowa.

I have been assured you will be made as comfortable as possible here on Earth for the balance of your stay, and that Shalaians on the other member planets are also being treated as honored guests by their hosts. Our scientists, as well as specialists from Earth and Orowa, believe that Shalaii will undergo potentially severe earthquakes and storms before she returns to normal, now that the singularity is no longer pulling at her. When

192

they feel it is safe to do so, Shalaians everywhere will be returned to their homes, or to temporary accommodations if their homes have been badly damaged or destroyed.

I thank you all for your patience and understanding during these trying times. I will inform you of every important development as it happens. In the meantime, please do your utmost to be considerate of your hosts, for they, also, have had very little time to prepare for your arrival. If you have a problem which cannot wait nor be otherwise resolved, Ablakan and I will remain on Earth with you, and can be reached through the manager of your accommodation.

Tweno nodded towards Ablakan to close the connection. "Set that up, will you? And I'd like Tix to go to Orowa. Kyollan can go to Lowen but cover the camps on the other worlds, since there are a lot fewer Shalaians on them than on Earth and Orowa."

"I'll take care of it," Ablakan promised. "Orowa next?"

"Please."

Through Ablakan, Tweno delivered the same message, almost word for word, to the Shalaians on each member world. When the last had been advised, Tweno leaned back with a groan.

"Once Shalaii stabilizes, all we have to do is rebuild almost every structure on her," he said ruefully.

"I know," Ablakan sighed. "I'm no economist, but I don't think we have the funds to do it all."

"If I know Earth and Orowa, they'll lend a hand, but we'll still be heavily in debt probably for generations to come." Tweno shook his head morosely. "I sure wish we could make Aq'Narl pay at least partial restitution."

"Not likely! Although, to be fair, they probably couldn't even if they wanted to. From what I gathered, Maxxift left them in a sorry state."

"It's a shame Maxxift isn't here to answer for it. I'd have liked to sentence him to hard labor rebuilding our homes till his dying day."

"He'd have just been more trouble than he was worth," Ablakan suspected.

"Probably." Tweno shook his head dejectedly. "When I took on the role of Primary, I never thought I'd be leading Shalaii from unprecedented wealth to the deepest depression we have ever known."

Ablakan placed a hand on Tweno's arm. "If anyone can ease our way through this, it's you."

"Let's hope so." Tweno shook his mane, as though trying to rid himself of the depressing outlook. They left the small conference room and nodded briefly to the security guards, who opened the door to the larger room for them.

"Ah, there you are," the U.S. President said, beaming broadly as he came forward to greet them. "We have been scheming behind your back." Several heads nodded smugly.

"Have you, now?"

The President gestured to Serapernan to take the floor.

The U.N. Secretary-General cleared his throat officiously. "The last of the member planets just reported in, directly from their respective leaders. The vote was unanimous." He paused a moment, obviously relishing the moment. "Primary Tweno, when Ablakan, on your orders, repossessed your uranium from Aq'Narl and moved your asteroid field out of Maxxift's reach, you were acting on behalf of us all. But yours was the only planet to pay the price.

Those mini-holes in each of our planet's space were not put there for no reason. Without our 'porters' timely intervention, the holer technology could have – and no doubt would have – been used against us, just as it was against Shalaii.

Therefore, we believe it is only fair that we all play an integral role in helping to restore your planet. That includes reconstructing your buildings, repairing roads, re-establishing your economy, and so forth. School, due to their physical nature, has not been asked to contribute, but considering their role in the evacuation and, they assured me, the resettlement to come, they will have assisted all they could."

Ablakan felt like the weight of their world had been lifted from his shoulders. A quick glance at Tweno confirmed that he, too, was almost speechless with gratitude.

"You have all already done so much," Tweno murmured, his voice husky with emotion.

"None of which would have been necessary if Shalaii hadn't had to bear the full brunt of Maxxift's retaliation," the President pointed out. "We could not stop the destruction, but at least we can do our part in the reconstruction. And indeed we will. Despite our friendships with you and your people, this is *not* benevolence. We are attempting to pay restitution of an enormous debt we owe you. Besides," he grinned cheekily. "Devastated economies make poor trading partners. We have to look out for our own interests, too, you know."

Abruptly, Tweno guffawed with laughter. "Leave it to you to camouflage generosity as capitalism. But I am in no position to refuse."

"Especially since you know you'd do the same, if the situation were reversed," Shownae put in knowingly.

"He's got you there," Ablakan chuckled.

Tweno nodded. "Besides 'thank you', I don't know what to say."

"It's good for us, too," Jan added. "It'll all but erase our jobless rate, and that's good for the economy. Beats doing it the historical other way."

Ablakan felt his face lengthen. "You mean, war?"

Jan nodded. "Sadly, yes. War and post-war economies are the strongest – assuming you win. But at what price?"

"Ow!" Tweno grimaced. "In that case, bring on your jobless!" That triggered a ripple of laughter.

The next hour was devoted to Tweno, through Ablakan, formally thanking those planetary leaders not in attendance, and finding out the living arrangements for himself and Ablakan. Tix and Kyollan 'ported themselves to Orowa and Lowen respectively. Although Lowen was the newest member planet, it was central to the others on which Kyollan would be fielding queries from the Shalaians temporarily housed there.

Not surprisingly, the U.S. President talked Tweno into staying at the White House, and Ablakan was delighted to accept Jan's offer that he and Juneli live with 'the gang', which now included the rambunctious felines. With Jan, Tom, Jack, Brenda, Billy and Wiki already in residence, it would be a bit crowded, but Ablakan could think of nowhere he would rather be except home which, at the moment, had been reduced to rubble.

"How are Wiki and Billy getting on?" Ablakan inquired, as he, Juneli and Jan left the conference room hand in hand.

"Wiki has the patience of an angel. And I think Billy has a crush on her. Which is good, as it makes him easier to handle."

"Ah, first love," Juneli intoned, her eyebanks glistening with mischief, as she glanced slyly at Ablakan.

He pretended not to notice, which was hard to do while blushing.

A moment later, he found himself standing in Jan's kitchen. Immediately he was set upon by a boisterous Jack, and an equally delighted Tom, both talking at once and clapping him on the back while trying to shake his uninjured hand at the same time. Brenda ducked under the outstretched arms and insinuated herself between the men and Ablakan, enclosing him in a bear-hug, Brenda-style.

"It's been ages," she cried, releasing him at last.

"I wish you wouldn't do that," Jan complained. "It just makes him shoot up taller."

Which was probably true. Ablakan grinned at their goodnatured teasing.

"While you folks were carousing around the galaxy, I was slaving over dinner," Tom stated. "Pull up a seat."

They didn't have to ask Ablakan twice. Now that Tom mentioned it, the smells in the kitchen were irresistible.

"Chinese food, Shalaian style," Tom announced.

"Wonderful." Ablakan smacked his lips in anticipation. Obviously, Tom had remembered which food items Ablakan had especially enjoyed during past visits, for most of them seemed to have made their way into the heaping platters being placed on the table. Ablakan guiltily considered how he could tactfully ask Chef to include the recipes in his repertoire.

While they were filling their face, the large black hole in Shalaian space pulled in a passing meteor and doubled in size.

* * *

Ablakan was preparing for bed when a quiet knock sounded at his door. He had been expecting it. Juneli and he needed to talk, and there had not been time earlier.

"Come in."

But instead, it was Wiki who entered, lighting up the room with her sunny smile. She was carrying a pitcher of lemonade – a personal favorite of Ablakan's. "I thought you might like this. Tom showed me how to make it."

"That's very thoughtful. Thank you."

A tentative quality insinuated itself into Wiki's smile. "I was also hoping to speak to you privately, if you're not too tired. If you are, it can wait."

"No, I'm fine, thanks." Ablakan motioned her toward the only chair in the room, while he sat attentively on the foot of the bed. He didn't want to give her the wrong impression.

Wiki was playing with a shapely digit, obviously ill-at-ease. "This is a bit awkward, but I was thinking, now that Juneli is a teleporter, she will no doubt be needed in that capacity, rather than as your assistant. Which means, once we are back on Shalaii, you will need someone to keep things running smoothly while you and Juneli attend to the rebuilding of Pantai. I would like to offer my services in that capacity, on a temporary basis until you can interview candidates for that position."

The speech sounded carefully rehearsed and formal. On some level he did not understand, Ablakan felt disappointed.

"An excellent suggestion. At the first opportunity, you, Juneli and I must discuss how to best set up operations when we return home. Thank you for your offer."

Wiki leaned forward in her chair, her eyebanks radiating intensity and hope. "Perhaps I shouldn't be saying this, but I just want you to know, sir: I am available in any capacity you need, at any time. I would very much like be your friend. As close a friend as you want me to be – and not just because you saved our planet from destruction."

Ablakan just stared at her, unable to think what to say. Wiki was by far the most beautiful creature he had ever met, and one of the most capable, but the effect she had on him had nothing to do with her qualifications. And she was offering . . .

He met her eyebanks then, trying to separate his 'leader' feelings from his personal ones. "Wiki, I don't know how we would have gotten through all this without you. You have my undying gratitude. And I would consider it an honor to have you as a friend. But right now, I'm still what the humans call 'shell-shocked'. It may take me some time to sort out my feelings. I hope you understand."

The smile was back, though not quite as bright. "Perfectly, sir. It has been a terrible ordeal. I had better let you rest now."

"Thank you. I'll see you tomorrow."

"Rest well."

Ablakan stared at the door for a while. He needed sleep in the worst way, but now he had two wonderful ladies – two friends – who appeared to be in love with him. Worse, he harbored deep feelings for both of them as well. Suddenly, black holes seemed a simpler problem by far.

* * *

Morning sunshine brought Ablakan awake. Considering how late he had gotten to sleep, he felt amazingly refreshed. He was just completing his waking rituals when a 'knock' sounded in his mind.

Greetings, School. Ablakan's focus sharpened. School did not call for frivolous reasons.

We greet you, too. The singularity in your former location requires your attention. It will soon cause a star to be formed in the sister universe and destroy the nearby inhabited planet.

Thank you for the warning. I will contact the others.

The connection went dead without so much as a 'goodbye'. Evidently, School considered the event imminent.

Ablakan mentally found the black hole, and was shocked at its size and 'pull'. He awakened Juneli, Jan and Brenda (which also alerted Tom and Jack), then placed a hasty call to his other 'porting cohorts. When everyone was assembled, he explained the problem.

Tix groaned. *Couldn't that stupid thing have given us one full night's sleep?*

Apparently not, Ablakan sighed. *School thinks it could blow up as a star any time. That means we have to move that antimatter solar system with the occupied planet in it somewhere safe. But we haven't had time to research it, let alone find a place to put it.*

Jan shook her head. *The other half of School is on that side. I'll ask them. Stand by.*

Ablakan felt Jan stretch out her focus to contact the multiplicity.

They opened to her just long enough to transmit a cryptic message. *Our other half said, 'Critical'.*

198

Which could only mean one thing. *It's about to happen,* Jan cried. *Follow me in.*

Scant moments later, with the others in tow, Jan crossed the line separating the two universes, and zeroed in on the planet, its inhabitants blissfully unaware of their imminent destruction.

I've got the sun, Jan reported. Somehow, it seemed almost natural to say that now.

The inhabited planet, Ablakan reported tersely.

One by one, the others confirmed they had the other planets ready for transport.

It's happening!, Shawnae gasped, as searing light burst forth from what had moments before been the expanding black hole.

NOW! Jan cried, enveloping her cohorts in a group 'port of the celestial bodies. She felt the immense energies which they fed through her as she threw the solar system obliquely away from the exploding new sun as far as she could fling it.

She leaned back, gasping.

"Are you okay?" Ablakan put his hand on her arm, his eyebanks large with concern.

"*I* am," she replied, horrified by the implications of her actions. "But I don't know where I sent it. There was no time to choose. I may have –" She couldn't bring herself to finish the sentence.

Somewhere in the vast other universe, a solar system had suddenly arrived. But to save one planet, had she destroyed others?

CHAPTER 14

We do not know, School-there reported soberly. *It is not in our neighborhood.*

Is there any way to find out where it is? I sent them that way somewhere. Jan projected a line from where they were mentally 'standing'. *But I don't know how far that way.*

School-there oozed reassurance. *We have reached them before. We should be able to locate them now, if they still live.*

Jan shuddered, horrified at the thought of what she might inadvertently had done. She could feel her friends' minds, tense with worry, 'parked' beside hers. All she could do now was wait for the verdict.

To Jan, it took eons before School returned. *They are alive, and their planet is intact.*

Did we put them in a safe part of space? Jan asked.

Yes. Most of space is empty, School confirmed. *Statistically, you were most likely to put them in a safe place, anyway.*

And the orbits look okay?

The multiplicity projected a smile without a face around it. *They are unconcerned, Jan, and unknowing. You have all done well.*

Relief washed over the small group in a wave, each feeling the others rejoice at the welcome news.

Thank you, dear friends, once again. Jan turned to the others mentally. *Home, James?*

You bet! Brenda answered for them all.

Making sure the group was all still attached, Jan said, *Here we go.* A quick mental twist, and they were back focused in the room.

* * *

It was Sunday, and most of the teleporters were off work. Ablakan, Juneli and Wiki accepted their hosts' offer of a tour of some of Earth's finest botanical and ornamental gardens. Ablakan's love of flowers had remained constant over the years – a passion shared by Tom.

That being the case, Tom was the group's human floral expert *pro tem,* and chose the locations they would visit. During the course of the day, Ablakan lost track of what marvel he saw where. But it was not only flowers which bloomed for him that day.

While they were exploring Butchart Gardens on Vancouver Island, Ablakan felt himself being gently steered down a more secluded path. He smiled at Juneli. He had been hoping they might have a few minutes alone.

A large bush to one side of the garden path afforded them relative privacy, and they both accordioned down onto the soft grass behind it.

"Wiki went to see you last night, which is none of my business, I know." She nipped a long blade of grass with her fingertips, making it of equal height with its brethren. "But you know how I feel about you. I just need to know if you'd rather I keep my feelings to myself."

She was asking if she still had a chance with him, Ablakan realized. He took her hand.

"I'm glad you brought that up; I've been meaning to talk to you. Wiki suggested she replace you temporarily as my assistant, since you'll be needed far more as a teleporter. She's right, there." Ablakan saw Juneli's face light up. "But she also expressed personal feelings towards me. And I'll admit, I like her a lot, even though she has been with us for such a short time. She is a remarkable woman."

Juneli nodded, looking down at the grass. "Yes, she is."

"But there is a difference between like and love," Ablakan went on, giving her hand a little squeeze for emphasis. "I should hate to lose her help and friendship, but I could not bare to lose yours."

Juneli went very still, her eyebanks searching his face. "You really mean that? Are you saying –"

"I'm *saying* I love you, June. I think I always have. It just took me a while to realize it."

"A long while."

They both leaned forward, closing the gap between them in more ways than one. Ablakan felt their kiss all the way down to his toes – an electric tingling followed by a flush of warm passion deep within him. He ached to love her more thoroughly and intimately, but he could hear footsteps approaching.

"Later," he vowed.

"A *soon* later."

"Very soon later." Ablakan helped her to her feet. They quickly brushed grass clippings from their clothes and manes before stepping back onto the path.

"There they are," Brenda pointed. "Thought we'd lost you guys."

Beside her stood Wiki, who gazed from one to the other, her expression a silent accusation. Ablakan flushed. Why did he feel like a truant child? The decision, after all, was theirs to make.

He cleared his throat as they approached. "Brenda, could I have a moment alone with my staff?"

"No problem. The others are meeting us at the fountain over there." She pointed toward the attractive display. "Join us when you're ready."

Ablakan headed for a bench a little ways down the path. No one seemed to be in the vicinity. It was as good a place as any to set things straight, if he could be quick about it. He deliberately sat next to Wiki, with Juneli seated beside her.

"Wiki, if you are still interested in being my assistant, at least temporarily, you would be taking a great load off my mind. As you said, we need Juneli too badly as a teleporter."

"Thank you, sir. I accept."

"Before you do, please understand: I consider you a friend, but Juneli and I have grown very close over the years. How close, I only just realized myself. Would you be comfortable working with us, knowing that we are becoming a pair?" Ablakan watched Wiki closely, trying to interpret the range of emotions that vied for expression on her face.

"I don't know."

"Please take your time. It will be a while before we can begin restoring Shalaii, and that is when we will need you most." He stood up. "Shall we join the others?"

Wiki nodded once and hurried towards the group. Ablakan sighed, wishing he had phrased it a bit more tactfully.

Juneli held back until Wiki was out of earshot. When she spoke, her voice was barely audible. "Let's always be very professional towards each other in her presence."

Ablakan nodded. "Yes, that should help." Leave it to Juneli to be considerate of the person who had been, albeit briefly, her rival. It made him love her all the more.

But the next day, Wiki let it be known through Jan that she was job-hunting. With her track record and trade connections on Earth, within an hour she was offered, and accepted, an embarrassingly lucrative position.

Ablakan was secretly pleased, as now he and Juneli were free to openly express their feelings for each other. That night, Ablakan knocked on Juneli's door once the house was in darkness.

She opened to him, clad only in moonlight. Silently, she took his hand, drawing him into the room, then closed the door behind him.

Within moments, they removed all his apparel save his arm sling. Ablakan felt his body tense, then his shoulders arched backwards, releasing the *abwa* cushioned between his abdomenal folds.

When the transition was complete, Juneli beamed in joyous anticipation and pulled him toward her and what was about to become their nuptial bed.

"I love you, Juneli," Ablakan whispered hoarsely, as he adjusted his body over her, carefully balancing his injured arm.

"And I love y–" She gasped, the rest of the sentiment cut off as he entered her.

He moaned deep in his throat, feeling passion course through his body, experiencing her urgency as intensely as his own. They moved in perfect rhythm, increasing the power and depth with their movements in a naturalness Ablakan would never have thought possible for two persons locked in their first coital union.

Every now and again, Juneli would emit a hypersonic cry of sexual ecstacy. And each time, it spurred Ablakan to greater erotic efforts.

When he felt like he must burst from the sensations, Ablakan heard Juneli's explosive scream and felt her constrict in a love-clench. At the same moment, he drove downward to meet her, shuddering convulsively at the massive release.

They held each other for a long time afterwards, spent but both reluctant to have the moment end.

At length, Ablakan chuckled, shaking his head ruefully. "How could it have taken me so long to know?"

"In fairness, when have you had time for anything but work, and the occasional game of golf?" Juneli murmured, stroking his mane lovingly.

"At least we'll have our nights." He said it as a question.

"Count on it, my first."

Ablakan nuzzled her neck, grinning at her deliberate double entendre.

And then she was doing exquisite things in the vicinity of his loins. Juneli smiled at him, her eyes at once mischievous and lustful. Ablakan stiffened, felt the classic response begin, and surrendered to rapture once more.